This book is dedicated to Cassy Hall and Jennifer Bryk, who were the winners of my website contest to name the palace in this series. Special thanks also to Tammy Warnick and Vee for the name of Hawthorne, which I used as Devon's title.

A simple twist of fate . . .

Four years ago, a mesmerizing stranger pulled Lady Rebecca Newland from her runaway coach, galloping to her rescue in a fog-shrouded forest. Though she was just seventeen, Rebecca felt an irresistible desire for the mysterious man, and swore that she would someday be his bride. But now she is betrothed to another man whom she detests—and Devon Sinclair, the future duke of Pembroke, and her hero, lies tantalizingly beyond her reach.

Haunted by an unspeakable past, Devon has no intention of taking a wife, not even the enticing Rebecca. But then his father rules that Devon must wed by Christmas or forfeit his rightful inheritance. Now, with his fortune at stake, Devon sets out to lure Rebecca to his bed . . . where their scandalous passion could prove they are destined for true love.

By Julianne MacLean

In My Wildest Fantasies
Surrender to a Scoundrel
Portrait of a Lover
Love According to Lily
My Own Private Hero
An Affair Most Wicked
To Marry the Duke

If You've Enjoyed This Book,
Be Sure to Read These Other
AVON ROMANTIC TREASURES

Bewitching the Highlander *by Lois Greiman*
How to Engage an Earl *by Kathryn Caskie*
Just Wicked Enough *by Lorraine Heath*
The Scottish Companion *by Karen Ranney*
The Viscount in Her Bedroom *by Gayle Callen*

Coming Soon

Untouched *by Anna Campbell*

Julianne MacLean

In My Wildest Fantasies

An Avon Romantic Treasure

AVON

An Imprint of HarperCollinsPublishers

AVON BOOKS
An Imprint of HarperCollins*Publishers*
10 East 53rd Street
New York, New York 10022–5299

Copyright © 2007 by Julianne MacLean
ISBN 978–0–06–081949–1
ISBN-10: 0–06–081949–9
www.avonromance.com

First Avon Books paperback printing: November 2007

Avon Trademark Reg. U.S. Pat. Off. and in Other Countries, Marca Registrada, Hecho en U.S.A.
HarperCollins® is registered trademark of HarperCollins Publishers.

Printed in the U.S.A.

10 9 8 7 6 5 4 3 2 1

Acknowledgments

Many thanks to Michelle Phillips and to Deborah Hale, for your friendship and support, helpful brainstorming sessions, and invaluable critiques. Thank you also to my editor, Erika Tsang, for all your great work at Avon, and to Paige Wheeler, my fantastically marvelous agent, whom I adore.

In My
Wildest
Fantasies

Chapter 1

Oxfordshire
August, 1870

A thick, gray mist moved through the darkening forest, creeping low along the ground like a twisting, rolling phantom. Rebecca Newland, dressed in black and seated beside her sleeping father in the dark confines of his carriage, was in a place somewhere between dreams and reality, her head tipped back upon the deeply buttoned leather upholstery, her eyelids falling closed briefly, then fluttering open again as the coach rumbled and bumped along the narrow, winding road.

They were on their way home from her uncle's funeral in London. Regrettably, he was an uncle she had never met before, but that was the story of her quiet life, she supposed. She knew very few people, cloistered away as she was in her father's secluded country house, built of old stone and cloaked in thick, leafy ivy, which hindered even the company of the sunlight.

The only thing that kept her from going completely mad in her isolation was the fact that she was seventeen now, and her first London Season was drawing near—next year perhaps? If she closed her eyes she could see the glitter and the gowns she read about in books, the sparkling jewels and hair combs; she could anticipate the balls and stimulating conversations. She longed for it, all of it, everything she had been missing in her father's somber home for as long as she could remember.

Oh, she prayed he would let her go next year. Surely he would say yes. It was not as if he relished her presence at home. They were hardly close. And her aunt had offered at least a dozen times to be the one to introduce her to society. . .

She was just beginning to imagine herself curtseying to a handsome duke, when suddenly, the coach swerved, and her belly lurched with panic. She sat forward, gripping the windowsill, then heard a heavy *thump*.

"Father, wake up," she said, sweeping her idle daydreams aside.

He stirred groggily, sat up and looked around, as if he weren't quite sure where he was. "What is it?"

"Did you hear that noise?" she asked. "The coach swerved, and there was a thump."

They were rolling along quite smoothly now, however, and her father sat back, unalarmed but annoyed with the interruption. "For pity's sake, Rebecca. One of the bags probably tipped over on the roof." He folded his arms and closed his eyes again.

She touched her forehead to the cool windowpane and tried to peer down at the ground passing beneath them, wondering if one of the bags might have fallen off when they'd swerved. Then slowly, the coach began to decrease speed, slower and slower until they were traveling at a snail's pace, then they stopped, and the horses whinnied and jangled the harness.

Her father opened his eyes and sat forward again. "Have we arrived?"

Rebecca was still peering out the window. "No, Father. We're surrounded by sycamores."

He frowned and leaned closer to the window on his own side. "Why the blazes are we stopped here? We're in the middle of nowhere."

"I think you were right. We might have lost a bag."

Growing impatient, he reached for his walking stick and folded his gnarled, rheumatic fingers over the ivory knob, waiting for the driver to appear at the door and inform them of the problem.

But there was not even the sound of movement from outside the coach.

"Maybe he's already gone back along the road to retrieve it," Rebecca said.

"Well, he could have told us, instead of leaving us sitting here like a couple of ducks, wondering what the devil is going on."

Rebecca peered out the window again, glanced up at the sky under the mist-shrouded canopy of leaves, and took note of the fading light. "I hope he is quick about it," she said, "or he won't be able to find it—or us—in the dark."

They continued to sit and wait in silence for something to happen, but nothing did. Rebecca watched the mist blow past the window, and felt rather uneasy. "May I get out to see what's going on?" she asked.

Her father grunted his displeasure and reached for the door handle on his own side, while she wrapped her shawl around her shoulders and did the same. The step had not been lowered, so she hopped the distance to the ground. She landed with a thud and turned to lower the step.

As she did so, a chill enveloped her and seeped like icy water through the sleeves of her black serge gown. She looked around. The forest was as silent and still as the grave, except for the mist drifting between the trees. She could smell dampness and moss and tree bark, but heard nothing. No wind, no birds, nothing.

She shivered, then one of the horses whinnied and shook the harness again. Turning and gathering her shawl more tightly around her shoulders, she looked up. The coachman's seat was empty. It was as if he had simply vanished.

Was this a haunted forest? she wondered ridiculously. Was there a troll who plucked coachmen from their seats and feasted on their tasty bones?

Her father came around the back of the coach and stopped to stare down the road they'd already traveled. "I'll have his hide."

Rebecca sighed, wishing her father's nap had not been interrupted. Now he would be irritable the rest of the day, and she would be the one to bear the brunt of it inside the coach.

"*Smith*!" he shouted, his voice swallowed instantly by the thick chill in the forest. "*Did we lose something?*"

No reply. Not even an echo.

Rebecca moved closer to him. "Should we go and look for him?"

Her father leaned his frail form upon his cane, but before he could answer, a noise from somewhere ahead caused them both to turn. It was the heavy, thunderous rumble of hoofbeats.

Rebecca's heart began to tremble. Someone was coming.

With her imagination getting the better of her in these eerie, deserted woods—*were they about to have their cold bones feasted upon, too?*—she slipped her arm around her father's as her heart continued to clatter in her chest.

A second later, an enormous black horse and rider emerged from around the bend, galloping toward them, hooves pounding hard and fast upon the ground. The man, like a dark phantom in the mist, was as dark and mesmerizing as the horse, broad-shouldered and cloaked in a black overcoat, a top hat perched at a rakish angle upon his head.

The instant he spotted the coach and team blocking the road, he pulled his great steed to a skidding halt. The horse reared up in protest, its hooves clawing at the air, its enormous muscles straining and flexing while it let out a sharp, angry whinny. The man shouted and fought to regain control, while the beast reared up a second time and turned on its hind legs in a complete circle.

"*Whoa!*"

His voice was deep and commanding, arresting Rebecca on the spot. For a brief second, she feared the man would be thrown to the ground, but he held firm, soon bringing the wild creature under control.

"*Easy now, Asher!*" he commanded. "*Easy . . .*"

While the animal huffed and stomped around on heavy hooves, Rebecca noted the luxurious quality of the man's overcoat. The collar and lapels were lined in chocolate-brown fur, all the way to the hem.

He sat back in the saddle and turned his striking gaze to Rebecca and her father. His eyes were pale blue like the dawn sky, penetrating like an arrow pointed directly at one's heart. His lips were full, his nose straight and aristocratic. It was a magnificent face with strong lines and sweeping splendor, and Rebecca was both captivated by his beauty and intimidated by his authoritative presence, high upon the massive horse.

"What's happened here?" he asked impatiently, glancing at the empty driver's seat, then back at Rebecca and her father, who were, she suddenly realized, staring up at him as if they had just encountered Lucifer himself.

The stranger urged his horse forward along the side of the road, approaching even closer until he was directly in front of them.

They backed up, and her father spoke harshly. "Get in the coach, Rebecca."

"But . . ."

"Do as I say, gel."

She supposed he was wise to be cautious. They knew nothing about this man or his intentions, so she dutifully stepped back into the coach, boldly meeting the stranger's gaze as she climbed inside.

She perched herself on the edge of the seat, leaning forward where she could at least peer out the open door and witness the conversation. But because the man's horse was adjacent to the door, she could see him only from the chest down. The top of the door was blocking his head and shoulders.

Consequently, knowing that he couldn't see her either, she let her gaze wander down the length of his muscular leg. She felt a strange, quivering curiosity in her belly as her eyes traveled over his thick thigh and strong knee, then down to the toe of his expensive black riding boot, polished to a flawless sheen. Even the stirrups were gleaming.

"Do you require assistance?" he asked her father.

Assistance . . . That at least sounded promising.

Her father leaned upon his cane. "No, we are quite all right, thank you."

"But father . . ." she protested, inching forward on the seat.

He gave her a stern look, which told her to keep quiet.

The stranger bent forward over the horse's well-groomed mane to peer inside at her. Her heart began to race again as she noted for the second time the striking color of his blue eyes, which seemed to see straight through her. She felt naked and exposed, and her blood seemed to burn with a dark, almost frightening excitement.

Heaven help her, she had never in her life encountered such a striking man. He took her breath away. She could not move.

Then suddenly, a crazed black raven swooped down from the trees, screeching and flapping its wings in front of the horses. The coach jerked under her, and she was thrown back against the seat, smacking her head against the leather upholstery. The horses took off like a shot, and before she knew what was afoot, the trees outside were whizzing by the open door in a dizzying blur.

Sheer fright blazed through her, and she clutched at the side of the coach, which continued to gain speed and bounced out of control over the bumps in the road.

"Stop!" she shouted, knowing it would do no good.

The coach swerved around a sharp bend in the road, and she was tossed to the side. She hit her head again, winced and shut her eyes at the pain, and when she opened them, she found herself gazing out the door at another blur of movement.

Something passed her by—a flash of black. It was the man on the horse, galloping even faster than the out-of-control coach. The heavy hooves thundered over the ground as he disappeared in front, and she heard the sound of his deep voice shouting, *"Hold up! Steady now!"*

The horses whinnied, the coach rocked and swayed, then the noise and commotion died away as they pulled to a gradual halt.

Overcome with panic, she scrambled across the seat to the open door, looked out at the gentleman who was still on his horse up front holding onto the harness, and said, "Thank you, sir!"

She threw a foot out to climb down.

"But, miss," he quickly replied, glancing over his shoulder. "Please don't—"

She didn't even have a chance to comprehend the warning before—*kersplash!*—she was hip-deep in a cold bog, her breath coming short from the shock of the chill.

"*Oh, bollocks!*" she cried, as the cold water seeped into her drawers and numbed her skin. "This is freezing!" She flapped her hands through the air, flicking glistening droplets of water in all directions.

The man quickly brought his horse around. "Give me your hand."

The plain words and firm voice of command moved her to action, and she reached out. Without delay he pulled her up out of the water, which was no easy task with her skirts dripping and heavy as a dead elephant. He set her sideways in front of him, then smoothly walked his horse out of the bog.

As soon as they were on dry ground, he dismounted, and she found herself looking down at those mesmerizing blue eyes again while he reached his arms up to her.

"Down you come, darling," he said. "Just slide yourself into my arms."

Darling.

Dear Lord . . . A runaway coach and a darkly handsome man who wanted her to slide into his arms. This was more than any socially sheltered seventeen-year-old could take. It was the stuff of fantasies and fairy tales.

Flustered and befuddled, she placed her hands on his broad shoulders and felt the soft fur of his wide lapels through her wet gloves as she slid down from the saddle into his solid male frame. She had never touched a man like this before, had never been so close.

He began to lower her down, and the whole front of her body pressed tightly against his firm chest. Her heart was pounding so fast it was making her lightheaded, and she wasn't sure if it was the lingering terror from being whisked away inside a runaway coach, or if it was the fact that she was being held by this man—this dangerous, exciting stranger with shoulders as broad and solid as an oak, and eyes that made her shiver inwardly with a strange curiosity she couldn't even begin to understand. She had never experienced anything as exciting as this. It felt wild and wicked and shamefully titillating.

When her toes finally touched the ground, neither she, nor he, made a move to step apart. He continued to hold her steady, his huge hands gripping her corseted waist while he looked down at her.

"Are you all right?" he asked.

She nodded. "I think so."

"Well, that's a relief," he replied, the corner of his mouth turning up in a sweltering grin that turned her brain to clotted cream. "For a minute there, I thought you were done for."

Despite the overwhelming shock of what had just occurred, and the fact that she was freezing cold from the waist down and *still* being held in his arms, she found herself letting out a nervous little chuckle.

His blue eyes warmed at her response, and he stepped back, appearing comfortable with the fact that she was indeed all right and would be able to stand on her own two feet without swooning.

But it was only early yet, she supposed. There was still plenty of time for swooning.

"Are you sure you're not hurt?"

This time, she actually thought about it, and felt a pain at the back of her head. She reached up to touch the sore spot. "I was knocked around a bit, I'm afraid."

"Let me see." He was a full twelve inches taller than she, so it was nothing for him to lean over her and examine the back of her head. His fingers slid into the loose knots of her thick, red hair and gently massaged her scalp, searching . . . touching . . . Then he stroked downward to the back of her neck and massaged the sensitive tendons there.

Every nerve in her body quivered and pulsed with a thrilling awareness and a hot jolt of pleasure. She drew in a slow, languid breath and held onto it.

"I believe you'll live," he said, lowering his hands to his sides and stepping back again. "But you'll have a bump or two."

"A bump," she replied, before she let out that long held breath and marveled at the indulgent wish to be pressed up against his hard body again and feel that strange, amorous pleasure inside her.

"Yes, a bump," he said. "Any other injuries?"

Still recovering from the exquisite heat of his touch, she considered it. "My elbow, I think."

He grinned wickedly at her, as if he were catching her at some kind of game. But she really had whacked it against the side of the coach when they'd taken off, and wanted only for him to touch it and rub it and stroke it with those magical hands of his. Oh, and of course make sure it was sound.

"Let me see that, too," he said.

His voice was heavy and smooth as velvet, and it sent luscious gooseflesh tingling down the side of her body. He reached for her arm and felt around the bones. "Does this hurt?"

"No."

"This?"

"No."

"What about this?" He massaged the muscle just above her elbow.

She hardly recognized the deep, sultry sound of her voice in response. "That feels quite nice actually."

His head was bowed down, but his eyes lifted knowingly. A dark brow lifted, and he grinned again. "Yes, it does feel quite nice."

He continued to work his hand over her elbow while his horse stood by in the quiet forest, discreetly tasting the grass and flicking his ears at insects. Rebecca's body grew warm and pleasantly weak from the gentleman's touch.

"Do you suppose this is proper?" he asked, lifting his eyes again with that same seductive expression. "We haven't been introduced, you know, and we are very much alone."

She wet her lips and pondered the fact that they were indeed alone in the forest and he was touching her intimately, and she had no idea where her father was. Anything could happen. He could seduce her. He could sweep her off her feet and into his arms, carry her to the coach and toss her down upon the soft, leather upholstery, kiss her neck and hands, overwhelm her with terrifying passions she'd never known, and *ravish* her without mercy. . . .

She swallowed hard.

"You are correct, sir. We have not been introduced, so I suppose it is not proper at all. I confess—you have me quite unsettled."

"I don't mean to unsettle you." He was quiet

while he tested her upper arm. "Please allow me to give you this reassurance—there is nothing to fear. I only wish to be certain you are not hurt."

But despite his assurances, there was still something so incredibly erotic about the way he spoke to her and touched her, and the way it made her feel hot and lazy inside.

"I do appreciate your concern."

He continued to massage down the length of her arm all the way to her wrist. "You're very lovely. Has anyone ever told you that?"

"No."

"No?" He sounded surprised, then his gaze narrowed. "How old are you?"

"I am seventeen, sir."

His hand went still upon her arm, then he gently lowered it, setting it away from him with a sigh. "Much too young for an elbow examination, I'm afraid."

"How old are *you*?" she asked, quite unable to restrain her curiosity.

"That's a bold question for a well-bred young lady like yourself."

"It's the same question you asked me," she argued.

"Yes, but I'm not a well-bred young lady."

She let her eyes sweep over the broad width of his chest and the visible power in his shoulders. "No, you certainly are not."

They stood gazing at each other for a moment

until he looked across the green bog, those powerful shoulders heaving with another sigh. "I suppose I must turn your coach around and return you safely to your father. He is no doubt concerned."

"Yes, I am sure he is." She realized with some chagrin that while this extraordinary man had been touching her, she had forgotten about her father completely. "I am fine now."

But her teeth had begun to chatter.

Without the slightest bidding from her, he removed his heavy, fur-trimmed greatcoat and slung it around her shoulders. "This will keep you warm."

She felt the heat from his body inside it and smelled the enthralling fragrance of his cologne. "Thank you," she said. "And thank you also for coming to my rescue."

He touched the brim of his elegant top hat before he swung himself up onto his horse again. "I assure you, it was nothing at all."

Oh, no, nothing at all, to come galloping after a runaway coach and pull a distraught young lady out of a bog, then make her forget all about the pain in her head and elbow and the fact that her skirts were dripping wet with that cold, sticky slime.

He clicked his tongue, walked his horse back into the water, and took hold of the harness. "Onward, now," he said.

While he led the team in a wide circle and back up onto the grass, Rebecca admired his form without the coat. Wearing a fine black dinner jacket and crisp white shirt with a dark, crimson necktie, he was even more perfect than she could have imagined, for there was an incredible strength and vigor in his shoulders and in the defined lines of his torso and hips.

As soon as the wheels were on dry land, he rode closer and dismounted again. "Allow me to assist you."

She glanced uneasily at the coach. "The horses won't bolt again?"

"Not while I am leading them."

He certainly knew how to instill confidence.

"Then I must thank you." She took his hand and stepped back inside.

She settled into the seat and covered herself with his coat to keep warm. He closed the door with a firm click, but opened it again a mere second later and said, "I am twenty-four."

She stared numbly at him as he smiled. He closed the door again.

A moment later, they started back along the road to where her father was surely waiting in a tizzy.

She shook her head when she thought about that. Her father's tizzy. Surely it could be nothing compared to hers, for it could never have been so frightfully wicked, yet so wonderfully breathtaking at the same time.

Chapter 2

"Thank the Lord!" her father said, looking her up and down from head to foot as she stepped out of the coach. "What happened? You're all wet!"

"I am fine, Father," she replied.

"The horses turned off the road and into a bog," the gentleman explained as he dismounted from his own horse. He removed his gloves and strode toward them, glancing briefly at her father's misshapen hand upon his cane. "May I enquire about your driver, sir? Where is he?"

"I am afraid I do not know. We thought he might have stopped to retrieve a bag that fell from the coach before you came along."

"Did he not tell you of his intentions?"

"No."

Tapping his fine leather gloves against his palm, her handsome rescuer looked up at the baggage tied down on the roof. "Everything appears to be secure, even after what just occurred." He turned to look in the direction from which they had come. "Wait here, please. I'll be back shortly."

He started walking.

"Well, at least you're all right," her father said, glancing briefly at her. "This gentleman, was he . . . Was he helpful?"

"Very helpful, yes," she replied, sensing her father's concern and doing her best to alleviate it with a show of indifference. She could not possibly tell him what *really* occurred, not to mention how much she'd enjoyed it. "I'm fine, Father."

A few minutes later, they heard footsteps returning, and curiosity compelled Rebecca to start walking toward the sound.

"Where are you going, child?" her father snapped. "Stay here beside me, if you please."

She stopped in the center of the narrow road, but remained exactly where she was with her back to her father, anxious to see her magnificent hero returning. At last he appeared, carrying Mr. Smith over his shoulder like a heavy sack of potatoes.

"What in the world happened?" she asked.

He continued walking toward her, but addressed her father, not her. "I regret to inform you, sir, it was not a piece of baggage that fell from your coach. Your driver has had too much to drink and tumbled over the side."

"How can you be sure?" Rebecca asked, following them back to the coach. "What if he is ill?"

He carried Mr. Smith around to the front of the coach and managed with a grunt to tip him over the driver's seat rail. The unconscious man fell backward across the cushioned bench, his arm falling limp and resting on the footboard. He snorted and groaned.

"I found the empty bottle a few feet away from him," her gentleman-hero explained as he wiped at his hands. "And he smells like a distillery."

Rebecca's father limped around the coach and stood beside her, leaning on his cane. "He is no good to us in the driver's seat. What the devil are we to do now?"

"May I ask your destination?"

"The Cotswolds Arms for tonight, then we're on to Burford in the morning."

The man turned and strode toward his horse. "You can expect to be there in an hour."

Her father limped after him. "But wait, sir! How are we to get there?"

Rebecca followed as well. After everything her handsome rescuer had done for them so far, was he going to abandon them now? Surely not.

"I beg your pardon, sir," she said, "but my father cannot drive. His hands cause him great pain."

The man had already reached his horse and was now leading the animal past them, toward the back of the coach. "I understand that," he said, "and it would be my pleasure to drive you."

Rebecca exhaled with relief, then marveled at the strangeness of this day and the miracle of how this extraordinary man seemed to have everything decided before she or her father even realized there was an issue to work out. And her head was still spinning from the wild carriage ride and the most unnerving memory of his touch. She would never forget it, not as long as she lived.

"That is most kind of you, sir," her father said, while the gentleman tethered his horse to the handrail above the page board. "But we don't wish to inconvenience you. Are you certain it is no bother?"

The gentleman stroked the horse's muscular neck, then his expression warmed as he bowed slightly at the waist. "As I said, it would be my pleasure. It's a perfect night for a drive."

She could sense her father's reluctance to accept the offer, as he did not enjoy being beholden to anyone for anything. God forbid that particular person might pay a visit to their isolated house in the country to provide him the opportunity to return the kindness. But under the present circumstances, they did not have much choice unless he would allow Rebecca to drive, and that was most certainly not going to happen.

Her father straightened his thin shoulders and finally resigned himself to the necessity of accepting the offer. "You are most kind," he said to the gentleman. "Allow me to introduce myself. I am Charles Newland, Earl of Creighton, and this is my daughter, Lady Rebecca Newland."

Introductions at last.

The gentleman held out his hand to shake her father's. "It is an honor to meet you, Lord Creighton, and a pleasure, Lady Rebecca." He bowed to her, revealing nothing of what had occurred between them earlier. Not a hint of a grin, wicked or otherwise. No mention of the way his hands had worked over her arms and down her neck.

"I am Devon Sinclair, Marquess of Hawthorne," he said. "My father is the Duke of Pembroke."

"Of Pembroke Palace," her father blurted out.

"That is correct."

Good Lord, they were in illustrious company indeed, and they were about to employ a marquess, the future Duke of Pembroke, as their coachman.

"The palace is not far from here," he said. "Just under an hour's ride to the north."

This was his father's property, all of it, miles and miles of prosperous farmland and thick, lush forests. And *he* was the Marquess of Hawthorne, and heir to one of the oldest, most prestigious titles in England. Rebecca could barely comprehend it. A thrill rolled up her spine, as thick and compelling as the mist all around them.

"But what about our driver?" her father asked. "I'm half tempted to leave him here."

"Father . . ." Rebecca admonished, glancing down at the ground as her cheeks flushed with embarrassment.

Lord Hawthorne smiled. She was so glad she finally knew what to call him.

"I might be tempted toward the same end myself," he said, "if he were my driver. But have no worries. I'll prop him up beside me, and he'll keep me company when the moon rises." Lord Hawthorne glanced up at the darkening sky. "Which will be very soon, so if you don't mind, I must insist we move on. Allow me?"

He opened the door to the coach and lowered the step, then straightened and held out his hand to Rebecca. A rush of butterflies invaded her belly at the thrilling notion of touching him again, and when she slowly wrapped her tiny, gloved fingers around his larger ones, she felt the strength of his whole arm and the rock-solid support he offered, which she already knew firsthand. She gathered her heavy wet skirts in her other hand, then met his gaze for a brief, fleeting second. His blue eyes were dazzling, captivating, disarming, and the whole world came to a shuddering halt on its axis.

She wet her lips and managed to say, "Thank you," in a quiet, ladylike voice. He bowed his head and handed her up.

Her heart was still racing when she sat down on the leather seat and watched the ducal heir assist her father up as well, holding him by the arm to steady his frail form.

How strong and capable he was, like a brave knight from a childhood story. None of this seemed real.

As soon as her father was seated, Lord Hawthorne raised the step, but Rebecca spoke up. "Your coat . . ."

He held up a hand. "I insist you take care of it for me until we arrive." Then he addressed both of them from the open door. "We shall reach the Cotswolds Arms in one hour, so settle in. I will see you when we get there."

He closed the door, and the coach bounced slightly under his weight as he climbed up onto the driver's seat outside. Rebecca and her father sat in silence, waiting while Lord Hawthorne lit the lamps, then the coach lurched forward. The harness jangled, and they began to roll on. They turned around in a clearing, back in the proper direction.

"I suppose we were lucky that young man came along when he did," her father said uncomfortably, folding both his hands upon his cane.

"He was very helpful." Rebecca took a deep breath and tried to settle in for the remainder of the journey, but it was not easy to relax when such a handsome, heroic man was sitting just outside, leading them out of the dense forest to their destination, after having saved her life and stirred her passions so unexpectedly. Her whole body was buzzing with delight under his warm, heavy, fur-trimmed coat, and it was a challenge just to sit still.

What a night, and, Lord, what a man. She couldn't wait to arrive at the inn just for the chance to be in his presence again, one more time, however briefly, before they said goodbye.

The coach came to a smooth halt outside the inn, and Rebecca heard voices in the dark outside. Within seconds the door opened and Lord Hawthorne was standing there in his black dinner jacket and elegant hat—more handsome than he was an hour before if that was possible—reaching a hand in to Rebecca.

"Here at last," he said, with more charm and appeal than any man had a right to possess.

"Yes, at last. Thank you." She accepted his hand, but before she could step out, he glanced down.

"Ah, forgive me, Lady Rebecca. I am remiss in my duties already. What a terrible footman I would make. I must lower the step." He let go of her hand and did just that, then straightened and met her gaze again with those enticing eyes.

He handed her down, then assisted her father as well. Pointing at a groom who was setting a bucket of water down in front of his horse still tethered to the rear, he said, "I've already spoken to Mr. Griffin here, an excellent young man, and he will take care of your horses. He will see to Mr. Smith as well, who will be escorted into the stable for the night."

"Will he be all right?" Rebecca asked.

Lord Hawthorne looked at her with pointed intensity, and she felt a sudden wave of dread, for the end was near. She would be forced to say goodbye to him, and who knew when she would ever see him again? *If* she would ever see him again.

"He will be fine," he replied. "He was mumbling quite lucidly the whole way here."

Her father shifted his cane from one hand to the other. "I cannot thank you enough, Lord Hawthorne. You have been most helpful. I don't know how I can ever make it up to you."

"Just see your lovely daughter home safely, sir."

Rebecca sighed with a strange mixture of joy and sadness. If only Lord Hawthorne knew this was the most exciting thing that had ever happened to her, and that she thought him the most captivating, attractive man in the world. If only he knew that she was wishing this moment did not have to end, and that she would not have to return to her secluded home and her impossibly quiet life with her reclusive father.

"At least join us for dinner here at the inn," her father said.

Yes, please!

"Or a drink at least," he added.

It was not like her father to wish to dine with a guest, for he was not a sociable man, which proved it. Lord Hawthorne *did* have more charm than was humanly possible, if he was able to turn her father into a convivial person.

"I appreciate the offer," Lord Hawthorne replied. "But I am afraid I must decline. I have a previous engagement."

Her shoulders heaved with disappointment. She wondered where he'd been going before he'd come upon them.

"I see," her father replied. "I hope we have not imposed."

"Not at all."

"Then let me extend an open invitation to you," her father added. "If you are ever near Burford, you must come to Creighton Manor for dinner. It would be a great honor to welcome you."

And that, quite frankly, was a miracle, and the best thing she'd ever heard her father say.

"Thank you, Lord Creighton," he replied. "Likewise, I shall see that you are invited to Pembroke Palace." He bowed to Rebecca. "It was an honor making your acquaintance, both of you. Have a safe trip home and enjoy your stay at the inn." He went to fetch his horse.

Rebecca continued to watch him, wishing she could know him better, and wondering about all the tiny details of his life. What did he like to do when he was not rescuing young maidens in the forest? Did he hunt? Did he enjoy politics? Dinner parties? Was he always this charming?

And had he found a bride yet?

She knew what her father would say to such a silly, romantic notion. *You're only seventeen—too young to be thinking of marriage.*

But she would not be seventeen forever.

They stood outside the inn while Lord Hawthorne mounted his horse. He turned the great animal around, then touched the brim of his hat. "Safe journey."

"Same to you," her father replied.

He kicked his boot heels and said, "Onward, Asher," then trotted down the hill in the moonlight. Rebecca watched him the whole way until the hoofbeats faded to silence and their brief encounter found a private, profound place in her memory.

She sighed when she considered how this night compared to the empty stillness of her existence back home, but supposed her life would not be so empty now. Not after what had just occurred, because she would have this to dream about and give her hope for the future. Yes, Lord Hawthorne would figure prominently in her dreams for a long time to come.

And soon she would be entering society as a

lady—the very next Season if her father permitted it—and it was entirely possible she would encounter Lord Hawthorne again in different circumstances. As a woman.

She quivered with excitement when she imagined it, and surrendered to the fact that she would spend the next year of her life fantasizing about that moment.

Chapter 3

Four Years Later
April, 1874

On the day Devon Sinclair, Marquess of Hawthorne, returned to Pembroke Palace after a three-year journey abroad, it was raining. In fact, it had been raining in every corner of England for six days straight. Bridges and roads had been washed away, rivers were rising, and the farmers were indoors—the idea of spring planting nothing more than a hazy dream in their heads until the weather passed.

Devon's coach was barely making it up the hill on the steep approach to the palace, for the road was slick with mud and the horses could not gain a proper footing. His driver was shouting and snapping his whip at them, and the sensation of the carriage wheels slipping and sliding put Devon on edge more than he cared to admit.

He gripped the side of the coach and looked out

the window. The rain fell harder still. The clouds hung low over the hilltops, thick and heavy, like a pillow coming down upon one's head. He ran a hand over the top of his thigh to his knee and squeezed at the deep, aching sensation of that old wound he preferred to forget, but it was impossible to ignore the pain on a damp day like this.

Springtime in England. How he loathed it. If it weren't for his mother's fiftieth birthday celebration and her flood of letters over the past six months imploring him to come home for the grand masquerade ball, he would still be in America, enjoying his freedom and his comfortable, homeless wandering.

He breathed deeply, closed his eyes for a moment, and cupped his forehead in his hand. He recalled the last letter she had sent, where she had tried so hard to sound cheerful. He knew, however, that there was a great deal she was not telling him about what was going on at home. He had recognized her anxiety in the white spaces between the lines.

Then again, perhaps it was simply the fact that she was coming to the end of another decade of her life and was feeling the weight of her regrets over how her life had unfolded. Or perhaps at this stage in her life, she was bidding farewell to impossible dreams.

He opened his eyes and looked again through

the glass, streaked with water and splattered with mud. He desired his mother's happiness, just as he desired Charlotte's, his sister, who had written him dozens of letters as well over the past three years, keeping him informed of her joys and tragedies, always asking when he would return, never mentioning why he had left. She was twenty-three now, and her life, like their mother's, had not unfolded as she'd believed it would.

But life was never predictable. He had learned that before he'd left.

And of course, there was Blake, the brother he was closest to—taking care of everything, as always, amidst everyone's hard luck at home.

As for Vincent and his father. . .

Devon had not received any letters from either of them, though he had never expected it. Frankly, he would be surprised if they were even home today to welcome him back. Vincent especially.

The coach reached the crest of the hill, and the wheels finally gripped the road and picked up speed. Devon drew in a deep breath, then let it out and leaned closer to the window.

There it was. He could make it out in the distance, even through the wash of rainwater down the grimy glass windowpane, obscuring his view. His home—that imposing, stately palace, materializing in the mist like an enormous dragon with wings spread wide across the land.

Despite the tension he felt in anticipation of seeing Vincent and his father again, he could not deny a sense of awe at the extraordinary grandeur, which was his birthright. Everything seemed breathtaking—the towers and turrets, the thirty-foot stone finials topping the central rooftop like coronets, and the triumphal arch at the entrance gate leading into the massive cobbled court. It was built to extravagant excess on the ruins of an ancient abbey, high upon a hilltop overlooking lush, green parkland studded with aging oaks. Altogether, it was a noble citadel and monument to the great glory of England, dominating the English countryside like a mighty sovereign.

He felt with surprise an unexpected surge of pride and sentimentality suddenly, remembering that this was his childhood home, and there was a time he'd been happy here, when he was younger, when things had been different.

Perhaps his mother had been right to press so hard to bring him home. Perhaps it was time to put the past behind him and mend what had been shattered and broken. If it could be mended. He was not sure that it could.

The coach drove across the cobbled court and pulled to a halt at the front entrance. A liveried footman came dashing down the wet steps carrying an umbrella, his buckled shoes splashing through puddles. He opened the door of the coach and lowered the step, then held the umbrella up for Devon, who emerged at last from the dark confines.

He would have liked to take a moment to gaze up at the enormous portico above the grand entrance and the sculptures on the clock tower, but the rain was coming down too hard, pounding on the ground and hissing like a beast while the wind gusted and threatened to pull the umbrella inside out.

"Welcome back, my lord!" the footman shouted into his ear.

What was it about the rain that made people think they needed to shout? "Thank you. It's good to be back."

It was partly true, at least.

He started up the stairs with the footman at his side holding the umbrella for him, but as soon as they passed through the open door and entered the grand hall, the servant was gone, and Devon's mother, the duchess, was striding toward him with a smile.

He stopped. She was as beautiful as ever with her golden hair swept into an elegant twist, her form-fitting gown the color of a ripe peach, the long, trained overskirt caught up at the sides and draped with pleats in the front. She was almost fifty, but possessed the slender, attractive figure of a woman half her age, and an ivory complexion few women could rival.

She crossed the hall to him. "Oh, my dear, you are home at last." She rushed to him and took his hands in hers. Her eyes sparkled. She seemed too excited to breathe.

Devon bent forward and kissed her on the cheek. "How wonderful to see you, Mother," he said. "You look exquisite. More lovely than ever, if that is possible."

She raised a mischievous eyebrow at him. "I see my son has not lost his charm. I'll wager those American girls were very sorry to see you board that ship back to England." He shook his head, and she slapped him playfully on the arm. "Don't be modest, Devon. You know I'm right. Oh, I thought this day would never come."

Another set of heels came clicking across the marble floor. It was his half sister, Charlotte. "Devon!" His mother had to step back to clear the way as she dashed straight into his arms. "At last! You're here!"

"Yes, Charlotte," he replied. He was pleased the past year with all its painful emotional heartbreak over her fiancé had not broken her spirit as well. She was still as boisterous as ever. He held her away from him. "Let me get a look at you." Charlotte was golden-haired like their mother, and equally as lovely with deep blue eyes, long lashes, and a flawless complexion. "What a beauty you have become."

She smiled. "And you are still the same handsome heartbreaker you were before you left. I must admit, however, I am surprised you did not come home with a rich American wife."

A wife? Him?

"It's been in all the papers lately," she explained, "about Lord Randolph Churchill marrying the Jerome girl from New York just last week. Did you hear about it?"

"Of course. The New York papers printed every detail of the engagement."

"They say she's very beautiful."

"I am sure she is, and I hope some day to meet her." He reached into his pocket and pulled out a small velvet bag. "My only wish at the moment, however, is to see you, my dear sister, wearing the gift I brought you."

"Oh, Devon." She reached for the bag. "What is it?"

"Open it and find out."

She slid her fingers into the drawstring opening, withdrew a pearl bracelet, and held it up to the light. "It's stunning. Help me put it on?" She handed it to him, and he wrapped it around her slender wrist, then fastened the silver clasp. "It's perfect."

"I have something for you, too, Mother," he said, "but it's wrapped up in one of my trunks."

"You didn't have to, Devon. Your presence here in the house again was the only gift I wanted."

He noted a slight melancholy in her voice, a weariness in her eyes, and recalled a similar look on her face the day he had left, when the family had seemed to split apart at the seams with heartbreak and hostility.

"Is Vincent here?" he carefully asked.

She lowered her eyes and shook her head. "No. He is still in London. I'm very sorry."

He watched her for a moment. "No need to apologize, Mother. I didn't expect him to be here."

Blake's voice sounded from the saloon. "Devon, you're back!"

He felt a swell of pleasure at the sound, then strode forward to shake his brother's hand, noting that the young man he had left behind three years ago had matured. At twenty-six, his looks had not changed much—he was still tall and dark and broad-shouldered—but something in the way he carried himself was different. He had always been a calming influence in the family, but now, he seemed to know it. He appeared relaxed and confident, and Devon felt certain that whatever problems had arisen while he was gone, they had been kept well in hand.

"Good God, man," Blake said, pumping his hand firmly and squeezing his elbow. "You've been in the sun. You look like a pirate."

Devon laughed. "I spent every possible minute

up on deck during the crossing, which I am sure you would have done, too, had you been there. This rain. . . ." He turned to direct his comment at Charlotte and their mother. "Will it ever stop?"

"We are all wondering the same thing," Blake replied, then his voice took on a twinge of resignation. "But the weather is a taboo subject around here. Isn't that right, Mother?"

She nodded. "Yes, it is."

Devon narrowed his gaze, looking at each of them in turn.

He faced his brother again. "You have all worked very hard to drag me home from America, and I can see you are itching to tell me something. Accompany me to the library, if you will, Blake. You know how I hate being kept in the dark."

Blake's face clouded over with uneasiness. He took a deep breath and let it out. "Indeed, there is much to discuss, and there is no point putting it off. The library it is, then. Is it too early in the day for a brandy?"

"Not by my watch," Devon replied. "Judging by the look of dread on your face, something tells me I'm going to need it."

"So here it is in a nutshell," Blake said, his voice somber as he handed a glass to Devon. "It's Father. I am sorry to be the one to tell you this, but he appears to be . . . Well, there is no polite way to put it. We all believe he is . . ." He paused a moment and took a drink. "Father is going mad."

Devon accepted the glass without looking at it, because it was all he could do to keep his eyes steady on his brother. "Mad, you say."

"Yes, mad. Rattled in the brain, nutty as a fruitcake, cuckoo, loony, out of his tree . . ."

Devon held up a hand. "I get the picture, Blake. Has the physician been summoned?"

"Yes, a few times over the past few months, but he assures us Father is in perfect health."

"But you believe otherwise," Devon said, watching his brother carefully as he sipped his brandy. "Did you tell this to the doctor?"

"Of course. Mother and I both have, but whenever he comes to perform an examination, Father is perfectly lucid and explains everything quite sensibly, so the doctor thinks we are overreacting, and that we simply do not understand his eccentric disposition." Blake strode across the room to the desk in front of the window and leaned back upon it. "Dr. Lambert's a bloody brownnoser if you ask me. He's been the family physican for thirty years and he expects something from Father in the will, no doubt. He doesn't want to cross him." His voice grew resigned. "Father is sixty-nine now, Devon. He is not going to live forever."

Devon gazed down at the brandy in his glass. "I

am aware." He took a slow sip. Outside the window, the rain came down harder, driving against the panes. "But tell me of his behavior. What evidence do you have to support your suspicions?"

Blake's dark brows lifted—as if he had a whole list of examples, but didn't know where to begin.

"About six months ago, he began to have trouble sleeping. Now, every night, he gets up and wanders the dark corridors for hours in his nightshirt and slippers. He often talks to himself and speaks about our ancestors and what he knows about their lives."

Devon went to the sofa and sat down. For a long moment, he considered what his brother was describing to him.

"I admit," he said, "that this is disturbing to hear, but perhaps the doctor has a point. You said yourself that Father is sixty-nine now. This sounds to me like nothing more than the eccentricities of old age. He is simply reminiscing about the past. Perhaps that is why the doctor is not overly concerned."

His brother took another sip of brandy. He looked tired all of a sudden and shook his head.

"You seem disappointed," Devon said, as a small twinge of displeasure nipped at his mood. "Were you expecting that I would come home and simply wave a hand and make the problem disappear?"

When his brother gave no reply, Devon studied

his expression carefully, then leaned back against the sofa cushions. "Or perhaps you are remembering that I am not the hero everyone always imagined me to be."

It was why he had left home in the first place three years ago—because he had disappointed everyone to impossible degrees. Vincent and Father especially.

No . . . *Disappointed* was not a strong enough word. Because of his own youthful passions, he had betrayed Vincent's trust and shattered and crushed his father's grand and lofty opinions of him. He had annihilated the man's unfathomable pride in his eldest son.

Devon remembered every word of their argument as if it happened only yesterday—how his father had told him what a useless failure he was as a son and especially as a man.

Why hadn't he been able to control the horse? he had asked. How could he have been so foolish as to take that slick, muddy path through the woods that time of year? And what had he been doing with MaryAnn in the first place? Had he no sense of honor or decency? She was his brother's fiancée.

Devon had listened to all of this at a time when he was leaning on crutches, when the stitches over his eye still burned, and when the guilt over what had occurred was worse than death itself.

Because MaryAnn—the woman Vincent had loved and intended to marry—was dead.

You are no longer my son, his father had snarled at him from behind the desk.

Their argument had ended there. Devon did not even say goodbye the next morning when he struggled awkwardly into the coach to leave for America. He had never written to his father, nor had he received any letters from him, but he had not expected it, such was the intensity of the man's rage that night.

"We need you," Blake quietly said, interrupting Devon's recollections. "You are the head of the family."

"No," he firmly replied. "Our father, the duke, is head of the family."

"Not if he is mad."

Devon stared uneasily at his brother, then set down his glass. "I am not yet convinced he is mad, Blake, nor will I be until I speak to him myself. As I said, it is probably just old age. There is nothing to be done about that except to be patient and tolerant as best we can until the end comes."

"Until the end comes, you say." Blake chuckled with some bitterness.

"Is there something amusing about that?"

Blake stood and walked to the window. "It is not amusing at all. I only chuckle at the coincidence of your remark. You see, I didn't get to the most distressing part of all this."

"Which is?"

Blake faced him. "Father has spoken of the *end* more than a few times himself over the past month. Come here." He waved Devon over to the window. "Look outside and you'll see what I mean." Devon stood and approached Blake, who pointed at the Italian Gardens. "There he is, out there in the rain."

Indeed, there he was—their father, the exalted Duke of Pembroke, powerful patriarch of this family, on his knees in the muddy garden. Or at least, what was left of it, for all the plants had been dug up, and there was nothing left but deep holes and piles of dirt. He was now digging up one last rose bush with a shovel.

"He's been moving all his favorite flowers to higher ground," Blake explained.

Devon felt his temper rising. "God in heaven, where is the gardener? Why is he not doing it? And why is there no one out there with an umbrella over his head?"

"Father won't let anyone help him," Blake said. "He insists on doing it himself, and just last week, he fired a footman who tried to push the garden cart for him."

"But what is he trying to accomplish?"

"He says he is saving the palace, Devon—his beloved gardens especially—because he believes we are victims of some ancient curse, and that a great flood is coming and we are all going to be swept away."

"A curse!" Devon blurted out. "Bloody hell, Blake, has he lost his mind?"

His brother sank down into the chair behind the desk and took a drink. "Now you're finally getting it."

Devon looked out the window again at his father, who had placed the rosebush in the wheeled cart and was struggling to push it across the muddy terrain.

"But the real reason we are thankful that you have returned," Blake said, "is because he believes you are the only one who can stop the curse."

"Me? *How*, for pity's sake? I'm the one he declared no longer his son."

"We do not know how," Blake replied, "but we are eager to find out, which is why we wanted you to come home. He will want to see you, Devon, the very minute he hears you are back."

Devon looked out the window at his father again. "I am no one's hero, Blake. Nor do I ever wish to be. Ever again."

"I know that. I remember what you went through. But that does not concern him. You'll have your work cut out for you, trying to convince him of it."

It would not be easy, he knew, and he doubted he could make a difference. But something had to be done. His father had to be brought in from the rain at the very least.

Devon set down his glass and strode to the door to get his coat. He paused, however, and turned back to face his brother. "I don't know what will happen out there, Blake, but I will at least bring him inside and, hopefully, I will return with answers."

Chapter 4

Dear Diary,

Heaven help me, I am doomed.

This morning, I woke in my bed in my father's house with the early morning sun shining in on me, and felt again those wicked sensations of need in my body. I fought to resist them, truly I did, but alas, I was weak. I slipped out from between the thin sheets, dressed quickly, and went into the woods again.

It was cool beneath the shelter of the trees, and the deeper I went into the forest, the faster my heart began to race with that wild and decadent excitement that will not release its hold on me. Soon, like all the other times, I did not even care how wicked it was. My skin was tingling with anticipation, and, oh, how I gloried in the cool perspiration that drenched my body! I pulled the pins from my hair and let it fall loose down my *back, then I began to run, shedding all my inhibitions and reservations along the way. All I cared about was the irresistible pleasure I knew he would bestow upon me when I came to him.*

I reached the clearing and he was there, lying naked on the grass, bathing in the sweet warmth of the sun. If only I could describe the overwhelming fire in my blood and the ferocity of my passions! I stood unable to move, blinded by my desire and bewildered by the impossible splendor before me. His smooth skin was gleaming, his long, muscular legs stretched out on the blanket, and that manly part of him I cannot bring myself to put in writing held me captive and burning with fascination. I could barely catch my breath!

Then I could not wait another minute. I removed all my clothes and left them in a careless pile on the grass, then walked naked across the lush, green clearing toward him.

He heard my soft approach and sat up. "Lydie," he said in a deep, husky voice that made my heated body throb. "I knew you'd come."

"I couldn't stay away."

He smiled at me with desire in his eyes. "Come closer."

When I stepped onto the soft, warm blanket, he rose up on his knees and touched his open mouth to my quivering belly, licking and suckling just below my navel until my—

A knock rapped hard at the door, and Rebecca slammed the musty diary shut, then stuffed it under the pillow.

Taking a few seconds to cool her thoughts and subdue her racing heart, she slid off the bed and crossed the small room of the Pembroke Village Inn. She paused briefly at the door, listening. "Who is it?"

"It's Grace," her aunt whispered from the other side.

Exhaling with relief, Rebecca smoothed out the fabric of her dressing gown before she opened the door for her aunt, who was barely visible beneath the flouncy mountain of costumes in her arms.

"I'm glad it's you." Rebecca struggled to distract herself from her wicked reading just now, by stepping forward to peer up and down the narrow corridor. "I panicked for a moment, thinking it might be Father."

She stepped back in.

"He has no idea where we are. We're safe for the time being," Aunt Grace said.

Rebecca looked more closely at her aunt's gown for the ball that evening. "This is beautiful."

Grace was going to the Pembroke Palace Fancy Dress Ball dressed as Mary, Queen of Scots. Before she'd lost her head, of course. "I can't wait to see you in it, Aunt Grace."

"And I cannot wait to see you in your costume. Shall we begin?"

Rebecca stepped aside to invite her aunt into the room, so they could assist each other in preparing for the ball. Neither of them, under the present circumstances, had dared to bring their maids.

Her aunt squeezed her plump figure along with the oversized costume through the door. "I wore this two years ago at the Summervilles' costume ball in London. I do hope none of the guests at Pembroke attended that particular evening, or I shall be quite embarrassed."

"There was hardly time to have new costumes made," Rebecca reminded her, recalling with a shiver how they had fled her home in the night like two thieves making their escape. "I'm sure it will be fine, Aunt Grace."

But would it really be fine? she wondered uneasily as she went to withdraw her own costume from her valise in the large armoire. Her whole life had been turned upside down in the past week with the devastating news that her father intended to marry her off to their neighbor, Mr. Rushton.

Though he was handsome by certain standards and could wield some charm when he wished to, she could never marry him, not in a thousand years, for he was a bully and a tyrant. He slapped his horses in the face when they were not quick enough to obey him, and once, not long ago, when she was out walking, she had seen him kicking his dogs into submission. She had boldly confronted him about it a day later when he paid a call to her father—for what purpose she never knew; they always conversed in private—but he denied doing any such thing and assured her it must have been one of his grooms. With a mocking, patronizing display of shock and concern, he promised to reprimand all of them.

Even now she felt her jaw clenching as she remembered the incident.

For her father's part in this . . . Well, she could only conclude that his pain was what had made him irritable these past few years—so irritable that he seemed to resent her very presence in the house, despite the fact that she was the only person in the world who still endeavored to cling to the tattered remnants of her affection for him.

She often asked herself why she continued to cling to them with so little return of affection, and the answer, she supposed, was simple. Because he was her father, and he was not well. She wanted to be a good and dutiful daughter, to be patient and understanding about his cantankerous moods. She did what she could for him. She wanted him to be comfortable. She genuinely did not want him to be alone in his discomfort, for there was a time, many years ago, when they had been close.

But now, because of this mad promise he had made to Mr. Rushton with no concern for her wishes, everything was different. His actions had chipped away at her compassion. Now, all she could do was accept that his isolation from the world had caused him to lose all sense of reality. He had not stepped outside his home in over a year, and therefore could not comprehend that there was life beyond the borders of his estate. He could not even fathom that there were other men in England she could marry. When she had suggested it, he had insisted her duty was *there,* near the estate—to him and the Creighton title, for it was one of the few earldoms that descended through the female line.

She laid her costume out on the bed, and thought about how difficult it had been to deliberately defy him by leaving without a word. A daughter was supposed to obey her father. She knew that.

But to marry Mr. Rushton?

She sighed. Perhaps in some ways, she should be grateful for this call to arms, for she had been living far too long in the thin, dwindling realm of her optimism, clinging to her dreams and bright hopes for the future, even when her life had become unbearable, while she had remained at his side.

She had never had a proper debut or a magical first Season like other young women her age, nor had she accepted a single invitation to anything outside the vicinity of her father's estate. A few country fairs and dances under the chaperonage of an elderly female neighbor were the most she had experienced.

Looking back on all of it now—from a very different and desperate vantage point—she wondered if she had accepted that life for so long because she had been living in a world of dreams, and experiencing passion through someone else's diary—the mysterious Lydie. Perhaps she might have fought harder for her independence if things had been different, if she'd never found that diary to keep her dreams alive—dreams of a particular gentleman who had left England for America three years ago.

Perhaps his absence was the very thing that had allowed her to be content in her small world, because she knew someday he would return, and she was perfectly willing to wait for the kind of relentless passion she had been reading and dreaming about. The kind of passion she had known once before for herself on a deserted country road not far from the inn.

Well, the waiting was over at least, she thought, struggling to regain her wounded optimism as she sat down in front of the mirror and watched her aunt sweep her wavy red hair into a knot on top of her head, then pull a single lock free to trail down her back. Lord Hawthorne had come home. He had arrived just in time for his mother's

fiftieth birthday celebration ball, and just in time
to give Rebecca hope again. She, with her aunt as
chaperone, would be in attendance at that ball,
because Rebecca needed him. Urgently.

"Do you think he will remember me?" she
asked, working hard to sound relaxed and non-
chalant as she looked at her aunt's reflection in
the mirror.

She was going to the ball dressed as Helen of
Troy, and had chosen the costume with the express purpose of attracting his attention. Helen's
beauty had launched a thousand ships, after all.

"I don't know, dear," her aunt replied as she
pinned Rebecca's costume more snugly over her
shoulder. "He's been gone for so long."

Rebecca wet her lips and nodded, trying not to
feel too disappointed.

Her aunt smiled at her in the mirror. "Oh,
what am I thinking? In the past four years, how
often could he have come to the rescue of a beautiful red-haired damsel in distress in a runaway
coach, whose driver had fallen down drunk from
his seat?"

Rebecca tried to smile. "You are right, Aunt
Grace. Surely he remembers that night, but what I
want to know is—will he remember *me*, or more
importantly, will he treat me differently, now that
I am older? I was only seventeen then. I am almost
twenty-one now."

Six days shy of her twenty-first birthday, to be exact. And six days short of her majority.

Her aunt toyed with the fabric of her Trojan costume, adjusting the way everything draped in the front. "He has kept you and your father on his family's guest list all these years, so that is a good sign."

"He probably put us there and promptly forgot about us, since we haven't gone to one single party."

At least now, she understood *why* she had never been permitted to attend any gatherings. It was why she and her aunt were here, registered at the Pembroke Inn under false names. It was why she had snuck away in the night like a criminal.

Just the thought of it filled her with sickening grief over her father's betrayal, and a genuine fear for her future. She could still hear the impatient tremor in his voice from three days ago. *You will not refuse him, Rebecca. He won't stand for it. Nor will I.*

She turned to her aunt. "Thank you, Aunt Grace, for helping me. I don't know what I would have done if you hadn't been willing to take this risk. It means so much to me."

Her aunt touched her cheek. "How could I possibly say no? Your mother was my beloved sister, and when she was alive, we would have done anything for each other. I could not let you be forced into marrying that man. Have you decided which earrings to wear?" Aunt Grace was clearly eager to change the subject, for the hour was growing late. She held both pairs up for Rebecca to consider.

She examined them only briefly. "I like these," she said. "They will bring out the color in my eyes and I will need all the help I can get from behind this mask. Oh, how I wish this was a regular ball, not a masquerade. He won't even be able to see my face."

"I disagree, dear," Aunt Grace said. "There is nothing more appealing to a man than a woman of mystery, and when we arrive, remember what I told you in the coach on the way here. If you wish to entice him, you must be confident and elusive. You cannot be presented to him like a drooling puppy with your tail wagging, or like a young woman who wants something from him. Being the heir to a dukedom, I am sure he encounters women like that every day of his life. You must tease him and lure him in your direction. Make yourself into a golden ring he cannot quite grab hold of, then at the end of the night, you will be the one he will remember. The one he will wish to see again. Then you, my dear, will be safe from Mr. Rushton, for you will have caught yourself the son of a duke."

Rebecca sighed and nodded, even though it was

not his station in life that had brought her here after fleeing her home and the prison of her future. It was the very man himself who had haunted her dreams for four difficult years. It was the memory of his touch, his strong and capable hands on her body that wild and dangerous night when she had met someone who was everything a man should be—confident, honorable, heroic.

She longed to see him again with every breath in her body. She wanted *him* to be the one she would marry, not Mr. Rushton. She wanted to feel passion for her husband, the kind of passion Lydie wrote about in her diary.

Perhaps, if the fates were kind, she would feel that passion tonight, and maybe even secure a happy future. She certainly hoped so, because if she were forced to marry a man she did not love, she might as well give up breathing.

Devon strode out of the palace doors into the cold, hard rain, and raised an umbrella over his head. He crossed the flagstone terrace to look over what had once been the Italian Gardens, but saw only a muddy ruin.

His father had completely destroyed the garden. He had moved the shrubs and hedges. He had dug up bulbs, leaving deep holes and large mounds of earth scattered indiscriminately. All that remained was the large fountain in the center and the beautiful statue of Venus, abandoned, left alone in a devastated wasteland. No wonder Mother had wished him to return.

Gathering his coat collar tighter around his neck and noting the fact that he could see his breath in the damp chill, Devon tightened his grip on the umbrella handle and looked toward the highest point on the property. There, he saw his father with a garden spade, digging another hole.

Devon left the stone terrace and walked up the gravel path, running a hand down his thigh to massage the pain out of his knee. When he finally reached his father, he stood quietly for a moment, watching him.

The duke forced the shovel into the tough ground and tossed the wet earth carelessly behind him. Water dripped from the brim of his hat, and his coat was soaked straight through. He did not seem to care, however. His only concern was the hole in the ground.

Devon cleared his throat. "Father."

The duke continued to dig, so Devon took a step closer and spoke again, louder this time. "Father!"

The duke stopped and turned and stared bewildered at him. "My son!" He dropped the shovel, rushed forward and wrapped his arms around him. "Thank God! You've come home!"

Devon managed to hug his father and hold the

umbrella over both their heads, while his emotions fell into turmoil. His father was not the same. He did not seem to recall the terrible fury and anger upon which they had parted three years ago. It was as if it had never happened.

"Yes, Father, I have returned," he said warily. When they stepped apart, Devon held the umbrella over his father's head, not his own. "Blake said you wished to speak to me about something."

"Yes, it's very important."

"Why don't we go inside to talk," he suggested. "It's pouring rain, and you're soaking wet."

"Not yet. I have to save the garden. Everything needs to be right here, exactly where we are standing. On high ground."

Devon looked at the disastrous layout of shrubs and hedges, which had been hastily transplanted with no sense of order or beauty. It was utter chaos, and mud was oozing everywhere.

He hated mud. He hated the look of it, the feel of it, the smell of it.

"Surely this can wait until tomorrow," he suggested. "Guests have already begun to arrive for the ball tonight, and Mother would like to have you with her to greet them. It is her birthday after all."

The duke glanced back at the half dug hole. "But I must finish. I must get that rose bush into the ground before the flood comes."

Devon swallowed uneasily. "There is no flood, Father. This is just a heavy spring rain."

"But there is a curse on us."

Devon stared at his father for a moment. "*No*, Father. It has been raining all over England. Not just here."

"But it is *our* fault it is raining." His father continued to stare doggedly at him, shivering in the cold. God in heaven. He was going to catch his death if he carried on like this. He had to be brought inside.

Devon looked down at the rose bush waiting in the cart, then back at his father.

"I'll plant it for you," he heard himself saying, "if you will hold my umbrella and explain to me what you told Blake—how you believe only I can stop this . . . this curse."

The duke reached a shaky hand out to take the umbrella from him. "Thank you, Devon. You're a good son. The very best."

Devon glanced briefly at his father while he moved to scoop up the heavy rose bush and its jungle of roots, caked in dirt. He carried it to the hole and got down on one knee to set it inside. Then he picked up the shovel and began to fill the hole back in, making sure to cover all the roots.

"I won't keep you guessing any longer," his father said at last. "You must marry right away,

Devon, and you must convince all three of your brothers to do the same."

Marry?

Devon stopped patting the mud around the bush and straightened. "I beg your pardon? Did I hear you correctly?"

"Yes. It will stop the curse and therefore stop the rain."

"How the hell will four weddings stop the rain?"

"They just will," his father said simply, sounding completely sane.

Devon stabbed the shovel into the ground with his boot and leaned a wrist upon the handle. Rain pounded onto his shoulders.

"You are not making sense, Father, and I will not succumb to this. I am going to send for Dr. Lambert immediately and insist that he prescribe something for you to take at night that will help you sleep."

His father shook his head. "No. Dr. Lambert's a man of science. He doesn't understand any of this, and it's not sleep I need, it is a legitimate grandchild. The palace is in jeopardy."

Devon's head drew back as if a ball had just been thrown his way. A grandchild to save the palace. Suddenly everything was becoming very clear.

"Father," he said, as gently as possible, "I assure you, there is no need to worry. You have four sons, and you have my word that one of us will eventually provide an heir. The ducal line will continue."

The duke laughed scornfully. "Rubbish. This rain is a warning, because you boys are all too busy playing cards in London or gallivanting about the world, never thinking about settling down and doing your duty. Except Blake, who's been taking care of everything in your absence, but for that reason hasn't had a single minute to look around and find himself a pretty lass. And you, Devon, you're the eldest, the future duke. You should set an example. At least be speaking of it occasionally, but I swear all you do is look at your mother's sour face and think to yourself, '*I am never getting myself shackled.*' And poor Charlotte. She tried, but what happened to her? The bloke went off and got himself stuffed into the ground, six feet under, and what is she to do now but cry herself to sleep?" He lowered the umbrella to his side, completely oblivious to the rain now pouring down upon his head and shoulders, streaming down his body. "I know everyone thinks I am mad, but I am not. The family is cursed, I tell you, and we must do something about it. There must be another generation begun in this house before winter."

"There is plenty of time," Devon assured him.

"As I said before, we will each marry when we are ready."

"No. You will marry now."

Devon slowly shook his head at him. "No, Father," he firmly said. "We will not."

The duke stared at him for long moment, then his face sank into a dark, angry frown. "I see nothing has changed."

Devon's gut wrenched with an agony he did not wish to feel. He had spent his entire childhood trying so very hard to be the son his father wished him to be, and had succeeded most of the time—until three years ago when he had failed miserably and his father had cast him out.

Bloody hell, he did not want to *care* that his father was disappointed in him. He could do that well enough on his own.

"I thought that might be the case," the duke said with the forceful, unwavering conviction Devon remembered so well from his youth. "So I took steps to ensure that you would do as I say. Events are already in motion. My solicitor was here four days ago and I have altered my will. It now states clearly—and legally I might add—that if all four of my sons are not married by Christmas, I shall leave my entire unentailed fortune to the London Horticultural Society." He gazed with agitation at the rose bush, then stomped on the dirt at its base. "So that they may replant my gardens after the flood."

Devon strove to curb the rage twisting and turning in his gut, while his father nodded triumphantly. "There now. You're not so happy now, are you, my wayward one, knowing you won't have your inheritance to squander on another continent. You will get the estate, of course. There is nothing I can do about that. But I warn you—without the fortune you will have little else. Land isn't what it used to be."

He started toward the garden cart and tossed the umbrella inside. "And don't bother trying to invalidate the will," he said, taking hold of the handles. "Dr. Lambert has deemed me quite fit, and my solicitor has assured me that I can leave my money to whomever I bloody well choose."

With that, he started down the hill. "Find a bride, Devon. You can begin at the ball tonight. I have invited a number of suitable young ladies, but there is one in particular who will be a good match. She is the daughter of a duke, so she will fit right in."

Tonight?

Bloody hell! Did his father think it would be that easy? That Devon would surrender to this ridiculous plan just like that? Surely a snowball was more likely to survive a full year in the burning furies of hell.

Chapter 5

By some miracle of God, the rain stayed away that evening, the downpour stopping approximately one hour before the guests from the village began to arrive. The cool air carried the fresh fragrance of early spring, reminding everyone of the brightness that normally touched their spirits and stirred their hearts at this time of year.

Everyone except for Devon, of course, for spring was the season he hated most of all. Not to mention the fact that he had just been told he must marry immediately or be disinherited, and he was now waiting to be presented to a young lady his father had already picked out. All in all, it had not been a good day.

While he wandered around the perimeter of the ballroom, dressed in the costume his mother had arranged for him—a highwayman's black cape and mask—he wished he had arrived the day before and had at least been given a chance to absorb what was happening and to accept this fate being forced upon him. Or perhaps find a way around it.

Right now, all he seemed able to do was look around the room at all the young English girls and their mothers, eyeing him with the same hungry purpose—to be the next Duchess of Pembroke.

It was hardly an aphrodisiac, when what he really needed right now was some plain and simple sexual attraction. A flirtation. The promise of pleasure. A bit of a challenge, perhaps. Maybe even a hint of seduction. Was it too much to ask, to be attracted to a potential bride?

If he was committed to finding one, of course. Which he was not.

Just then—surely by some second miracle of God—a woman waltzed by him, passing by so fast, he felt a slight breeze ruffle his cape. Her hair caught his eye—flame red, one single lock trailing thick and wavy down her back. She was dressed as a Roman, or a Trojan . . . Helen of Troy perhaps? He turned and watched her circle the room with her partner, Dr. Lambert's son, who resided in the village.

But who was the woman? He did not recall her being announced, though he might have been outside taking some fresh air at the time. To avoid complete and utter suffocation inside.

His mother approached. "Devon, I've been looking for you. Where have you been?" She brought two women with her. A mother and daughter, ravenous with high hopes, no doubt.

"Good evening, Mother," he said. "I was outside on the terrace, enjoying the air and marveling at the notion that one could do so without becoming thoroughly drenched." He smiled courteously.

"Oh, yes," his mother said, "how we all appreciate this welcome respite from the rain." She turned to Devon and gestured to the others. "Allow me, if you will, to present the Duchess of Swinburne and her daughter, Lady Letitia. They came all the way from Cornwall to join us this week. Ladies, this is my son, Lord Hawthorne."

And this was the young lady his father had selected—a striking beauty to be sure. He bowed. "It is an honor to make your acquaintance," he said. "I hope this weather did not make your travels unduly difficult."

Her Grace, a small, plump woman with dimples, brown hair, and round spectacles, shook her head. "Not at all, Lord Hawthorne. Nothing could keep us from your mother's birthday celebrations, not even weather such as this."

Devon turned his attention to the dazzling daughter, who was not small like her mother, but tall and slender with shiny black hair and a flawless ivory complexion. She was dressed as a fairy with wings, gazing at him with interest. "May I compliment you on your costume, Lady Letitia? It is most becoming."

Her eyes, from beneath her sparkling white mask, revealed her pleasure at the compliment. "Thank you, Lord Hawthorne. You are most kind."

His mother then engaged the duchess and her daughter in a conversation about orchids. While they discussed the pretty flower, he let his gaze wander discreetly until it came to rest on Helen of Troy again, who had been returned to her chaperone and was now standing with her back to him. This allowed him the opportunity to admire the curve of her hips and backside.

Her hair—that striking, shocking red hair—stirred his masculine senses, for he was consciously aware of the fact that although it was swept up in an intricate twist, that long, curling lock he'd noticed before fell to a sharp point at the precise juncture between the center of her lower back and her bottom. He liked the shape of that bottom, to be sure. It was very easy to imagine her standing there completely nude.

He could not contemplate such ideas further, however, for Helen of Troy turned to be presented to someone, and he was struck by an odd familiarity.

Good God, he had met this woman before. But where? When? If he had, it would have been a long time ago, before he'd left for America. In London perhaps? If only he could place her. If only she weren't wearing that mask.

She turned to face him and her gaze traveled about the room, just as his had a moment ago, as if she were looking specifically for someone. Then her eyes found his. He wished again that she were not wearing a mask because he would dearly love to see her whole face. Not that he had any doubts about her beauty. Her lips were full, her skin creamy white, her nose tiny and straight. And that hair—Lord that hair. It was her crowning glory. What he wouldn't give to comb his fingers through it and see it splayed out on a pillow.

She reached up and fiddled with an earring, never taking her eyes off him as she did so, and he felt another stirring, this time in his groin when she confidently wet her lips with her tongue.

He liked confident women. Women who were capable and could handle themselves in any situation.

"Devon?" his mother said, and he realized he had not been listening. "Were you sorry to leave America?" She was repeating a question the duchess had asked.

Devon politely answered, then gazed at Lady Letitia, who smiled at him again.

He wondered if she might have a fiery spark like Helen of Troy, then sought to discover it for himself. "Will you do me the honor, Lady Letitia?"

"I would be delighted," she replied as she took his proffered hand.

He led her onto the floor for a country dance, and she engaged him in polite conversation throughout the steps, offering one-or-two-word answers to his questions. She then asked a question of her own concerning the weather, which was now a subject thoroughly exhausted. He replied courteously, however, reminding himself that this was the nature of casual discourse, and in that regard she was displaying her perfect manners.

There was not much to think about while he danced and spoke to her, so he found himself glancing away every so often in the direction of the red-haired woman who made no secret of the fact that she was watching him as well.

He could not count the number of times their eyes met across the crowded floor, nor could he deny the pleasure he gleaned from it. And he was all for pleasure tonight, looking for a diversion from all his responsibilities.

The dance came to an end, and he escorted Lady Letitia back to her mother. His own mother was now with Charlotte on the other side of the room, so he excused himself and immediately set off in their direction.

He reached them and lowered his voice. "Do either of you know that woman with the red hair? See there, she is speaking to Sir Charles."

His sister and mother both looked in the direction he implied.

"Do you mean Helen of Troy?" Charlotte asked. "Why, that is the Earl of Creighton's daughter, Lady Rebecca. She is here with her aunt, Lady Saxby. We were all surprised she attended this evening. It's the first time she has accepted one of our many invitations, which we've been sending to her father for years. Though I cannot, for the life of me, remember why."

Devon listened to all of this with astonishment and remembrance, for his ravishing Helen of Troy was none other than Lady Rebecca Newland, the young girl from that very intriguing night on the old coach road years ago. He recalled it well. She and her father had been stranded, and he'd pulled her out of a bog.

She had been dressed in black that day and had seemed older and more experienced than her years. He remembered lifting her down from his horse. Ah, yes . . . He would never forget that soft, lush bosom sliding down his chest.

He would also never forget how frustrated he had been to learn she was too young to touch, because there had been something about her eyes and the sumptuous sound of her voice that aroused him. He remembered the exact way her lips had puckered when she spoke, and the way she looked at him with a very obvious sexual curiosity.

And here she was, standing across a ballroom. A woman now. A confident, coquettish woman with enough sexual charisma to stop a train. How old would she be? Twenty-one? Why was she not yet someone's wife? Were the men of England blind? Perhaps she was too much for them. The thought made him smile.

"Is her father here?" he asked.

"No, just her aunt," Charlotte replied. "Evidently, her father is somewhere in India."

"Which is very surprising," his mother added, "considering the earl's reputation. He's been described as a bit of a hermit. I once heard he chases visitors off his property with a pack of dogs, but I'm sure that is overblown gossip. Look at his daughter. She is lovely, is she not? How could she blossom so beautifully under such depressing circumstances?"

"I met her father, once," Devon told them. "They were stranded on the road near here, and I offered assistance. The earl possessed a serious nature, to be sure, but he was nevertheless gracious and invited me to his home, so you are right, Mother, that must be gossip."

He was completely aware that he'd been watching Lady Rebecca the entire time he was conversing with Charlotte and his mother, and saw no reason to put off the inevitable. "I would like a proper introduction," he said, though it seemed silly after how intimate they had been so long ago. But she might not remember him, and a ballroom had its rules. "If you would be so kind, Mother."

"Certainly," she replied, starting off in that direction. "She is indeed a prestigious young lady, Devon. Despite her father's odd reputation, his title is very old, and it descends in the female line, which will make her a peeress in her own right one day, for she is an only child."

"How nice for her," he replied.

His mother sighed with frustration. "What did you think of Lady Letitia, then? Your father was adamant that you meet her this evening."

"A lovely girl as well."

"She made her debut last Season, and has an exquisite singing voice. She is Swinburne's eldest daughter, and has already turned down two marriage proposals. Mind you, these came from gentlemen who were quite beneath her, from what I understand, but *you*, Devon . . . Oh, your father would be overjoyed if . . ."

Devon leaned close to his mother's ear. "Let us not put the cart before the horse. Despite Father's demands, I am not ready to be matched up with a bride just yet. I only arrived at Pembroke this morning. Let me at least catch my breath and get my bearings."

"My apologies, Devon."

She led him around the edges of the ballroom until they reached Lady Rebecca and her aunt, then made the appropriate introductions. "Allow me to present Lady Saxby, and her niece, Lady Rebecca Newland, whose father is the Earl of Creighton. Ladies, my son, Lord Hawthorne."

Now that he was closer, he could see the rich green color of her eyes behind the sparkling mask, and remembered again how striking he had thought them to be that night years ago in the forest.

"It is an honor, Lady Saxby." He bowed to her, then turned to Helen of Troy. "But Lady Rebecca, we have met before, years ago. Do you recall?"

Those moist, cherry-red lips puckered into an alluring smile. "Of course I recall, Lord Hawthorne. My father and I were stranded in the woods not far from here, and you offered your assistance. How could I forget?"

Everyone in the room seemed to disappear for a moment, while he and Lady Rebecca gazed openly at one another, as if there were no secrets or pretenses between them. There was a spark of attraction, potent and exhilarating. It had been pulsing between them since their eyes had met across the room earlier that evening, and neither was about to deny it.

God, he loved how direct and forthcoming she was. He wasn't in the mood to dance around the obvious. He had desired pleasure and excitement tonight, and, by God, here it was without point-less preamble.

His mother stammered slightly. "Was . . . Was your journey . . . I beg your pardon, Lady Saxby, was it a difficult trip from Gloucester, with the recent rains?"

He regretted that his mother was uncomfort-able with his blatant flirtation right under her nose, but there it was. The evening had hit a high note, to be sure, and thank God for that.

Lady Saxby described the condition of the roads while he and the lovely Lady Rebecca continued to openly observe each other. What was going through her mind right now? He would dearly love to know. What a wonderful flirt she was.

And twenty-one. Thank God for the passing of time.

At last the right moment presented itself. There was a break in his mother's conversation with Lady Saxby, and he was able to request a spot on her niece's card. As it happened, she was free for the next one, a Strauss waltz, which began right away.

He held out a gloved hand, and Lady Rebecca's eyes glimmered enticingly as she took hold.

Chapter 6

Rebecca had been right about how she would feel upon seeing Lord Hawthorne again after all these years. Her entire body was pulsing with excitement and desire, for he was even more handsome and compelling tonight than he had been upon their first meeting in the woods four years ago.

And there was something different about him. Perhaps it was the way he looked at her. Though she had almost no experience with men, her instincts told her it was because she was no longer a seventeen-year-old girl. She was a woman now. A woman whose senses were blazing with untested desire. Could he see it? Sense it? Recognize it?

Lydie's lover in the woods had always known what she'd wanted. He'd been instinctive that way. Lydie had said so.

The notion that Lord Hawthorne was instinctive in a similar way excited Rebecca beyond any imagining.

They reached the center of the room, and he slid his arm around her corseted waist, never taking his eyes off hers. Her blood coursed even faster through her veins from the thrill of his touch, which she had longed to feel on her body on so many dark, lonely nights alone. Was it possible to die from the painful restraint of passion? She almost felt faint.

Then he spoke. "My sister, Charlotte, mentioned this is the first time you have accepted one of our many invitations. I'm glad you chose a time when I would be here to pay my respects."

He held her firmly but moved with grace around the floor, and she had no trouble keeping pace with him as he turned her about the room. "I dare say, Lord Hawthorne, it is the first time, and I am quite overwhelmed by the grandeur of the evening. I apologize for our absence over the years, but I am sure you have heard that my father enjoys his privacy. He is a quiet man and we do not engage in many society gatherings."

That was putting it mildly. But Lord help her. She had not intended to sound so provincial. Surely Lord Hawthorne preferred a more sophisticated woman, a woman who could match his knowledge and worldliness. She had seen him dancing with a duke's daughter earlier.

"But your father is out of the country?"

"Yes, and I confess, my aunt has been waiting for this opportunity to steal me away."

"Remind me to thank her, because you have brightened my evening, Lady Rebecca. I only just arrived back at Pembroke this morning, and to be honest, after the day I've had, I would have been just as content to go straight to bed an hour ago. I'm glad I did not."

"I am glad, too. I am also flattered that you remember meeting my father and me all those years ago. As for myself, I never forgot it, the way you came to our rescue. It was a very . . . *exciting* evening for me. I don't know what we would have done if you hadn't come along."

"It was my pleasure, truly."

"But you were on your way somewhere at a very swift pace. I hope we did not make you late for an appointment."

"I assure you it was not important. Even if it had been, any concern over my poor punctuality would have been overshadowed by the unexpected adventure, and the very pleasant trip we took to the bog, you and I."

Despite the tension she felt—because so much of her future happiness depended on this single, vital dance—she somehow managed to laugh. "Pleasant?"

He leaned closer—so close, she could feel the

heat of his moist breath in her ear. "I greatly enjoyed the perfect curve of your elbow that night."

A delicious shudder of surprise danced through her. She had come here to secretly entice him, but suddenly *he* seemed to be the one enticing *her*. Could it be, that after all she had been through lately, the fates were finally smiling down on her?

"You're the only man in the world," she confessed, "who has ever touched my elbow."

God help her, she felt as if she had just bared her soul to him. Perhaps it was too much. Her aunt had told her to be elusive.

But then he chuckled, as if he found her reply very witty, when it had not been a joke.

He spoke close to her ear again. "I wonder if one of these days I might be fortunate enough to touch it again."

She wanted to say, *"Yesterday wouldn't be soon enough,"* but thankfully, she had more sense than that, and managed to simply smile daringly at him as he guided her around the outer edges of the dance floor, keeping perfect time with the music.

"Pardon my ignorance," he said, "but are you and your aunt staying here at the palace tonight? If so, I hope you have found your accommodations satisfactory."

"No, Lord Hawthorne, we are not staying at the palace." Did she detect a hint of disappointment in his eyes? She hoped so. "We only decided to come at the very last minute, so we are staying in the village."

"The Pembroke Inn?"

"Yes."

His voice, soft and low, filled her with quivering anticipation. "How unfortunate for me that I won't see you at breakfast in the morning. I believe the sight of you over coffee would be a most promising start to my day."

"Why don't you picture me in your mind," she suggested with a sensual lilt in her voice—the kind of lilt Lydie had once written about. "I will be wearing a rose-colored gown with white trim when I order my toast with strawberry jam, and I will ask for milk in my tea. Perhaps even a little sugar if I feel in the mood for something sweeter than usual."

He smiled again. "I promise you, I will think of nothing else all night, Lady Rebecca."

She felt a moment of triumph as he swept her past the tall tree fern near the orchestra, then toward the open French doors that led out onto the flagstone terrace. She caught a whiff of the cool, nighttime air and inhaled deeply as they passed by, feeling rejuvenated by their open flirtations and hopeful for her future once again. Mr. Rushton seemed a thousand miles away. He didn't even exist for her now, when she was being swept around the room in Lord Hawthorne's strong arms. She wished she could dance with him until dawn.

Sadly, however, the orchestra soon finished the piece, and she was forced to step out of his arms.

But that couldn't be it. It couldn't be over. She prayed for another opportunity to converse with him before they said goodnight.

He escorted her back to her aunt, then bowed to both of them. "Thank you, Lady Rebecca. May I hope to escort you to the dessert table later this evening?"

Her prayers had been answered, and her heart drummed with delight. She accepted his invitation.

"I presume it went well," Aunt Grace said, speaking quietly after he left.

"It appears so."

They watched him circle the room. He stopped to speak to the young lady he had danced with earlier—the duke's daughter with the strikingly dark features—and Rebecca let out a sigh.

"Perhaps I am dreaming, Aunt Grace. Look at him. Surely he must prefer a woman like that—tall and graceful, with a neck like a swan. A woman who knows how to behave in society. I feel like such a novice."

"Maybe that is your charm."

Lord Hawthorne joined his younger brother, Lord Blake. They spoke briefly, then left the ballroom.

"Do not worry," Aunt Grace said. "He will return, and he has promised you a trip to the dessert table."

"But then what? Dancing with a man is one thing. Getting him to propose is quite another. And there are so many other attractive women here tonight. It appears I have quite a bit of competition."

Her aunt considered it. "You must have patience, darling. Rome wasn't built in a day."

Just then, Devon's mother, the duchess, approached again, and Rebecca turned to find herself gazing up at another handsome gentleman—tall and dark like Devon, with shiny black hair. His eyes were brown, however, instead of blue. The strong, attractive angles of his face resembled Devon's closely, but there was something very different about this man's demeanor. There was a bold, rather callous look in his eye.

The duchess gestured politely with a hand. "Lady Saxby and Lady Rebecca, since this is your first visit to Pembroke Palace, I thought you might like to meet another of my sons, who only just arrived from London this evening." She turned to him. "Allow me to present Lady Saxby of Gloucester and her niece, Lady Rebecca Newland. Ladies, my son, Lord Vincent Sinclair."

"Charmed," he said, before turning immediately to Rebecca. "May I request a dance?"

Caught off guard, she glanced uncertainly at her aunt, who nodded at her.

"I would be delighted," she replied, allowing Lord Vincent to lead her out, and wondering how this unexpected development was going to affect her plans for this evening.

"He arrived an hour ago," Blake explained as he left the ballroom with Devon. "Mother just told him about Father's demands upon us to find wives. I thought you should know."

They strode to the gallery to speak in private. "So he knows I have returned."

"Yes. Charlotte told him before he had a chance to remove his hat and gloves, but evidently he had nothing to say about it, and went straight to the billiards room with some local chap for a drink and a game before dressing for the ball."

"Then his hostility toward me has not waned."

"Were you hoping it had?"

Devon considered it. "Hoping? No. I rarely have hope. I'm too much of a realist. I knew I would not be welcomed back or forgiven, at least not by him."

He had only himself to blame, he supposed, for there had been a time when they had been not only brothers, but friends as well, sticking up for each other when trouble was at hand, laughing together, and later, drinking and gaming together.

Vincent had always been loyal, even through the blinding glare of Devon's overprivileged position as heir, when their father had favored him and denied Vincent the respect and affection he'd needed and deserved.

Devon had never wanted to be treated differently at Vincent's expense. His guilt over that had reached a pinnacle on the day MaryAnn had written him that letter.

She had told him he was the most extraordinary man she had ever known. He wished he had burned it.

Devon jumped when Blake touched him on the shoulder and brought him back to the present. "Do not let him get to you," he said. "Vincent enjoys his anger and does not wish to let it go. You would do best to remember that and resist the urge to mend fences, at least for the time being. You'll only frustrate yourself because he will find a way to knock them down again. In fact, I think he has been anticipating your return for that very reason, and in that regard, I must warn you. He enjoys a fight these days, with anyone who will oblige him by raising a fist."

Devon gazed with regret at his younger brother. "It pains me to know that."

"I know."

He sighed deeply. "If Vincent enjoys a fight, Blake, you are the opposite. You keep the harmony."

Blake lowered his hand to his side. "We all have our purpose, I suppose."

"And what is mine?" Devon asked. "To be Duke of Pembroke and take care of this estate and all the people who reside here, when I am not to be depended upon? I have proven that with both my actions in the past and my prolonged absence." He shook his head. "I have often thought it should have been you. You're the diplomat. While I have deserted my post, you have remained here in my stead and kept the machine running."

"Not really, Devon. All I did was grease the wheels occasionally, when what we need is a new axle."

Devon thought of the once beautiful Italian Gardens and the melancholy in his mother's eyes, and knew his brother was right on that point. Something had broken down here. There had been too many betrayals and tragedies. He felt no hope in these rooms. He felt no hope inside himself.

"Shall we go back?" Blake asked, and Devon could not help but notice again that his brother seemed weary. It was no easy task, he supposed, keeping the peace in this family.

"Yes, I want to see Vincent," he said. "Despite the wretched history between us, and the fact that he despises me, and quite rightly so, he is still my brother. We must at least look each other in the eye before we venture into a new decade of open hostilities."

* * *

Lord Vincent, like his older brother, was a confident, skillful dancer. His shoulders were broad and his movements smooth. He was a handsome man and possessed a good deal of charm, but otherwise, Rebecca knew very little about him, except that he was the duke's second son, only one year younger than Devon, and that he spent most of his time in London away from Pembroke Palace.

Oh, and she had once read in the society pages that he was an incorrigible scoundrel.

"You must be pleased to have your brother back in England," she said, seeking to establish some polite discourse while they danced.

"Yes, we are all overjoyed," he replied. "Father especially. Though sometimes I wonder if my brother should be forgiven at all for staying away as long as he did. How helpless we have all been, living our lives without him."

Rebecca stiffened at Lord Vincent's obvious sarcasm, and almost missed a step. She did not know what to say.

He smiled. "I've shocked you, Helen of Troy. Please accept my apologies. I will confess the truth. My brother and I have been at odds in the past, and shameful brother that I am, I have not yet welcomed him home. I did see him, though, from across the room, dancing with you. That was when I decided I had to dance with you as well."

Rebecca frowned at him. "Your confession is hardly flattering, my lord. If you are at odds with your brother, what does that make me? The rope in your tug of war?"

All at once, the fairy-tale palace of her Prince Charming seemed not such a perfect world after all. There appeared to be battle lines drawn in the house. But real life was always more complicated than fantasy, she had recently discovered.

Lord Vincent smirked at her. "Why have we not met before?" he asked. "You're very lovely and very clever."

"I rarely visit London," she replied. "My father has always preferred the country."

"Pity for us Londoners," he said with a blasé tone, looking over her head. "But may I be so bold as to ask, are you spoken for? Betrothed? In love?"

She swallowed over her shock. "You are indeed bold, Lord Vincent."

"Is that a yes or a no?"

She was feeling rather aggravated by his blatant cheekiness. "No to everything."

"Delighted to hear it."

Not quite sure what had just happened, she somehow managed to make light conversation for the rest of the dance, and when it ended, they stepped apart and he offered her an arm to escort her off the floor.

As the crowd cleared in front of them, dispersing in all directions, Rebecca spotted her aunt in the very place she had left her, but she was not alone. Beside her, watching attentively from the edge of the ballroom, was Lord Hawthorne.

His strength and power seemed to fill the room—and to fill Rebecca simultaneously with the exhilarating notion that he had been watching her. Her intuition told her he'd been making sure his presumptuous younger brother was not overstepping those battle lines—whatever and wherever they might be.

Lord Vincent halted, forcing Rebecca to halt as well. She glanced up at him. His face had gone pale. He did not seem quite so confident now. He appeared rather shaken in fact.

Lord Hawthorne on the other hand, stood with one hand behind his back, the other at his side, his eyes beneath the black mask fixed upon Rebecca. It felt as if they were the only two people in the room.

She and Lord Vincent started off again.

"Lady Rebecca," Hawthorne said when they reached him, and though he did not say it out loud, there was a question in his eyes. *Is everything satisfactory?*

She had never spoken to anyone without words before, but believed she succeeded in assuring him that all was well.

He bowed to her, then directed his gaze at his brother. "Vincent, it is good to see you."

"And you."

A long, uncomfortable silence weighed heavily upon them. Rebecca glanced at her aunt who watched the exchange with some dismay.

Lord Hawthorne asked, "How is London these days?"

"It is the same as it was before you left," Vincent replied. "Only wetter."

The brothers continued to stare heatedly at each other, until Lord Hawthorne turned to Rebecca and her aunt. "Pardon me, ladies, but if I recall, I promised you both a guided tour of the dessert table, did I not? Shall we see what delectable treats await us?"

The tension in the air drained away with the pleasant tone of his voice, and Rebecca let out a deep breath.

"That would be lovely," Aunt Grace said, accepting the arm he offered with a flirtatious smile of her own. It appeared Aunt Grace was not immune to Lord Hawthorne's charms, either.

Rebecca took his other arm and resisted the urge to look over her shoulder at Lord Vincent, when she could feel the heat of his scorching gaze upon their backs.

They left the ballroom and reached the dessert table, which was adorned in lace and covered with gleaming silver platters covered in cream cakes and sugared fruit in every color of the rainbow.

Rebecca wandered around the table, eyeing everything before she removed her gloves and tasted a raspberry bonbon, then a chocolate tart with whipped cream on top. She was licking the cream off the tip of her baby finger when she noticed Lord Hawthorne was not enjoying any of the sweets. He was merely watching her with heavy lidded eyes from the opposite side of the table.

She felt a quivering thrill in the pit of her belly and stopped what she was doing, for she knew these moments at the dessert table were pivotal. Her instincts were telling her to *do* something in order to capture and hold his attention. She had to tempt him, beguile him, perhaps even seduce him, but for the life of her, she had no idea how to do it.

He turned to converse with her aunt. A moment later, Aunt Grace left to go and speak with an acquaintance who was sipping champagne on the other side of the dessert room.

Rebecca raised an eyebrow at him, encouraging his approach. Virile and striking in his black costume, he came around the table to stand before her.

"So you met my brother," he said matter-of-factly.

A footman appeared beside them with a tray of

champagne, and they each helped themselves to a glass. Rebecca took a sip. "Yes, my lord, and he is very different from you."

"In what way?"

She pondered the question, not quite sure how to articulate what she meant. "You make people feel safe. He has quite the opposite effect."

Lord Hawthorne's pale blue eyes became expressionless as stone, then he bent forward slightly and spoke with a hush that sent a shiver of awareness through her. "What makes you think you are safe with me?"

Her body trembled, and she marveled at the peculiar panic he evoked in her. Then he turned and casually strolled around the dessert table, looking at everything but sampling nothing. Rebecca followed him and tasted a lemon jelly candy, then a sweet red grape.

When he came around again, having circled the table, he faced her, hands clasped behind his back. He couldn't have looked more relaxed if he were basking in the sun.

"So tell me," he said, "what did you and my brother speak about?"

"He asked if I was betrothed."

"Did he, indeed? And what was your reply?"

"That I am not, of course." She paused, watching his reaction, then continued. "He also asked if I was in love."

Lord Hawthorne shook his head with disapproval. "Tsk, tsk, Vincent. Such bold questions. And what was your reply to that?"

"No again. But the night is still young."

She wasn't quite sure where that clever but risky response had come from. She could only credit it to her provocative reading of late.

His smiling eyes glanced down at her body. "Did you enjoy dancing with him?"

"He is an excellent dancer."

"That's not what I asked."

She recognized a fire in his eyes—was it jealousy?—and decided not to answer the question. She simply took another sip of champagne and strolled to the other side of the table.

"Is that why you were waiting for me after I danced with him?" she asked. "And why you escorted me here to the dessert table? To protect me from your brother, the alleged scoundrel?"

"Yes."

Her view of him was briefly obstructed by the tower of lemon cakes. She tilted her head to the side. "It seems you are always coming to my rescue, Lord Hawthorne. First a runaway coach, now a scoundrel of a brother. What next, I ask you?"

The corner of his mouth curled up in a grin, and when he spoke, the whispery quality of his voice tingled across her body, as if he had stroked her with a feather. "I suspect there will have to be something, Lady Rebecca. Any chance there might be a monster under your bed tonight that I can save you from?"

The implications of that question shocked her to her core, and she felt quite decidedly out of her depth. "Are you sure it is your brother who is the scoundrel?" she asked. "Perhaps I should be warned about the masked highwayman before me, who wants to peek under my bed."

He watched her turn and stroll to the end of the table. She reached for another grape, but did not eat it right away.

"What a night," she said. "I've danced with two scoundrels, and now I've been scandalized by a shocking comment about a monster under my bed. Lord Hawthorne, you are a very, very bad man."

And he excited her to the depths of her soul.

She popped the grape into her mouth, and something in his eyes changed. His searing gaze swept down her body again.

"You must come and stay in the palace with the other out-of-town guests," he said. "They are all staying until Friday."

The very air around them seemed to snap with electricity, and she began to believe that whatever she had said or done during these crucial moments around the table had worked. "But we have already unpacked at the inn," she explained.

"Tomorrow, then. My mother will speak to your aunt tonight before you leave."

Rebecca could not smother the great fire of triumph now burning inside her. "You have everything worked out, I see."

Her aunt appeared at her side, and Hawthorne turned his eyes to her. "You have returned, Lady Saxby. Rest assured, your charge was in good hands. I rescued her from the chocolate kisses. She did not have a single one."

"Gracious, my lord," Aunt Grace said, "I do owe you my deepest gratitude, because we all know that one kiss is never enough, and they are, oh, so dangerously sweet. A lady must watch herself."

He smiled with amusement at Aunt Grace, then bowed to both of them. "Good evening, ladies."

Her aunt watched him leave. "My, what an incredible man, Rebecca. No wonder you never forgot him."

"And you are terrible, Aunt Grace! What you said about the chocolate kisses! I could brain you!"

Her aunt ignored her admonishment. "I suspect he never really forgot you either, dear, and I predict you will be seeing him again."

Rebecca leaned close. "Sooner rather than later, it appears, because he has invited us to stay at the palace for the week."

Grace shot her a quick look. "You don't say. In that case, I suppose I don't need to be giving you any more advice, do I, child? You obviously have a natural talent." She lovingly patted her hand. "Well done, Rebecca. We have crossed the first threshold. I believe we are one step closer to your future happiness."

But after all the deprivations in her life so far, it had almost been too easy, Rebecca thought, with a strange and unexpected niggling of doubt. She thought of the old adage: *too good to be true*, and hoped it would not apply to her fairy-tale dreams of this man—and of the grand, passionate, perfect love she desired.

That night, after all the guests and family members were asleep in the palace, the duke, wearing only his nightshirt and cap, slid quietly out of bed and lit the lantern. Carefully picking it up by the squeaky handle, he padded across the dark chamber to his slippers by the door, then slid his bare feet into them and gazed anxiously about the room. He raised the lamp and peered through the dim golden light at the wood-paneled walls. His brows pulled together in a frown, his mouth fell open. His breath came faster in the chill of the night air.

He hastened to the door and ventured out into the dark corridor, looking both ways before he stepped softly to the right, quickening his pace while he checked over his shoulder. Carrying the lamp to the end of the hall, he stopped there and held it high before the massive gilt-framed portrait of the second Duke of Pembroke.

His Grace stared at it for a moment, then quickly shook his head before starting off toward the south wing. He passed a number of the guest chambers, glancing briefly down at the brass knobs on the doors as he passed.

"Yes, it is a very good time," he said.

He continued on, reaching the main staircase and hurrying down to the ground floor, his thin nightshirt flapping about his legs as he went.

He raised the lamp again and looked around the great hall. "No, Brother Salvador, not that way. This way." The duke slowed his pace at last and shuffled into the gallery. "Now let me tell you about young Rupert," he said. "He was a very good boy, but no one seems to remember him. No one except for me."

He walked the long length of the gallery, and the glow from his lamp seemed to bring the portraits back to life in the dark.

Chapter 7

"**A**t least we have until winter," Blake said to Vincent over the breakfast table the next morning, before any of the guests joined them in the room.

Vincent chuckled bitterly. "Good God. Leave it to you to find the silver lining in hell."

Devon walked into the room and met Vincent's dark gaze. His brother, seated at the white-clothed table with a plate of eggs and sausage before him, paused with his fork in midair, then lowered it with a noisy *clink* upon the fine china. "I believe I've lost my appetite."

Exhausted—for he had been up all night, his thoughts bouncing back and forth between his father's insane demands and the stimulating allure of Lady Rebecca—Devon went immediately to the sideboard for coffee. "Don't miss out on a hot breakfast on my account, Vin. You know I'm not worth it."

He could feel his brother's gaze at his back while he poured himself a cup, then he took a seat at the table across from him. They glared at each other. Vincent picked up his fork again and resumed eating.

"We were just discussing Father's intentions to see all four of us married by Christmas," Blake said.

Devon curled his hand around his hot coffee cup. "I have news about that. Early this morning, just before dawn, Father came to my room and informed me that he would offer a reward to each of us if we marry before the end of the Season. Five thousand pounds in a lump sum on the wedding day."

Blake whistled. "That's a hefty sum. He *is* losing his mind, isn't he?"

"Five thousand pounds you say," Vincent sat back in his chair.

"Garrett must be informed of the situation as soon as possible," Devon said.

"The last time we heard from him," Blake replied, "he was somewhere in the Greek Islands enjoying the Mediterranean wine. He won't be pleased to hear this."

"I doubt he'll even care," Vincent said. "He's already declared he wants nothing from Father. He'd be just as happy to stay in Greece and let us all drown in the bloody flood."

Devon brought his hand down flat upon the table. "*There is no flood.*"

"You don't say," Vincent replied with sarcastic bite. "Look, it's your fault the old man went so nutty in the first place," he said. "You weren't here to witness his wrath after you left. He probably burst something in his brain from all the ranting he did."

Devon gazed out the window at the rain pelting down upon the devastated garden terrace, filling the deep holes with water, the wind howling through the trees.

Yes, perhaps part of their father's madness was his fault, for he had disappointed him more than ever that last day, walking out after what he'd done and leaving the country without a word. He had abandoned them all.

You are no longer my son.

He was not proud of his prolonged absence from England, he never had been, but he'd always known his exodus was necessary. He'd needed to go off alone and suffer for a while, to wallow in his shame before he could finally distance himself from certain events. He'd had to do that before he could return home and fulfill his duty to the family.

He looked at his brother—the brother he had betrayed. "You are correct in that regard," he said. "I *am* to blame for the sorry state of affairs here at Pembroke."

Vincent set down his fork again and leaned back in his chair. "Bloody well right."

"*No*, Devon," Blake said, interrupting. "Our father's madness is not your fault."

Devon shook his head. "I suppose we'll never know, will we? But in the end, that is not the point."

"And what is the point, exactly?" Vincent asked.

Devon tapped a finger on the table, thinking for a minute. "Whether Father is sane or mad, he has taken legal action to change his will, and it appears we are all in a bit of a bind."

"Brilliant deduction," Vincent said.

Devon met his brother's burning gaze across the table. "I've been awake all night thinking about this and what must be done. I have been absent for the past three years and have avoided my responsibilities." He paused a moment, looking up at his mother's portrait over the fireplace, which had been painted just before her wedding day. "But I am home now, and I will do what I must. I will remain here at Pembroke to marry and produce an heir." They both stared at him with surprise in their eyes. "What the two of you decide to do is your own choice. I will not force a future upon you because of our father's preposterous belief in a family curse." He took another sip of coffee, then spoke quietly and pensively. "Perhaps in time the promise of a grandchild from me will be enough to pacify him, and I will be able to talk him out of this nonsense about a curse, and get him to change his will back to the way it was. Perhaps we can get him proper treatment. That is what he needs above all."

Blake stood up. "Do not let father do this to you, Devon. Do not let him put guilt on your shoulders and use it to steer you where he wants you."

Vincent gestured toward Devon with a wave of his hand. "That's not what's happening here."

"And what do you think is happening?" Blake asked, while Devon merely waited in silence for his brother to state his opinion.

"What's happening is that he is manipulating things to make everyone forget what he did three years ago. Instead we will all grovel with gratitude because he came back to save us all from utter ruin." He glared at Devon. "Maybe we should both just drop to our knees right now and thank you. What a martyr you are—the good son who sacrificed so much for his younger brothers. Someone get me a bucket so I can retch."

"Vincent," Blake said. "For God's sake, is that really necessary right now?"

"It's all right, Blake," Devon said, holding up a hand. "Let him speak his mind."

Vincent pointed a finger at the table. "Our father said it plainly. We are all named in the amendment to his will, and I have no intention of losing my inheritance, so I, too, shall marry."

"You never fail to surprise me," Devon said.

There was no warmth in Vincent's eyes. "I suppose, if we're going to be dragged by our ears to the altar, we should at least make it interesting. What do you say? I, for one, will fare better if I can call it a race."

Blake pinched the bridge of his nose. "God help us all."

"I will not play that game," Devon informed him.

"Why not?"

"Because I will not compete with you, Vincent, just to feed your hunger to knock me about. Besides, such a challenge hardly leaves room for romance, does it?"

"Then a swift seduction it will have to be," Vincent replied, "with the first decent-looking female who crosses my path. Speaking of which . . ." He stood up and strolled to the window. "Didn't I see Helen of Troy driving up with a coachload of bags this morning? How very convenient."

Without so much as a mere second to think about the finer implications in all this, Devon heard himself say, "Stay away from that one, Vincent. She is mine."

Vincent eyed him shrewdly. "Is that a fact? I didn't think you paid any heed to boundaries where women were concerned."

Devon's gut turned to ice at the sudden memory of that letter he had carried in his pocket three years ago.

"Do you already have an arrangement with Lady Rebecca?" his brother asked.

"No," Devon replied. He had lied to his brother once before and paid the price. He would not do so again.

Vincent laughed at that. "Well, I don't see why *you* get to have first choice."

"I have not yet made my choice."

"It sounds like you have. You just said she was yours."

Devon stopped for a minute to consider his intentions. Did he actually mean to choose Lady Rebecca as a bride without even considering Lady Letitia, or without taking a look around at the other young ladies who were sure to be in London for the first ball of the Season? He barely knew the girl. And that's what she was—a girl. She'd been out in Society for what, a day?

And what of Lady Letitia? he wondered. She would certainly appease their father.

"I have known Lady Rebecca for quite some time," he explained nevertheless, "and I have met her father. For that reason, there is some connection between us."

God help him, even now, some deep, guilt-ridden part of him was pushing him to step aside and let Vincent have first choice—because he owed him that. Didn't he? He certainly owed him something.

But *could* he step aside?

He thought about it, and found himself growing tense.

His brother stared intently at him. "Have you no interest in Lady Letitia? She is the daughter of a duke, and from what I understand, Father handpicked her."

Devon made no reply.

Vincent turned away, waving a dismissive hand. "All right, all right, you can have the Trojan. Perhaps I shall consider Lady Letitia, just to make Father happy because I adore him so." He faced them again and spread his hands wide. "What a noble son I am."

Vincent left the room, and Blake seemed to breathe a sigh of relief, while Devon merely squared his shoulders, going to refill his coffee cup and preparing himself for the week ahead, as it appeared he was suddenly in the market for a wife and had already voiced his preference for one woman in particular.

Who would ever have thought he would find himself herded into a future so soon after returning home? Who would have thought he would give in to the pressure to take a wife in such a swift, calculated fashion?

But what did it matter, he supposed as he stood next to the sideboard and sipped his hot coffee, when all was said and done? He'd always known he would marry one day, and he had come home to make amends and fulfill his duty as heir. He had never been eager to combine marriage with love. Love brought a fleeting, temporary joy, then it inevitably soured into a lifelong hell. He'd seen it countless times before. His parents were no exception, and he'd experienced it quite plainly for himself.

What he needed and what he must look for was someone uncomplicated. Someone who could be a proper duchess, provide heirs, and run this household. Lady Rebecca had been running the house at her father's estate for years, and he was most certainly attracted to her, which would at least make the duty of producing an heir a pleasant one. Unlike Lady Letitia, she had not been out in society for long, so she was a clean slate, so to speak, and would be easily molded to fit into his life at the palace the way he wanted her to. She had no scandals in her past, no other gentlemen sniffing around. Outside of Vincent, that is.

And she was *here*, which was convenient above all else.

Ease and convenience was all he could ask for, really, for everyone knew his opinions about un-

dying love and fairy-tale endings. They were contemptuous at best.

Maximilian Rushton had just pressed his stamp
into a sticky bead of red wax to seal a letter, when
a knock sounded at his door. Irritated by the interruption when he had other letters to write, he
set the stamp down and shouted across the room,
"What the devil is it?"

The maid answered him uncertainly from the
other side of the door. "You asked to see the
room, sir? When it was prepared?"

He stared at the door for a brief moment before
he slid his chair back and stood. A few seconds
later, he was walking into the bedchamber that
would belong to his bride. He stood in front of
the fireplace and let his diligent gaze pass over everything—the fresh bed coverings, the thickness
of the pillows, the quality of the very expensive
rug beside the bed. He assessed the color and design of the wallpaper he had chosen, as well as the
drapes and upholstery on the chairs. The white
bassinet with gilt trimmings in the corner was
spectacular. It would be an effective reminder of
his wife's duty in this room, and would likely give
her some pleasant dreams, imagining a child of
her own one day.

She would be happy here, he decided. At least
until her father was dead, at which time she

would no doubt be pleased to return to her childhood home as Countess of Creighton, with the Creighton heir. His own son. Maximilian would be pleased to relocate there as well. He had been waiting a long time.

Turning toward the fireplace, he inspected the interesting knickknacks he had selected for the mantel. He had chosen ornaments his mother would have approved of—a tiny, ceramic statue of a dog and a delightful fabric box covered in seashells. She'd had a seashell collection of her own, he remembered.

He also had found a small, framed print of a sailing ship. She had always wanted to travel abroad. He was especially proud of the ebony jar designed to hold hatpins—his mother had owned dozens of them—and the sterling silver puff box.

Yes, it was a lovely room for a lady. A bride. A mother. He turned to look at the bassinet, and his gut began to roll with hunger. Tomorrow. She would arrive tomorrow.

His trousers tightened abruptly over a sudden erection. He gritted his teeth with annoyance, just as his gaze shot to the plump parlor maid, who entered the room at that moment with a vase of fresh flowers. He watched her set the vase down on the table close to the window and toy with the arrangement.

Maximilian crossed toward her. The woman

was lazy as the day was long and smelled of stale cabbage, but she would know what he wanted and she would be repulsively eager. It was why he kept her in his employ.

After moving into their rooms at the palace and unpacking their things, Rebecca and her aunt enjoyed an informal luncheon with the female guests, while the gentlemen engaged themselves in a political debate in the library.

They were sitting in the drawing room afterward, sipping tea and eating chocolates, when Lady Letitia rose elegantly from her seat by the piano to join Rebecca at the window.

"Your costume was quite the thing last night," she said, holding her cup and saucer in her slender, long-fingered hands. She towered over Rebecca, who had to crane her neck to look up at her. Letitia's ebony hair was clean and shiny, swept into an ornate, braided twist in the back, which flattered the delicate bone structure of her face. Her complexion was impossibly soft and dewy-looking, altogether feminine, but there was something aggressive in her eyes, which Rebecca noted with caution.

"And your costume was delightful, Lady Letitia. You were lovely in it."

They looked out the window. A lengthy silence ensued.

"I didn't think you were staying at the palace," Letitia said. "In fact, it was my understanding you arrived at the last minute, only to attend the ball."

Rebecca nodded. "That's right. We had rooms reserved at the Pembroke Inn, but last night, Lord Hawthorne was kind enough to invite us to join the family for the rest of the party."

Letitia's eyes narrowed. "How very chivalrous of him. He is a generous man, don't you agree?"

"Yes, very."

They both sipped their tea, saying nothing for another minute or two, then Letitia gestured toward the front of Rebecca's gown. "I must say, you have your own sense of style, don't you? Your dress is very . . . Oh, how can I say this without insulting you? It's very daring for a ladies' luncheon."

Rebecca touched her neckline. It was not so very daring. No worse than any other dress in the room.

Nevertheless, she glanced around just to make sure.

"But you still look lovely in it," Letitia added brightly. "The color is quite nice. Not a shade I would choose, but . . . It looks pretty on you just the same." Her eyes raked over Rebecca from head to foot, then she smiled, but Rebecca detected a hint of scorn.

She resolved to be careful around this woman.

Later that afternoon, everyone gathered together in the conservatory for a poetry reading, where chairs had been set up facing a small dais of stone. The roses and gardenias were in full bloom, and the scent of spring flowers was almost strong enough to distract everyone from the hissing downpour of rain onto the glass ceiling over their heads.

Lady Charlotte was first to read Browning's *Two in the Campagna,* and Rebecca listened to the moving elegance of the words and was lulled by the musical tone of Charlotte's voice as she recited. She was soon distracted, however, by a pair of eyes upon her, staring. She turned her gaze to the left to discover Lady Letitia's head turned in her direction.

Rebecca nodded at her. Letitia nodded in return, then faced front again, lifting her chin as she raised her hands to applaud the reading.

Charlotte lowered her book, and appeared so deeply moved by the poem she'd recited, that she was on the verge of tears. She quietly took her seat in the front row.

Lord Faulkner stood and read *Summer Dawn,* by William Morris. His deep, masculine voice resonated throughout the conservatory. Rebecca listened to every word of the poem, realizing just what she had been missing in life by staying home with her father and never learning the joys of society and other people outside her own small world. She felt as if she were seeing a sunrise for the first time.

When Lord Faulkner finished his reading, she joined the others in enthusiastic applause, then turned her eyes toward the grove of tree ferns where the duke stood, and noticed he was not clapping, but picking at the leaves, tasting them and spitting them out.

Rebecca discreetly glanced over her shoulder at Lord Blake in the row behind her, who had already noticed the duke's strange behavior and was rising from his chair to intervene. When Blake touched his father's shoulder, the man turned his back on the tasty tree ferns and joined his son in applause.

Rebecca looked to the other side of the conservatory where Lord Hawthorne stood alone, leaning upon a low wall of stone around a bed of roses. His long legs were stretched out before him, crossed at the ankles. He had already been watching her. When their eyes met, his expression did not change. He did not smile. He merely watched her with hooded eyes, and she could not move or think or even breathe.

She remembered suddenly why she had come here in the first place when she thought she would be forced to marry Mr. Rushton. She had believed this man could conquer any foe, solve any predicament, and she still believed that was so.

He continued to hold her captive in his cool gaze, and a hot tingling erupted in the pit of her belly. She knew she should look away, for the next guest with a poem had already risen and moved to the front, but she could not, especially when he pushed away from the stone wall and came to sit in the chair beside her.

He said nothing. He merely crossed one leg over the other and listened to the reading.

Lord Faulkner concluded his recital, and while everyone was clapping, Devon leaned a little closer to her. "Are you comfortably settled in?" he asked.

"Yes, thank you," she whispered.

The readings were finished, and the other guests rose from their chairs and murmured in conversation. "You did not have a poem you wished to read?" she asked.

His blue eyes swept over her whole face. "I prefer more intimate surroundings for the reading of poetry."

"I see." Her cheeks flushed with color when she realized how breathlessly she had spoken.

Just then, there was a commotion behind them, and Rebecca turned to see Lady Letitia sigh and stagger, then begin to crumple to the stone floor in a billowing heap of silks and satin.

Devon had already pushed past and caught the young woman in his arms just before she hit the ground. He dropped to his knees and lowered her gently.

"Oh, my word!" Letitia's mother fumbled through her reticule and handed him her vinaigrette.

"Thank you." He flipped open the gold case and waved it under Letitia's perfect, tiny, aristocratic nose.

She gasped and blinked up at him, befuddled. "Good gracious, whatever happened?"

"You must have gotten up from your chair too quickly," Devon replied. "Are you all right?"

"Oh," she said with a sigh, touching her forehead with the back of her hand. "I do beg your pardon, Lord Hawthorne. How mortifying."

"Do not trouble yourself," he said. "Just lie still for a moment until you feel strong enough to stand." A footman approached with a glass of water on a tray, which Devon picked up and handed to Lady Letitia.

The others had crowded around them, gaping down at her, and when it was clear she was going to recover, they began to chatter and disburse.

Aunt Grace came to stand beside Rebecca. "That was quite a performance," she whispered.

Rebecca glanced at her aunt. "Do you really think so?"

Grace raised an eyebrow and shrugged.

"You are so kind, Lord Hawthorne," Letitia said, taking his hand in hers while she continued to blink up at him. "How can I ever make it up to you?"

"Nonsense." He helped her to her feet and began to escort her out of the conservatory, walking past Rebecca and Aunt Grace without so much as a single backward glance. "All I ask is that you feel well enough to attend dinner this evening."

"Oh, yes," she replied. "I'm sure I will be better by then, thanks to your gentlemanly assistance. And I will count every minute."

"As will I." He exited the conservatory with Letitia on his arm, while her mother trotted merrily along behind them.

It was becoming dreadfully apparent to Devon as he mingled through the drawing room reception before dinner, that Lady Letitia and her mother were conniving shamelessly to attract his attention, and to prevent any opportunity that might arise for him to speak to any of the other young ladies in the room, most notably the flame-haired Helen of Troy.

Devon's father was not helping matters either, for he was the one who encouraged Blake to escort Lady Rebecca into dinner, leaving Devon with no choice but to offer his arm to Letitia.

As if he weren't already being maneuvered enough into his future as it was.

Nevertheless, he did not wish to act too hastily in either direction. There was his father to consider, and his inheritance. He had to keep the old man happy.

They took their places at the table, and the meal was served. All the while, Letitia continued with her bold tactics to win his favor. She managed to boast about everything from her beautiful singing voice to her superb skills at archery, while her mother openly supported every narcissistic word that spilled out of her pretty mouth.

"And don't you agree, Lord Hawthorne," she said, when her dessert was set down in front of her, "that any lady of good breeding must have superb conversational skills? That she should have some experience moving about in society? A good hostess cannot hide away in the country, after all."

God help him, her chattering voice was like some kind of nightmare from which he could not awaken.

"You are quite right," he replied. "A lady of true accomplishments must possess some measure of charm."

"Oh, yes. That is how a lady can best serve the needs of her husband."

She gazed across the table at him with amusement in her eyes, as if they were sharing a private intimacy.

After dinner, the ladies retired to the green drawing room for coffee while the gentlemen enjoyed their cigars in the smoking room. Later they all converged in the blue saloon where one of the matrons took a seat at the piano and began to play for an informal country dance.

Devon was not in the mood for dancing, however. Nor did he have any desire to laugh and joke with the gentlemen or spend any more of his time with Lady Letitia, listening to her go on about her first-rate education and awe-inspiring travels to Paris and Rome. He was exhausted from all that had occurred over the past two days—the tension he had come home to, his father's madness, Vincent's hostilities, and his promise that he would be the first to marry. On top of it all, he was experiencing a persistent, aching desire to converse with another woman tonight. He'd had enough interruptions.

At that moment she entered the saloon in a yellow silk gown and pearls, her scarlet hair swept into an elegant twist adorned with sparkling combs. She looked like a welcome ray of sunshine in a room full of thunderclouds.

Their eyes met. She smiled with genuine warmth and crossed to the window, not far from where he stood. He took the liberty of approaching.

"Good evening," he said. She turned and smiled again, as if she had been waiting just for him. "Permit me to say, you look ravishing."

"Shameless flatterer." Her green eyes glimmered with teasing.

A footman strolled by with a tray of sherry, and Devon picked up two glasses and handed one to her. He leaned a shoulder against the wall and slowly sipped his drink, savoring the potent flavor and the pleasant effects of the vision before him—Lady Rebecca, in all her feminine glory.

"Did you enjoy the poetry reading this afternoon?" he asked.

"Yes. I found it very moving."

"You must not be referring to the comedy, then," he whispered, "which took place, stage left?"

"My lord?"

He leaned his head a little closer. "Just so you know, my father hasn't *always* had a penchant for leafy ferns. That is a recently acquired taste, I'm afraid."

She sipped her sherry and took a moment to consider her reply, then gave him a quiet smile. "I thought I was the only one who noticed."

"I hope you were."

They both shook their heads to refuse the offerings on a tray filled with chocolate cookies and squares, brought round by another footman.

"May I presume your father is experiencing some symptoms of old age?" she asked, as soon as the footman moved on.

"You presume correctly."

"It is not uncommon," she assured him, "but difficult for the family nonetheless."

Taking another sip of sherry, she looked away and watched the duke for a moment, while he warmed his hands in front of the fire. Devon saw compassion in her eyes, or was it melancholy? He wished to observe everything about her with great care.

"If there is anything I can do while I am here," she said, "I would be happy to assist. I quite enjoy your father's conversations actually. He is very passionate about his gardens, and I admire his spirit."

"That is most kind of you, Lady Rebecca."

"Well . . . My father has not been well either," she explained. "Though his ailments are more physical. He suffers from rheumatism, which has made life difficult for both of us. It has always hurt me to see him endure the pain." She paused and lowered her gaze while she took a deeper sip, then spoke in a low, somewhat defeated voice. "I am afraid he has not been himself lately."

Could it be she understood exactly what he was going through? Devon felt a connection to her suddenly, and wanted to know more about her.

He wanted to know everything. "I am sorry to hear that."

She lightened her tone and lifted her gaze again. "I am sure it gives your father great comfort to have you home again, Lord Hawthorne. It was good of you to return."

After all his own self-inflicted punishment over the past few days—for all the ways he had not lived up to his responsibilities in the past—her plain assurance was like a balm to his senses. "Those are generous words."

"They are not generous," she said. "It is simply the truth. Your family is fortunate to have you among them."

Before he had a chance to reply, his sister Charlotte joined them, and Rebecca's whole face lit up.

"Lady Charlotte," she said with a warm smile, "I cannot tell you how moved I was by your reading this afternoon. Your voice carried so well, and you read with such confidence and emotion. Your poem was my favorite of the day."

He studied his sister's expression. He had not seen such a smile on her face since before he had left for America. Not even his gift of a pearl bracelet had evoked such joy in her eyes.

"Oh, Lady Rebecca, you are so thoughtful," she replied. "I worry I might have sounded too tragic."

"No, not at all. I mean, you did sound tragic,

but that was what made it so special. There was such sincerity and integrity in your voice. It moved us all and reminded us of the beauty in the world, even when life seems grim."

Charlotte took hold of both her hands. "Thank you, Lady Rebecca. You have made me very happy."

Devon watched the two women, so close in age, as they discussed the other readings, and recognized an immediate connection between them as well. It pleased him to see it, for Charlotte was the only daughter among four sons in this family, and she had not often had a female friend to confide in. She had surely needed one in recent years.

He glanced across the room at Lady Letitia, who had been watching him with a frosty look on her face, but she smiled the instant their gazes met.

Lord Faulkner's son approached and asked Charlotte to join him in the next dance, which left Devon alone with Lady Rebecca again.

"Your sister is very beautiful," she said, as she watched Charlotte move to the center of the room with the young man. There was genuine affection in her eyes. "She has your mother's coloring."

She certainly did not have their father's.

"I will tell her you said so," Devon replied. "But before I do, will you do me the honor?" He held out a hand.

"I would be delighted." Her green eyes held a

hopeful, encouraging gleam that no other eyes could rival.

Indeed, she was making a first-rate impression on everyone, including him. Unlike Lady Letitia, she was a pleasant infusion of fresh air and warm sunshine, wholesome and unselfish and without a cartload of problems trailing along behind her. He was not only attracted to her, but felt some affection toward her as well. Practically speaking, she would be a good choice for a wife.

He glanced briefly at Lady Letitia again as he passed her by. It was highly unlikely *she* could ever win his esteem or fire his passions the way Rebecca did. But that fact alone gave him pause, so much so, he almost fumbled his steps.

He supposed—when one considered his jaded outlook on love and marriage—Lady Letitia would be a good choice as well, in a completely different way. With her, it would be easy to become a husband, yet change very little about the way he lived. He could remain detached.

With that in mind, he decided he would do well to keep his options open.

Chapter 8

The following evening, Rebecca dressed in a formal off-the-shoulder gown of deep blue satin with sapphire jewels and long white gloves, and sat with Aunt Grace in the music room, waiting for the classical quartette to begin playing.

Quietly, she gazed around the room—at the musicians with their instruments and music stands in front of them, at the shiny parquet floor beneath her feet, and finally up at the dazzling brass chandelier over her head. It was quiet in the room except for a few hushed murmurs of conversation toward the back.

"I must admit something, Aunt Grace," she said. "I feel rather dishonest under these circumstances. I came here because I want Lord Hawthorne as my husband, yet I wish to escape another man I do not wish to marry. That, above all, is what has brought me here so hastily. I wish I could simply tell him the truth about my life."

Her aunt clasped her hand. "You simply cannot ask a man to marry you in order to do you a favor. He must *want* to marry you, preferably because he loves you. And if he does, it will be his greatest desire to protect you from every unpleasant thing in the world, whether it is Mr. Rushton or a bumblebee flying around your bonnet. That is when you will be able to tell him everything, dearest, and he will embrace every challenge you represent."

"Let us hope it will come to that."

She checked over her shoulder and saw Lord Hawthorne enter the room with his sister, Lady Charlotte.

"There he is," her aunt said, "and I must say, he is looking very handsome. Good gracious."

Tonight he wore a fine black evening jacket with white waistcoat and tie, and his dark, wavy hair was slicked back, gleaming in the lamplight. The style accentuated the strong, rugged lines of his face.

He met Rebecca's gaze and inclined his head at her. She smiled in return, then faced front again, struggling to overcome the uncontrollable beat of her heart when the evening had only just begun.

"Oh, Aunt Grace, who am I trying to deceive?" she said. "I want to marry him for love and a grand passion, nothing else. I want the fairy tale with my charming, handsome hero. Mr. Rushton does not even exist for me now that I am here."

Her aunt leaned close and whispered, "I assure you, my dear, Mr. Rushton *does* exist, and he could be searching for you at this very moment. For that reason, it is imperative that you do what you must to secure the man you really want. A man who can protect you."

"Do what I must . . ."

"Yes," her aunt plainly replied, flicking open her fan and fluttering it in front of her face. "You saw what Lady Letitia resorted to in the conservatory yesterday."

"Are you suggesting I should pretend to swoon? I couldn't, Aunt Grace. I would feel like a fool."

"That is not what I am talking about. You know what I mean, do you not?" She raised an eyebrow.

Thanks to Lydie's most illustrative diary, Rebecca had a feeling she knew *exactly* what her aunt was referring to.

"You must touch his arm once with your closed fan when you are speaking to him," Aunt Grace whispered.

Touch his arm with her fan. "That is all?"

"What do you mean, that is all? It is a very bold maneuver."

If that was what most women considered bold, Rebecca was definitely out of touch with what went on in society. Clearly, she had been reading too much lately about sin and debauchery and the pleasures of the flesh. It was a very wicked pastime. She should stop, she really should.

She glanced over her shoulder at Lord Hawthorne, and felt that familiar stirring of desire, warm and intoxicating, heady and erotic. . .

Clicking open her fan, she sighed, because she knew the minute she returned to her room, she would be dashing to her bed and reaching very quickly for that wonderfully wicked diary, for more instructions on how to proceed. And if there was to be any swooning in her immediate future, it would be completely legitimate.

Devon entered the music room with his sister, Charlotte, and immediately spotted Lady Rebecca already seated with her aunt in the front row. She turned around and clicked open her fan, met his gaze over the top of it and smiled at him with her eyes while she fluttered it.

God help him, that russet hair and green eyes set his impulses fluttering as well, and he became instantly uncomfortable with the fact that despite his desire to remain detached and practical-minded, he was becoming more and more inclined to charge forth blindly and impulsively in order to ensure she would be his. He wasn't in danger of falling in love, was he?

No, it could not be that. He simply had a duty to fulfill and promises to keep, and he was trying to make the best of it by focusing on his physical attraction to a woman who might one day be his duchess and provide the dukedom with an heir.

He certainly had no reservations about succumbing to *that* part of his duty.

Taking seats near the front on the opposite side of the room, he and Charlotte conversed about the quartette and the evening ahead. His sister leaned forward slightly in her chair.

"I see Lady Rebecca is here. Oh, she is lovely, I must say—so pleasant and sincere and agreeable. And what I wouldn't give for hair like that. She is so different from every other woman in the room, and so very becoming. Don't you think?"

Devon leaned forward as well and admired the loose sweep of Rebecca's hair over the back of her slender neck, and the graceful line of her soft, creamy shoulders. "Your own hair is exquisite, Charlotte. You take after Mother, who has always been regarded as a great beauty."

They both looked toward the back of the room where their mother was greeting the guests. Their father, the duke, entered and pumped the hands of all the gentlemen standing at the back, then went and spoke to Lady Letitia and her mother.

"Well, I certainly don't take after *him*," Charlotte said with more than a little resignation.

"Neither you nor Garrett do," he said. "But look on the bright side. At least you haven't inherited his propensity to believe in curses. I, on the other hand, might one day believe the palace is being overtaken by leprechauns."

He was not surprised when Lady Letitia and the Duchess of Swinburne approached and claimed the seats beside him. The young lady began to immediately go on about the quartette, and how she had heard them play once before. As soon as the music began, she prattled on with a dozen insignificant little criticisms, implying of course that she could do better.

"It is a shame this quartette does not have a soloist to sing for your guests," she said far too loudly, between pieces, while the players turned the pages of their music sheets and pretended not to hear her. "Wouldn't you like to hear someone sing, Lord Hawthorne? Surely you enjoy an accomplished vocalist, do you not?"

"The music of an accomplished vocalist is always a great pleasure," he replied. "Perhaps you will consider singing for us later this evening, Lady Letitia?"

Her eyes beamed with satisfaction. "I would be delighted, Lord Hawthorne." She gave him that look again, as if they were secret paramours.

After the concert, the guests moved to the red drawing room where champagne and hors d'oeuvres were being served. Devon mentioned to his mother that Lady Letitia would be showing off her vocal talents later, then he conversed his way through the crowd to where Rebecca and her aunt stood tasting pastries.

"Good evening, ladies." He bowed to each of them. "I trust you enjoyed the music this evening."

Lady Saxby quickly swallowed. "Yes, very much, Lord Hawthorne. And may I personally thank you for inviting us to stay at the palace under such short notice?"

"It was my pleasure." He turned to her niece. "And you have everything you require, Lady Rebecca?"

"Yes, thank you. Your family has been most welcoming. And the palace itself . . ." She looked around the room. "Well, there is no possible way to describe its beauty, Lord Hawthorne. It absolutely takes my breath away."

All at once, he found himself a little short of breath as well, and spoke before he considered any outcomes or ramifications. "In that case, may I be so bold as to escort you to the gallery, where I might show you my family's collection?"

Bold, to be sure. He might as well have declared himself right there. Strangely, however, he didn't care if he was charging past the point of no return. He just wanted to be alone with her.

"I would be delighted, Lord Hawthorne." Her voice was soft and velvety, and sank into his masculine impulses like fine wine.

He escorted her out of the drawing room and down the long, vaulted corridor under the keystone arch to the gallery, where his ancestral history could be revealed in less than fifteen minutes.

"Let us begin," he said, "with this portrait of the first Duke of Pembroke."

They looked up at the life-size painting. The duke stood with feet apart, hands on hips.

"The pose is very similar to the famous portrait of King Henry VIII," she said.

"Yes, but this was painted by a different artist."

He watched her profile in the dim light from the wall sconces as she looked up at the portrait with a charming sense of wonder. "There is great courage in the artistry," she said, tilting her head to the side. "I am beguiled by the variety of brush strokes. It almost seems like a revolt against the classical balance of High Renaissance art. It's willful and anxious."

Devon continued to watch her, feeling rather beguiled himself.

"Am I correct," she asked, "in my knowledge of your family's history—that the title of duke was a gift to this man from King Henry himself?"

"Indeed, you are. My ancestor chose this site as the palace location for personal reasons, which at the time were deemed quite scandalous."

"You have inspired my curiosity, Lord Hawthorne. What was the scandal?"

They began to stroll to the next portrait. "It is quite an intriguing story," he explained, "because the palace itself, to this day, sits upon the ruins of an ancient abbey. The east courtyard is the old cloister."

"Yes, of course," she replied. "I strolled there this afternoon."

"Well," he went on, "in 1522, the prior was murdered by two of his own canons, who had discovered his secret love affair with a local woman." He leaned a little closer. "In case you are wondering, that is the scandalous part."

"Obviously."

"After the prior's death, the woman had his son, then years later, the abbey was dismantled during King Henry's Dissolution of the Monasteries, and all the monks were sent away. The boy grew up and surprisingly went on to become one of the king's trustworthy allies, and was later awarded the title of duke."

"Which means your ancestor was the murdered prior's son," she said with some fascination. "You are correct, Lord Hawthorne, it is a most intriguing story. Though it does pain me to know that there is tragedy in your family's past."

"Rest assured, the wounds are healed," he replied. "It was many generations ago." He stopped and pointed at the small, oval portrait before them. "This is all we have of the first duke's mother, who died when he was still a boy."

"She was lovely."

"Yes. It is unfortunate that she never knew what her son would accomplish. Shall we move on?"

"Please."

They continued up the long gallery, looking at the other family portraits and discussing the estate's collection of French and Italian works.

"I am impressed with your knowledge of art," he said when they started back toward the drawing room. "You have a very sophisticated eye."

"But I confess, Lord Hawthorne, that most of my knowledge comes from books, as I have rarely been away from my father's estate." She gazed up at him again with those stunning green eyes, and he felt almost weak in the knees, awaiting her next confession.

"So I am yearning," she continued, "to experience real life for myself. I wish to know all its many pleasures—pleasures I have never known. Sometimes I fear I am going to collapse from the pressure of all my pent-up desires."

He studied her face, trying to decide whether she was a supremely accomplished flirt with no inhibitions—which he doubted—or if she was so incredibly innocent, she had no idea of what she was implying with such silky words and sensual looks. How did she know to say things like this?

He supposed it did not matter. The effect was

the same. He found her irresistible in the most basic carnal way. He was even tempted to pull her into his arms right here in the gallery and taste the flavor of her lips and satisfy those pent up desires she had just mentioned. The urge almost knocked him over. He had never met a woman so sexually alluring, yet so remarkably innocent at the same time. What a contradiction she was, and how very convenient that he had found such a woman when he was obliged to take that long dreaded walk down the aisle.

She was an innocent, he wanted to bed her, and maybe, just maybe he could.

He stopped on the soft carpet and held both her gloved hands in front of him. "I am pleased you decided to join us for the week, Lady Rebecca."

Her eyes lit up like the morning sun, and she spoke with fiery passion. "I am pleased, too. More than you could ever know. You see, I have never forgotten that night in the forest four years ago, and I have thought of you so many times since then. And when you left for America, all I did was yearn for you to return."

His head drew back in surprise. Only then did he realize his smile had reversed itself.

Not that he was angry or unhappy with her. Quite the opposite in fact. He felt rather swept away by a very romantic twisting of fate that had brought them together a second time—at a very

convenient time—after that intense first meeting.
Here he was, listening to her bold declarations
of yearning, suddenly giving in to romantic notions when he was the least romantic man in the
world.

"What exactly did you yearn for?" he asked in
a low voice, feeling a shameful compulsion to lure
her out of her innocence, when he had not yet of-
ficially declared himself.

She wet her lips. "I longed to see you again,"
she told him.

"So now that you've seen me," he said, taking
a step even closer to her—so close, it was beyond
propriety—"is there anything else you want?"

Her eyes glistened with anticipation. "Yes. A
great many things."

He was experienced enough to recognize the
heated tone of her voice, and for that reason, she
did not need to elaborate. It was enough that he
could feel the pull of her desires flanking his own.

He looked over the top of her head, down the
length of the gallery. Ascertaining that they were
alone, he took her hand and led her to the edge
of the room. He spun her, as if taking a step in a
dance, and the next thing he knew, he had her up
against the wall with his hands braced on either
side of her. She was looking up at him with eager
eyes and parted lips, and he could smell the flow-
ery fragrance of her perfume.

"Is *this* what you were longing for?" he asked.

"Yes."

He looked down at her moist and tempting lips. "Have you ever been kissed, Lady Rebecca?"

"Never in my life."

"Then you might want to prepare yourself," he said in a low whisper, "because I intend to be your first."

He dipped his head and tasted at last the flavor of that warm, sweet mouth.

A tiny whimper escaped her and she slid her arms up over his shoulders and wrapped them around his neck, urging him to press his upper body to the lush swell of her breasts and pin her tight to the wall. She was surprisingly eager, which was by no means a complaint.

Her thumb stroked the line of his jaw. His body quickened, and he deepened the kiss and swept his tongue into her mouth. She kissed him in return like a seasoned lover, though he knew she was not. Her sexuality simply came naturally, he suspected. He had picked up on it from the beginning.

She tipped her head back and he kissed and suckled the side of her soft neck.

"What if someone comes?" she asked.

"There's no one here," he assured her, bending at the knees and sweeping his pelvis upward in a scooping motion that almost lifted her off her feet.

"Oh, Lord Hawthorne, you have no idea how many times I've dreamed of this."

"What else have you dreamed of?" he asked. "Tell me and I'll do it for you."

"I couldn't possibly say."

He pressed his mouth to hers again and tasted her lips and tongue, then brushed his open hand down the front of her neck and kissed the skin just above her low neckline, where the swell of her breasts was driving him mad with lust. He simply could not resist her. "I really wish you would. I want to hear you say wicked things."

She blinked up at him and tipped her head back against the wall, as if she did not possess the strength to keep it upright on her own. Her eyes were lazy with desire. "I've dreamed of what it would be like to feel you on top of me, and I like to imagine how heavy you would be. Every time I imagine it, I can almost feel you inside me. I've grown to crave the sensations."

They were hardly the words of a virgin. But she had said she'd never been kissed. Was she lying?

Whether she was or wasn't, it hardly mattered. In fact, he would almost prefer it if she were not a virgin, so he could take her to his bed this very night—with or without a wedding ring.

"What a coincidence," he replied with a smile, gently thrusting his hips toward hers. "Right now I'm craving all the sensations as well."

She whispered with breathless anticipation. "I'm still afraid someone will come."

He brushed his lips against her ear. "Don't be afraid. No one will see."

"How is it you always have everything under control?"

"But I don't," he openly replied, lowering himself onto one knee and looking up at her while she rested her hands lightly upon his shoulders.

"What are you doing?"

He gave no answer. He simply kept his gaze locked on hers as he slid his hands down her waist, feeling the shape of her hips beneath all the layers of her shiny, satin gown. He moved his hands over her thighs and knees and down her calves until he reached the lacy hem. He continued to look up at her, noting by the rise and fall of her luscious breasts how quickly she was breathing.

He reached under the gown and wrapped his hands around each tiny foot, his grip gently pulsing.

Another whimper escaped her, revealing a mixture of shock and fear and delight. "This is *very* wicked," she said.

"Yes." He slid his hands up to her slender ankles, feeling the fine texture of her stockings while he stroked the inner bones with his thumbs. Still, he did not pull his gaze from hers, for it gave him great pleasure to watch her eyes roll back slightly as she inhaled.

She was leaning forward now with more of her weight resting on his shoulders. He slid his hands up a little farther to the warmth at the backs of her knees, drew two figure eights there on each one, which made her quiver, then he ran his fingers like feathers down the length of her calves to her ankles. He lingered there a moment, then returned to her knees again, rubbing his thumbs in tiny circles over the soft flesh.

"Higher?" he asked in a husky voice.

"Yes."

He slid his hands up the front of her thighs until the tips of his thumbs slid into her split drawers and touched her soft, wispy curls. The heat and moisture there was intoxicating, and he paused a moment, considering his options. Dare he go farther? Was it even necessary? He'd already done more than enough to require that he propose and she accept.

But the fact was, at the moment, this had nothing to do with that, and everything to do with the fierce yearning taking over his body. He wanted to touch her and feel the creamy heat of her womanhood. Marriage proposal or no, he wanted her salty scent on his fingers long after they'd returned to the drawing room.

He slid the pad of one thumb into her heated folds, and shuddered with his own burst of pleasure from the inviting wetness.

"Step wider," he said, and she moved her feet apart.

He continued to look up at her beautiful face while he stroked her slick opening, searching, feeling. Then he found it. Her maidenhead. She was indeed a virgin. Not that it mattered at this point, because he wanted her regardless of anything.

And he would have her.

Her eyes had fallen closed, and her arms were locked straight, braced upon his shoulders while her soft, pulsating body swayed to and fro. "Oh, that is heavenly," she gasped, squeezing his shoulders tighter and tighter until she was clutching the fabric of his jacket in her fists. "I'm going to have an orgasm."

He felt his eyebrows pull together in a frown.

Virgin, yes. Innocent, most definitely not.

Struggling to hide his dismay, at least for the time being, he continued until she shuddered and quivered and gasped with delight—he was not sure he'd ever made a woman climax so quickly—then her upper body tipped forward, and she rested her head upon his shoulder. "Oh, that was magnificent," she said. "You know *just* what you're doing."

Evidently, so did she.

He checked again, left and right, to make sure there was no one about, then gave her a moment to recover in that position.

A minute or two later, he withdrew his hands from under her skirt, smoothed it out, and rose to his feet. She opened her eyes and smiled lazily at him.

"I thought you told me you'd never been kissed," he said.

She appeared somewhat surprised by the remark. "I haven't."

"Then may I ask . . . ?" He paused, not quite sure how to articulate himself in a respectful way. "How do you know the things you do?"

"What do you mean?"

"Surely you've had some experience," he continued, prodding her. "You used the word orgasm without modesty. I'm not criticizing. I'm just a little . . . perplexed."

"Isn't that what all women say?" she frankly asked.

"Perhaps *some*," he replied with a chuckle of dismay, quite unable to believe his ears. "But only after they'd been to all four corners of a gentleman's bed, if you understand my meaning."

"Oh." Her face drained of color. "I understand," she said, "but I assure you that I have not been to any of those four corners."

He couldn't help but smile. She seemed very prim and proper all of a sudden. "I believe you." He rested his hands on her hips. "I think."

"But you must," she insisted. "There is a very

simple explanation. You see, I . . . Oh, this is all very strange to be talking about. I found an old diary a few years ago, not long after we met that night in the woods, and every entry is about . . ." She hesitated.

"What we just did?"

"Yes, and other things."

He nodded his head. "Ah, the mystery is solved."

"Do you believe me?"

"I think so. But where in the world did you find such a diary?"

"Under a loose floorboard in my father's stable," she replied. "It was written in 1828 and was covered in dust, so it had obviously been there for quite some time."

"Do you know who it belonged to?"

"No, only that her first name was Lydie. She describes her love affair with a young man named Jess. I think he might have been a servant who worked for my grandfather."

He ran a finger lightly over her cheek. "I must say, that sounds like very compelling reading. Do you have it with you?"

"It's in my room."

In her room. Indeed.

"Might I borrow it?" he asked.

"Definitely not," she said. "It's dreadfully wicked. You would be shocked. Horrified."

He grinned again at her charming innocence. "I think I can manage the upset."

Her lips pursed with shameless chagrin. "We are behaving very badly, my lord."

"Without question. And please, call me Devon," he said, knowing that to encourage the use of their given names was yet another clear indication of his intentions.

"And I hope you will call me Rebecca," she replied, indicating her intentions as well. She slowly blinked up at him, and the effect was pure seduction. "But how should I give the diary to you?" she asked. "I don't want anyone else to see it."

"I'll come to your room tonight and pick it up."

She raised an eyebrow. "I may lack experience, but I do know that that would be highly improper."

"And this wasn't?" he reminded her with a chuckle. "Trust me, darling, it will be our little secret. No one will know."

She glanced around the gallery, as if to make sure they were not being watched. "All right," she whispered. "But wait at least an hour after I retire."

"Whatever you say." He pressed his lips to hers again and willed his tremendous erection to diminish—at least for the time being. "I am going to want more of you," he said.

"And I, you," she replied, resting her hands on his forearms. "But I do hope you believe that I've never done anything like this before. I don't want you to have the wrong impression of me."

"I have the exact impression I wish to have," he assured her, as he raised her hand to his lips and kissed the back of it, realizing all at once that he was not only attracted to her sexually, but quite enamored with her as well, which was not what he'd had in mind when he imagined choosing a bride in such a rush, for he was not a romantic. He was a realist, and he had certainly never imagined desiring a woman who would remember a simple rescue years earlier, and view him in an idealistic fashion. As if he were some kind of hero.

He had experienced such a thing before with disastrous consequences, and it had shaped him into the man he was today—a man who was exceedingly cautious with women and their emotions. A man who did not seek romantic, all-consuming love.

No, he had never wanted to be the sun, the moon, and stars to a wife, yet for some reason he could not seem to kick free of the wave that was carrying him into his future. It was all happening so fast, and after what just occurred, after the liberties he had taken with her and the things he had said and implied—and what might very well happen later tonight when he visited her room—

this would all have to be decided upon and arranged quickly. There could be no turning back.
No escape.

He had, for better or worse, closed the window
on his options.

Chapter 9

The instant Rebecca entered the drawing room with Devon at her side, Lady Letitia fixed her scalding eyes on them both and pursed her lips.

Devon escorted Rebecca back to her aunt, who asked about the artwork they had viewed, but when he turned to go and mingle with the other guests, he nearly stepped on Lady Letitia's toes, for she had approached him from behind.

"Lord Hawthorne, I would be pleased to entertain your guests now. I have already selected a piece of music I think you will enjoy, and my mother has offered to accompany me on the piano."

She looked past Devon's shoulder to glance smugly at Rebecca.

"That would be splendid," he replied. "Please, take your places whenever you are ready."

She strode to the piano, and her mother joined her. The guests found places to sit, while Devon moved to the fireplace and leaned an elbow upon the mantel. Lady Letitia looked to him for a signal, and he nodded to begin.

She sang the timeless classic, "Home, Sweet Home," showing off an insistent vibrato in her voice and furrowing her brow with a dramatic outpouring of emotion.

Letitia curtsied deeply when she finished, and the applause began. "Thank you so much. You are so kind." She cupped her hands together in front of her and gestured toward Devon at the mantel, suggesting he deserved applause as well, for arranging her performance.

He shook his head at the generous show of appreciation and directed everyone's attention back to Lady Letitia, who thanked them all again.

Not long afterward, the young woman found Rebecca alone on the sofa. She sat on the edge of the cushion with her spine as stiff and straight as a hot iron poker. "Do you not have any talents to display?" she asked, eyeing Rebecca with scrutiny over the rim of her wine glass.

"How could anyone possibly follow your brilliant performance this evening, Lady Letitia?"

They sat in silence, looking around at everyone else, not at each other, until Lady Letitia spoke in a low voice. "In case you are wondering, I saw you go off with Lord Hawthorne earlier, and I fear I would be a very bad friend if I did not inform you that you are making quite a spectacle of yourself."

Rebecca's heart began to pound a little faster. "How so?"

"By being too pushy. I don't know how young ladies are brought up where *you* come from, Lady Rebecca, but here in polite society—which you obviously know very little about—behavior like that can get a lady into trouble."

Rebecca frowned. "I was not pushy. He invited me to view his family portraits, but I hardly need to explain myself to you."

Letitia wet her lips, and finally met Rebecca's gaze. "I really wish you would leave."

"I beg your pardon?"

"I said I wish you would leave. You were not invited to this party, and you are getting in the way."

"In the way of what?"

Letitia lifted her chin and spoke in a low voice again. "Of my future."

Rebecca openly scoffed. "And the whole world revolves around your wishes and desires, does it?"

"*I* am the one the Duke of Pembroke chose to be the next duchess. That is why we came all this way through the putrid rain and muck. You are dreaming if you think you can walk in here and turn Lord Hawthorne's head. You are nothing but an unsophisticated country girl." She stood.

"Lord Hawthorne might be willing to *amuse* himself with you in a dimly lit gallery," she added in an angry whisper, "but he knows what his father wants. He will never propose."

With that, she turned and strode to the piano to entertain the guests with another merry tune.

Rebecca remained in her seat with a sick knot in her belly, while she glanced uneasily around the room.

"All is well?" Grace asked, probing discreetly for information about what had occurred between Rebecca and Devon in the gallery, and why Rebecca had suddenly lost interest in the party and wished to retire.

"Everything is fine," she replied.

Her aunt did not seem willing to accept such a vague answer. "Exactly *how* fine, darling? You mustn't leave me wondering, or I won't be able to sleep tonight. What happened while you were in the gallery?"

Rebecca hesitated while she considered how to satisfy her aunt's curiosities, without confessing the shocking, wicked and depraved details. She had behaved inexcusably in the gallery because she could not restrain her out-of-control desires, and now she was troubled by Lady Letitia's warnings.

She leaned closer and whispered. "He asked me to call him Devon."

Her aunt placed both hands over her heart. "Gracious me. That is as good as a proposal."

"Let us not be overly optimistic, Aunt Grace."

"But he is a gentleman. Surely he would not trifle with your affections in such a way. I am certain his feelings have become engaged."

"I shall go to sleep hoping," Rebecca said.

Grace smiled and hugged her. "You are a gem, darling. Everything is going to work out just the way you want it to. I am certain of it."

With that, they said goodnight, but Rebecca remained in the corridor for a moment, watching her aunt enter her own bedchamber next door.

She hoped she had not made a mistake, surrendering to her passions so openly with Lord Hawthorne and giving in to every erotic suggestion he made. Now he wanted to come to her bedchamber personally and borrow her scandalous diary, which she had never shown to anyone. He was actually going to read it and know all the things she had fantasized about over the past four years. It was beyond scandalous—far worse than being simply *pushy*.

Just thinking about such things, however, caused something to quiver and pulse inside her, and she realized that even if she *was* handing over the whole cottage and sheep herd to Devon without so much as a shilling in return, she couldn't possibly turn back now. She'd already said yes to his every request, and he would be knocking at her door in an hour. She could only hope it would lead to a proposal, but it was a risky game she was playing.

With a sigh, she put her hand on the doorknob and turned it, wondering further about the logistics of this. Should she dress for bed or remain in her formal evening gown until he came and left? She couldn't imagine answering the door in her dressing gown. That would only add to the appalling list of sinful improprieties this evening.

She supposed, if she wanted to redeem herself, she could just hand him the diary though a crack in the door, then quickly shut it in his face.

Quietly crossing the threshold, she entered her dark bedchamber, but left the door open for some light while she moved to the lamp on the bedside table. She found the matches and struck one, then removed the glass chimney and touched the flame to the wick. The room took on a golden glow, and she replaced the chimney on the lantern and looked toward the large *armoire*, where she kept the diary hidden inside her valise.

"Did you forget where you put it?" a masculine voice asked, causing her to gasp and whirl around to face the bed.

There he lay, stretched out at his ease with one long leg crossed over the other, his arms pulled back behind his head. He had taken off his dinner jacket, which was tossed over the footboard.

She laid a hand over her thumping heart. "Good Lord! What is the matter with you, scaring me like that? And how did you get up here so fast?"

"I know every secret passageway in this house like the back of my hand."

"There are secret passageways?"

He pointed at a life-size portrait of an ancestor on the wall. It was slightly ajar. "I came in through there."

She studied it curiously, then hurried to shut the bedchamber door before someone walked by and discovered him laid out like a pleasure god on her bed. "Keep your voice down," she said. "And you promised to wait an hour."

"I was bored."

"You were randy, more like it, wanting to see what's in that diary."

She shut the door and faced him. He leaned up on an elbow. "You have me pegged. But let me hear you say 'randy' again."

His teasing tone sent a tremor of excitement through her. Oh, she was doomed.

"*Randy*. Now please get off my bed."

He sighed with resignation, then swung his legs to the floor, but continued to sit with his hands curled around the edge of the mattress. "Do you know that you are the most exciting woman I have met in a very long time?"

"More exciting than Lady Letitia?" she boldly asked.

His eyes darkened with desire. "Far more."

It was exactly what she wanted to hear, but now was not the time to be bringing up another woman.

"I asked you nicely to get up," she reminded him, determined to at least *try* and behave respectably, even though she'd already chopped and burned and utterly annihilated that bridge behind her.

He smirked, then stood up and spread his hands wide. "There. How's that?"

"Better. Now go over there." She pointed to the fireplace on the opposite side of the room.

"Don't you trust me?"

"Frankly, no."

He chuckled and sauntered to the hearth, while she went to the *armoire*.

"It's damp in here," he said. "Allow me to light a fire for you."

"Thank you."

She knelt and reached into the lining of her valise for the old diary, then rose to her feet and turned to watch him lay out the kindling and strike a match. He was crouching down, his shoulders broad, his torso narrow, his buttocks muscular beneath his formal black trousers, stretched taut.

Holding the diary at her side, she suddenly understood why Lydie had needed to write about her lover and her passions on each glorious page of her diary. She hadn't wanted to forget what it felt like.

Rebecca was tempted to start a diary of her own. Surely, with this man as her subject, it would be a masterpiece. For her eyes only, of course.

He picked up the poker and shifted the logs around, drawing out the flames, sending sparks snapping and floating up into the black chimney, then he straightened and wiped his hands together. He turned to face her, gesturing toward the book she held at her side. "Is that it?"

"Yes," she said.

"May I look at it?"

Her heart began to pound as she held it out. For some reason when they had agreed to this earlier, she had imagined he would take the diary back to his own room and read it in private—for it was, needless to say, a very private kind of book. But she now understood that he intended to read it here.

He moved across the thick oval carpet and took it from her, keeping his gaze locked on hers the entire time until he turned and moved away, back toward the fireplace where the light was better.

He opened the book and read the first page.

Rebecca remained where she was, speechless and paralyzed, as if she were sharing her own diary with someone, for no one else had ever read this treasure she had kept hidden away since the day she'd found it.

Devon stood in front of the fire for a few minutes, then he slowly lowered himself into the wing chair and continued to read.

Eventually Rebecca moved to the bed and sat down. The only noises in the room were the sparks snapping in the fireplace, the mantel clock ticking, and the sound of pages turning.

She removed her earrings and necklace and set them on the bedside table, then sat quietly, trying to stay calm while she watched Devon read.

A short time later, he closed the book and looked at her. "This is indeed compelling reading, Rebecca. I think I should stop."

"Does it make you feel guilty, because it's someone else's private thoughts?" she asked. "I certainly felt that way at first."

"It's not that." He rose to his feet and came to stand before her. "May I ask you something?"

"Yes."

"When you read this book, do you fantasize about doing all the things Lydie does?"

Heaven help her, she wanted him to know. She'd *always* wanted him to know. "Yes."

"Do you ever fantasize about it with me?"

"Always with you."

His blue eyes warmed, then he held out the book. "Read something to me."

She slowly took it from him. "I'm not sure I can."

"Why not?"

"Because I don't think I could bring myself to say aloud some of the words Lydie uses."

His voice was quiet. "You said some colorful things in the gallery, remember?"

"Yes, but that was when I was . . ." She hesitated.

"Aroused?"

A passionate fluttering began low in her belly. "Yes."

A log dropped in the grate, and she looked toward it, feeling strangely mesmerized by the dancing flames.

"Why don't you turn to your favorite entry," he said.

Seated on the edge of the bed, she looked up at him. *I should not let this go further*, she thought. *I should ask him to leave*. But despite her fears of spoiling everything, she could do nothing but surrender to his will because she wanted him. She wanted this.

She opened the book and flipped through the pages near the start, and began to read aloud.

"Dear Diary,
"Today was my birthday, and Jess gave me a beautiful white stone he had found on a beach

when he was a boy. He told me he'd been keeping it all these years just for me, even though we met only six months ago. I will never, ever part with it, Diary. Not as long as I live.

"But that is not all that happened today, for I was very, very wicked, and if Mother and Father knew what I had done, they would surely send me away.

"Tonight, after they went to bed, I locked my door, put the lamp in my window, and waited for Jess to climb inside. We could not speak a word to each other for fear of being caught, but we did not need words, such is the depth of our bond to one another."

Rebecca stopped reading and glanced up at Devon, who was listening attentively. She cleared her throat to continue.

"I never felt such wild desire and passionate yearnings in my body. My blood raced with need as I looked down at his enormous erection. How I longed to touch it and feel the silky heat in my hand. I sat down on the bed, and he sat beside me."

Rebecca stopped reading again when Devon slowly sat down beside her.

"Continue," he said.

Feeling the heat of his muscular thigh touching hers on the bed, she fought her own dizzying desires and swallowed nervously.

"He kissed the side of my neck while he eased me onto my back."

Devon leaned closer and pressed his open mouth to her neck, just below the line of her jaw. His warm, wet tongue sent gooseflesh tingling down her body, as he suckled downward to the juncture at her shoulder.

She went weak all over, and was powerless to resist the lure of erotic sensation as he laid her down on the soft mattress. She knew she should not be giving in so easily. This was not how she'd intended to win his heart, but she could not stop herself. She could not.

"Keep reading," he whispered between kisses as he tasted the base of her throat. Rebecca barely managed to hold the book open in front of her.

"He unbuttoned the top of my nightdress and kissed and fondled my breasts, taking my firm, sensitive nipples into his mouth and sucking greedily upon them, until I was filled with such hunger, it was all I could do to keep from crying out."

Devon had already begun to unbutton her gown, and quivering as she was with desire, she could not continue to hold the book. She let it fall to the bed and reached up to touch his face. He kissed her mouth, thrusting his tongue inside, then pushed her bodice open and probed with his tongue into her cleavage at the top of her corset. It was all too much. She wanted him so desperately. She could not stop.

"Sit up," he whispered. "I need to take this off you." He began to ease her bodice off her shoulders.

She did not argue, for she was floating in the exotic realm of her sexual fantasies, even when she knew she should be thinking about more practical matters—like whether or not this was wise when she wanted a marriage proposal from him.

But she had wanted this for so long, and it wasn't as if she had just met him this week. He had been living in her heart for four lonely years. She was eager and aching with desire. She could not let go of this.

Soon she was nude from the waist up, feeling no modesty as she lowered herself onto the bed again and inched up onto the pillows.

With dark, mischievous seduction in his eyes, he crawled over her on all fours, then he tasted a nipple, teasing it with his tongue and squeezing it gently between his teeth. He began nuzzling her breasts with his lips and cheeks, tickling her with his hair, dropping wet kisses down the center of her trembling belly until she gasped with delight.

"What happens next?" he asked.

She didn't have to open the diary because she had every word of that entry memorized. "He removes her gown completely, then takes off all his clothes and mounts her, his body slick with sweat in the summer heat while her heart is racing with excitement and fear, for she'd never felt his shaft between her legs before. She'd only held it in her hands."

By the time she'd finished describing it, Devon was already unfastening her skirt buttons and untying the tapes of her white split drawers. She raised her hips while he pulled them down and tossed everything to the floor.

She was completely naked now. Her body melted in the excruciating pleasure of all her wild, erotic fantasies coming true.

He slid off the bed and stood to remove all his clothes, too, and when he was nude in the warm, golden light of the fire, Rebecca let her gaze float down to his enormous manhood, standing straight out, thick and long and shocking to her virginal eyes.

She was captivated.

He watched her with some amusement, then smiled knowingly, as if he recognized her fascination. It was a sexual grin, relaxed and full of cool confidence. "You might want to hold it in your hand first, if you want to know what Lydie knows."

"I do."

He came to lie beside her again, stretching out on his back, naked and magnificent like a great work of art. It seemed he was laying himself out for her benefit, to allow her time to satisfy her curiosity and explore the secrets of a man's body. He presented himself to her without modesty.

More than eager to begin her exploration and discovery, she sat up on her knees beside him and wrapped her hand around his erection, which was so much hotter than she'd ever imagined it would be.

She stroked and massaged him in the firelight, then slid her hand lower between his legs to toy with the rest of his tremendous, masculine anatomy, the way Lydie had described doing on so many incredible occasions.

"Please lie on top of me now," she whispered, brushing her lips lightly over his. "Mount me, like Jess does to Lydie in the book."

"Honestly, darling," he said as he rose to the task, "the things that come out of your delicious mouth . . ."

She lay down with her head on the feathery pillows. He rolled over onto her, massive and heavy, pressing her into the soft mattress. She spread her legs wide and felt the intimate tip of his penis against her hot, waiting core. Sizzling tension filled the air.

"Lydie's heart begins to race even faster," she said. "She is terrified, but at the same time overcome by her passions."

Rebecca ran her hands through Devon's thick, black hair and shivered with pleasure as he blew gently into her ear. "But her young lover does not take her virginity that night. He does not exert pressure, nor does he push or thrust into the depths of her body."

Devon went still, then lifted his head. "He doesn't?"

"No," she replied. "He simply lies on top of her with the silky tip of his erection poised against her maidenhead, holding her and looking into her eyes with love and affection."

"For how long?" he asked, sounding rather baffled.

"Until he rolls off her and she rests her head on his shoulder."

He rose up on one elbow. "Are you sure that's what it says?"

"Yes. Do you want me to read it to you?"

She could see his chest heaving, as if he were out of breath. "When *does* he take her virginity?"

"Weeks later, after he vows to make her his wife."

"Weeks, you say."

She nodded.

He held his weight on both elbows, propped over her. His hot stomach pulsed upon hers. He said nothing. He merely looked off to the side.

"But you want to make love to me now," she said in a low, sensual voice, for she was not a fool. She understood what was happening. He had expected more.

He met her gaze. She wiggled her bottom, rubbing gently against the tip of his erection. . .

He spoke in a raspy growl. "It's killing me not to. My hips have a mind of their own. They want to push."

"Then push," she said, appreciating the consequences of such a remark, knowing she could be ruining everything—herself included—for he had made no promises.

But she wanted what she wanted. She wanted sex—with *him*—and she wanted it now. She wanted to belong to this man and no other, no matter the consequences.

He did not move. "If I do that, Rebecca—if I take you now—you will belong to me. No other man will ever have you or even look at you the way I look at you. Do you understand?"

Had he been reading her mind? It was exactly what she wanted. Exactly.

"I want no other man," she told him. "I've never wanted anyone but you."

It was the truth, every single word, and right now, she didn't care if he married her or not. She didn't care about what she was running from, only that she was here in his arms. Nothing mattered but the blinding, searing passion in her heart, and the love—was it really love?—in the deepest realms of her soul.

He was breathing hard. She could feel the pounding of his heart against her chest.

Never taking his eyes off hers, he slowly began to exert pressure, but it seemed she would not let him inside. He was too big. She could not possibly accommodate him, even though she wanted to. Lord, how she wanted to.

"Relax and push against me," he said, "with the muscles inside you."

She tried to concentrate on the workings of her body while his strength and power over her made her want him all the more. He was a hero, a warrior. He could do anything, and she wanted to give him everything she was as a woman.

She closed her eyes and did as he suggested, pushing until he began to stretch and fill her. It hurt for a moment, and she sucked in a breath. Then a new kind of joy swept through her. The pain gradually diminished. He began driving in and out of her, growling with pleasure just as she'd always imagined he would.

He sank his fingers into the cheeks of her behind, lifting her so he could compel himself deeper, and she began to grind her hips around, wanting more and more of his triumphant, male form.

He bore down on her again, his body slick with sweat, the rippling sensations of pleasure playing lustily into her depths. The sensations were feverish and intoxicating. Her emotions were spinning and whirling. It was everything she'd imagined it would be.

He whispered close, and she shivered at the touch of his soft lips upon her sensitive lobe, the feel of his hot, humid breath in her ear. "I'm going to come inside you, then you will belong to me. No turning back."

"Yes."

He drove in hard and fast, shuddered and groaned, then she felt the hot liquid surge of his climax pour into her. She wrapped her arms around his shoulders, wanting to tell him she loved him, but she bit back the words because they seemed foolish, even to her. They barely knew each other. She was in love with the romantic fantasy she'd been nurturing all these years.

But it was real now. . .

Wasn't it?

He rested on top of her for a time, then rolled onto his back.

"Did I mention you are a very exciting woman?" he said.

"Yes." She stared up at the ceiling—amazed, bewildered, and terrified. She had just been made love to. By her hero, Devon Sinclair. Her body would never be the same. Nor would her heart, her mind, her life.

He sighed heavily. "I am spent." He lay quietly for a while, then he turned his head on the pillow to look at her. "Are you all right?"

It was all she could do to manage a nod.

"It always hurts the first time," he said.

"You didn't hurt me. It was wonderful. I am fine."

But was she?

He turned his gaze to the ceiling again. "How long do you think I've been here?"

She tried to guess, but time seemed immeasurable. "An hour perhaps?"

"Will your aunt come to check on you?"

"No," she replied. "But even if she did, the door is locked and she always knocks."

"I would have to hide under the bed, I suppose."

She managed a chuckle, while she struggled to get her mind around this light tone of their conversation. This was all so foreign to her. "If you wish to avoid a caning from her, yes."

He rolled to face her, resting his cheek on a hand. "I intend to speak to her in the morning. Is that agreeable to you?"

Her heart stumbled inside her chest. "Speak to her?"

"Yes, Rebecca. I will have you as my wife and duchess."

Strange panic exploded in her belly—for there it was. He had said it. He had put into words the thing she had dreamed of since she'd met him in the forest. Just the sound of the word on his lips—*wife*—was enough to dry up all the rain outside and bring sunshine into the room even though it was past midnight. He was offering her marriage.

But of course he would. He was a gentleman and she was a gentleman's daughter. He could not have made love to her without knowing the consequences and requirements.

How could it have been so easy?

"Are you certain that's what you want?" she asked, knowing it was a foolish question. "There are other women here who . . ."

"I don't care about them. You have enraptured me, Rebecca, and so much of this seems like destiny, don't you think? But are *you* sure you want me for a husband? I suppose I should have asked you that before I made love to you."

"Of course I am sure," she said. *Could there be any other answer?* "I confess, I have secretly wanted this since the moment I saw you galloping toward me on your horse. I cannot begin to describe how I desired you that night, and how I have wanted to feel your hands on my body every day since. I wanted what we just did, and I will want it again and again."

He smiled. "How is it possible I have found the perfect wife, only days after my return home to England?" He ran a finger lightly down her front—from the base of her throat to her navel.

She shivered with pleasure, even while her mind was reeling with disbelief. She had not expected any of this to happen so fast.

"Perhaps it truly is destiny," she replied.

Perhaps she was meant to be happy after all.

Devon's gaze followed the trail of his finger down to the triangle of her curls below, then his eyes lifted. "If this had not been your first time tonight, it would be my pleasure to satisfy your desire for 'again and again.' But I will make the proper arrangements first and give you time to recover. We shall have a respectable engagement, Rebecca, and save any further wicked antics for the wedding night."

He rolled off the bed and bent to pick up his trousers, which were lying in an untidy pile on the floor.

She leaned up on her elbows. "You're leaving?"

"Yes," he replied, pulling them on. "I don't want to risk gossip if I am missed."

She felt some uncertainty suddenly, and wished he did not have to go.

He wasted no time pulling on his shirt and buttoning his waistcoat. She supposed this sort of thing was easier for a man. He had no doubt done it before. Dozens of times, probably, or maybe even hundreds for all she knew.

He stepped into his shoes and pulled on his dinner jacket, then leaned forward to kiss her on the forehead. "Sleep well," he said. "We'll talk again in the morning."

He left her alone in the empty bed and dying firelight to contemplate her dream of a happy future. A moment later, the fire flickered out, leaving only a few smoldering embers. A chill came into the room, so she drew the covers up to her shoulders and hugged her knees to her chest to keep warm.

Devon walked out of Rebecca's bedchamber. He closed the door quietly behind him and strode down the corridor before someone had a chance to encounter him in this wing where he had no reason to be. Other than to debauch a virgin and seduce her into becoming his wife with immediate haste.

As soon as he entered the corridor that housed his own lodgings, he stopped and rested a hand over his stomach. He swallowed uncomfortably and backed up against the wall, then tipped his head against the dark oak paneling and closed his eyes.

He had wanted Rebecca tonight, there was no question about that, and he wanted her still—with every primal, pounding urge in his body. The troubling fact of the matter was—he had forgotten himself. He had allowed romance and desire to overshadow his intellect.

Marriage. He'd known he would have to succumb to it eventually, he just hadn't expected to be swept away so quickly and impulsively without even attempting to swim against the current. He had been home for only a few days, and already he was back in that familiar saddle, doing exactly what his father wanted him to do. This, when the man was clearly out of his mind.

Devon wondered how he would be dealing with this situation if Rebecca had not come to the ball. He certainly would not have been deflowering Lady Letitia tonight, or any of the other women who had attended. He would have been thinking things through more carefully, maybe even swimming upstream in the opposite direction. He would not have been so full of lust and desire as to thrust himself recklessly past the point of no return.

There was no going back now.

So it was *her* fault then, he told himself, with an embittered chuckle and cynical shake of his head. Her fault entirely, for being so inconceivably alluring, like some beautiful, magical nymph sent here to bring him to his knees.

Maybe it was a test of some kind to see if he'd learned anything from the past and had strengthened his will. If it was, he was failing it. Miserably. He would try to do better.

He pushed away from the wall and headed toward his own room. Tonight he would focus on practicalities. He would plan a swift and efficient wedding to the woman he had just bedded.

That very night, far from Pembroke Palace, beyond the Cotswold Hills, Rebecca's father, the Earl of Creighton, rose from his desk and sat down in front of the fire in his bedchamber.

He held a letter in his hand. The ink was barely dry. He had signed his name to it only seconds ago.

Rushton would not be pleased when he received it. What would he do? Would he come here straight away, or would he give up his plan to have Rebecca as his wife and simply back down?

Unfortunately, the earl knew that Rushton would not be so easily defeated. He had spent his entire life working toward this goal, climbing and clawing his way back to this tiny, secluded part of the world. He was not going to give up, and he was not going to be happy.

The earl took a sip of brandy and stared into the hot, dancing flames. His daughter was gone.

Damn her for her independence. She was too much like her mother.

But perhaps it was that very spirited nature that had attracted him to his wife more than twenty years ago, and later that young woman Rushton had brought round. . .

Serena.

For a brief fleeting second, he thought he could see Serena's pretty face in the flames, her golden hair flying in the wind, but then she was gone, and he became quite certain that he was looking into the very portal to hell.

Chapter 10

Devon hesitated in the doorway of the break-fast room when he spotted Lady Saxby standing by the sideboard with a cup of tea in her hands. She was laughing and conversing with one of the other female guests. Lady Letitia was on the opposite side of the room with her mother.

Rebecca sat at the table next to Charlotte. He looked at her lovely face and recalled the tantaliz-ing warmth of her voice when she'd read to him from the diary the night before, and the mindless lust that had driven him to make love to her and propose. Something lurched in his chest and all at once his feet seemed fixed to the floor.

A muscle clenched in his jaw. He wondered suddenly if Lady Letitia might have been a safer choice, for there would never have been any dan-ger that he might lose his heart to her.

But, no, there was no point wondering about what might have been. He had amends to make to everyone in this family, and he would make them. He had made his choice last night. He would go forward.

He stood for a few minutes more, then entered the room and approached Lady Saxby.

"I beg your pardon," he said, "but if I could have a word with you in private, madam?"

Her smile disappeared and was replaced by a look of surprise. "Of course, Lord Hawthorne."

He bowed to the others, then escorted Lady Saxby out of the breakfast room and through the wide doors to the blue drawing room, which boasted the best tapestries in the palace. He gestured toward the two striped chairs facing each other in the corner and spoke courteously. "Please."

She took a seat.

He sat down facing her. "May I enquire without pretense, madam, about your niece?"

"Certainly."

He hesitated a moment to allow her time to comprehend what he was about to ask, then spoke without ambiguity, determined to say what he must, but being careful not to reveal that he had already secured Rebecca's hand, quite irrevocably in fact, in the most dishonorable way possible.

"Has she given any thought to her future? Does she wish to marry?"

The woman stared at him for a moment before a clear understanding reached her eyes, then she spoke with complete discernment. "Yes, of course, Lord Hawthorne. What young lady of good breeding does not desire such a future?"

"In that case, may I enquire about her father? Is he available for discussions on the matter? Can he be reached during his travels?"

Her lips parted slightly, and she hesitated before she answered. He supposed this was an unnerving conversation for any woman in charge of a younger woman's future.

"He could be," she replied, "but it might take some time for a letter to reach him." She shifted in her chair and tilted her head to the side. "But would it be of interest to you, Lord Hawthorne, to know that my niece is only a few days away from her majority? She will be twenty-one on Saturday."

"Ah, that is indeed helpful," he said, for Rebecca would not require parental consent in order to marry. That would speed matters up considerably. "But I would of course still wish to communicate with her father about any important decisions regarding his daughter's future."

"I understand," she smoothly replied. Then she tilted her head again. "But allow me to inform you also that Lord Creighton has left his daughter in my capable hands with the express purpose of attending the Season in London, and shall we say, *solidifying* her future. As you know, he is not a social person, but he desires his daughter's happiness. So I have therefore been entrusted with his blessings, so to speak."

Devon studied Lady Saxby's expression with great care. She was eager, there was no doubt about it, but he supposed that was to be expected. Any woman in her position would consider it a great personal achievement to match her niece with a man of his rank. It was a plain and simple fact. He was heir to a dukedom.

He inclined his head at her. "In that case, I wish to appeal to you for the honor of your blessing, Lady Saxby, so that I may request a private moment with your niece this morning and speak to her directly about a shared future."

She appeared to have some trouble speaking.

"If that is agreeable to you, of course," he added.

With a quick breath, she said, "Yes, it is most agreeable, my lord. And of course, you have my utmost blessing with my own assurance that my niece, Rebecca, is very capable and mature and kindhearted. I feel comfortable leaving the two of you alone to discuss any matters of importance, as I trust her judgment entirely. You will find that she is most pleasant to talk to, and very honest and forthcoming."

"You do not have to convince me of anything, Lady Saxby. I have already discovered all of these things for myself. She is an extraordinary woman."

Her expression warmed knowingly, and he had

the distinct feeling this woman was very shrewd.
"And may I please say, Lord Hawthorne, that I
believe you are an extraordinary man. I am delighted we were able to reach an understanding
this morning."

He simply bowed his head. "Thank you,
madam."

When they arrived back in the breakfast room,
he turned his attention to Rebecca, who was still
sitting beside his sister. Charlotte looked up at him
with wide eyes, as if she knew exactly what was
about to happen and was completely astounded
by the velocity of it.

He circled the table. "Lady Rebecca, may I request a word with you in private?"

A hush fell over the room, and all eyes turned
to him. Vincent walked in just then and stopped
in the doorway.

Rebecca cleared her throat and stood. "Of
course, Lord Hawthorne."

He glanced across at Vincent, whose expression
was impossible to read, then escorted her around
the table, choosing not to meet his brother's gaze
again as he passed by.

Exactly one minute later, back in the blue
drawing room among the fine tapestries, Devon
dropped to one knee, proposed, and Rebecca
accepted.

"Your aunt informed me that you will be celebrating your birthday on Saturday," he said, rising to his feet but still holding her hand. "Would it please you to celebrate our nuptials on the same day?"

On Saturday? Rebecca's head was spinning. Even though this was exactly what she'd wanted when she'd fled her home in desperation, she still felt uneasy about how quickly everything was unfolding. It reminded her of how she had felt in that runaway coach all those years ago, how she had been thrown backward against the seat. "So soon?"

"I don't see any point in delaying," he said. "Not after last night."

After last night. Yes, the memory of it had swirled amorously through her mind and body and kept her awake and aroused in her bed until dawn.

"You're right, of course," she said. "But this has all happened so fast, I can barely catch my breath. May I ask . . ." She hesitated, not quite sure why she needed to know this, when she had come here to Pembroke Palace with a clear purpose of her own to make him her husband. "Was it your intention to find a bride so quickly the other night at the ball?"

He took a moment to put together a reply. "It's been my intention to find a bride my entire life," he told her. "I've always known I would marry one day."

She stared up into his striking blue eyes, searching for understanding, needing to hear something more. She wasn't sure what, exactly, but she wanted to feel as if she knew what was in his heart.

Not that she expected him to tell her he loved her. She wanted him to, of course, in time, but it was too soon for that, she knew. She only wanted some truth and honesty.

Somehow he seemed to recognize her need for both those things and kissed her hand. "Yes, Rebecca. It was my intention to search for a wife that night."

She pondered that. "Is that why you came home to England when you did? To settle down and marry? I am not naïve, Devon. I understand that as the future Duke of Pembroke, you have responsibilities. You can be honest with me."

Again, he took some time to answer. He seemed to be choosing his words with great care. "Indeed I do have responsibilities, and it pleases me that you have these practicalities in mind. If you must know, my father was exerting some pressure upon my return, and given his age and his rather unfortunate state of mind, I felt it my duty to oblige him."

"I see."

Was she disappointed? Had she truly imagined

it was instant love that had moved him to propose? That he had been utterly swept away by his passions, as she had been?

"Rest assured," he said, as if he could read her thoughts, "that I would not have married just anyone. I was drawn to you the other night, no one else. I wanted you in the most basic way a man can want a woman, which I am sure you saw for yourself last night in your bedchamber." He smiled at her. "You have warmth and charm, my family already adores you, and on top of all that, you have been managing your father's household for a number of years, so I am confident you will make an excellent duchess. I am very pleased with this arrangement, Rebecca."

Pleased with this arrangement.

So, she had not been the only one with specific ambitions the past few days. He had been holding the reins, too, controlling their speed and direction toward matrimony.

Not that it mattered, she supposed. She had gotten what she wanted. She should be thankful that the fates had overlooked her shameless, wicked behavior and been so very generous. Her luck had been incredible.

"It appears I chose the perfect time to finally attend a gathering at the palace," she said uneasily. "You were looking for your bride, which is exactly what I wanted to be."

"Yes. Did we not say it was destiny?" He kissed her hand again.

Perhaps it was, she told herself. Perhaps she should even be thankful that her father had betrayed her and promised her to Mr. Rushton. Perhaps she had needed that cruel but firm push to force her to take charge of her life once and for all. Otherwise, she might still be back home reading Lydie's diary, living through someone else's passions instead of experiencing her own. And Devon might be proposing to Lady Letitia this morning.

"That is very romantic," she said. "I shall remember it always."

And she would not fret over the new direction her life was taking, even though it was happening so fast, it was making her dizzy.

The slap across his face came without warning and stung like the devil.

"You, sir, are no gentleman."

Devon stood in the center of his study, allowing Lady Letitia this moment of fury, because she obviously felt she deserved it.

"You used and misled me," she said.

"How exactly did I *use* you?" he asked, touching his cool hand to his burning cheek.

She glared at him with a blaze of fire in her eyes. "You led me to believe there was an understanding between us."

Her jealous fury he would allow. Lies and accusations, he would not. "I beg your pardon, Lady Letitia. I did no such thing."

"But you did! You flirted with me and charmed me, and invited me to sing for your guests."

"An invitation to sing does not signify a courtship. Nor is it a marriage proposal."

She slapped him again, harder this time. "It appears my ladylike behavior was not to your tastes. You preferred an improper seduction."

He sighed. "I did not seduce anyone."

"Not *you*, Lord Hawthorne. *Her.* That woman used immoral tactics to trap you, didn't she? I could tell by the way she looked at you. It was appalling."

He swallowed over the ugly, sour taste of this conversation. "No one has trapped anyone, and that is the future Duchess of Pembroke you are speaking of, so I suggest you hold your tongue. I believe we are done here."

She began to tug at her reticule, as if she wanted to rip it apart. "We are most certainly done, Lord Hawthorne. My mother and I are leaving the palace this morning."

"I'm sorry to hear that."

She turned to leave, but paused at the door and spoke over her shoulder. "Permit me to say, sir, that you chose the wrong woman to be your wife. And I will wager my grandmother's diamond tiara that one day, you will live to regret it."

* * *

"I hear congratulations are in order," Vincent said to Devon as he entered the stable on a large, dappled gray horse and swung down from the saddle. Soaking wet after a morning ride through the driving rain, he handed the reins to a groom. "They say the wedding is to be held on Saturday. And to think you were worried about not having time for romance and a proper courtship." He strode across the hay-strewn floor and removed his gloves, tapped them a few times on his thigh, then leaned against a post at the corner of the stall. "You always could sling the rubbish."

Devon was not in the mood for this. He had come out to the stables for a few minutes to be alone with his thoughts and to see Marlow, the horse that had been a yearling when he'd left for America three years ago. Marlow had been sired by Asher.

Asher was gone now, of course. Vincent had seen to that. He had been the one to take the shotgun to the hill that day.

"I had a duty to this family," Devon said, "and Lady Rebecca was a practical choice." He ran a brush over the coarse hair and the firm bands of muscle on Marlow's neck. "There was no point beating around the bush."

"Oh, but I'd wager you did just that," Vincent said. "You probably beat around her bush at least once, just to make sure she'd have no other options but to—"

"Stop right there." Devon strode out of the stall and pointed a finger. "I'm warning you, Vince."

Vincent didn't move. "Why? Because she's your betrothed? Your future wife?"

"Yes, damn you. She is the future Duchess of Pembroke, and I will not tolerate your slander."

His brother's eyes narrowed, and the hatred he saw in them was deep and unmistakable. "She won't be your wife until Saturday, and a lot can happen in the final days leading up to a wedding. You know that better than anyone."

Devon dropped his hand to his side. "If you lay one hand on her . . ."

"You'll what? Make me regret it?"

Devon turned away and went back into the stall, then began grooming Marlow again with firm, angry strokes.

"Oh, for God's sake," Vincent said, ripping his hat off his head and speaking with impatience and irritation. "You know *I* would never break up a wedding, much less harm a woman."

Devon did know that. It was *he* who had harmed someone once, and supposed Vincent was relishing the opportunity to remind him of it. "What happened three years ago was an accident, Vince. You know I regret it."

"I will accept that MaryAnn's death was an accident, Devon, but your betrayal . . . That was not."

Devon stopped what he was doing and faced him. "I apologized, and you know damn well I suffered. Why keep punishing me?"

A muscle in Vincent's cheek twitched. "Because you are about to embark upon a new life with a charming, beautiful woman, your future duchess. Your suffering appears to be at an end, and you are going to be blissfully happy, while I will continue to suffer."

Vincent turned around and headed for the open stable door, where the rain outside was coming down in sharp, horizontal lines. He stopped and turned to say one more thing. "I still have that letter, you know. The one she had in her pocket. The one she wrote to you. I can't help reading it sometimes, even though it kills me to do it. I don't know why. I wish I could burn it, but I can't. It is all I have left of her. So I guess you'll just have to keep living with that."

Devon remembered the agony of that day on the hill, and the look on Vincent's face when he learned what had happened.

Devon would indeed keep living with it. Every day for the rest of his life.

Chapter 11

❧

Dear Diary,

Sometimes I wonder if the fates are determined to punish me for all my wicked thoughts and deeds—for today, the most wonderful thing happened, followed by the very worst.

Jess gave me a ring he made from a daisy in the clearing and told me he wanted to marry me. He said he would find a way somehow, then he cupped my head in his hand and pulled me close and kissed me deeply, sweeping his hot, delicious tongue into my mouth until I was sure I would melt into ecstasy right there in his arms. He made me promise to come to him in the clearing in the morning, and I said I would. I said I would do anything for him.

But tonight Father told me he was going to send me to live with Aunt Beatrice, for there was a man in her village who wanted a wife. Father said *he was a successful merchant, and that it would be best for me. I think he knows about Jess.*

   I hate him, Diary. I hate my father. And I will go to the clearing tomorrow to see the man I love. I will not be forced to marry another.

Rebecca closed the book, laid it down on the bed beside her, and touched a finger to her lips. She knew exactly what Lydie's future held, for she had read the diary so many times over the past few years, she knew it all by heart.

Knowing the outcome of Lydie's life gave her some reassurance that she had done the right thing by fleeing her father's home and coming without delay to Pembroke Palace. She was also thankful that Devon had returned to England when he did. Now there was hope for her future happiness.

She could not help but wonder, however, if she should have told him about her situation and her father's plan for her to marry Mr. Rushton. Lydie had certainly told Jess. He had known all about it and done everything he could to keep her at his side. But they had already been deeply in love.

If she had told Devon right away, would he have chosen her over Lady Letitia, or gone so far as to propose? Perhaps he would not have, for he might not have wished to become involved in a complicated family matter, at least until it was all settled and he was sure she did not belong to another man.

Which she did not. She had never, ever belonged to Mr. Rushton, no matter what her father had said to him. Her heart had always belonged to Devon, and it always would.

She would tell him about Mr. Rushton when the time was right. She promised herself she would, and she hoped with all her heart that he would understand.

That same night, a shiny black coach approached Creighton Manor. The ominous clouds overhead began to shift and roll, and thunder rumbled somewhere in the distance. The wind picked up, hissing and blowing through the trees and hedges.

The coach rolled to a stop, the door swung open, and two heavy black boots pounded down upon the walk, where weeds grew in the cracks between the stones.

Maximilian Rushton, standing tall and slender as he stepped out of the coach, looked down at the weeds with disdain and spit into the overgrown garden of wildflowers. He lifted his head to look up at the front of the medieval house cloaked in ivy, and felt a distasteful mixture of frustration and loathing.

He had expected a celebration of victory today and had been anticipating his vengeance with great delight. Instead, he was here at Creighton Manor with nothing but a note of apology in his pocket, his purpose hindered, his anger inflamed.

He strode to the front door and rapped hard on the brass knocker.

"Get the earl out of bed," he said to the young maid who answered. He shoved the door open and pushed past her into the main hall. "And tell him I am not happy."

"Yes, Mr. Rushton." She curtsied and scurried up the stairs, while he watched the tempting curve of her plump backside until she was out of sight.

He removed his gloves and strode slowly across the stone floor toward the central hearth, eyeing the stained-glass window at one end of the vast hall and looking up at the timber ceiling, reaching to a high peak overhead.

This old feasting room looked too much like a church, he thought, glancing toward the three arches that led to the pantry and buttery, and turning his nose up at the plain medieval furnishings.

He stood in front of the hearth, where a few embers still smoldered in the grate, though mostly, it was just ash. He hated this house. At least, he would hate it until he was master here. Then it would be his greatest achievement.

He walked to the window where he could look outside to the south wing where the ballroom was located. Possession of that, he supposed, was his foremost ambition.

A few minutes later he heard the sound of the earl's cane tapping down the stone staircase, then he appeared, breathing heavily and clutching a woolen shawl around his narrow, hunched shoulders.

"How dare you keep me waiting," Rushton said.

Creighton made his way across the hall. His face was pale and gaunt. "May I offer you a drink?"

"No."

The earl approached him warily. "I assume you read my note?"

Rushton reached into his breast pocket and withdrew it. He held it up between two long fingers, wiggled it in the air, then tossed it onto the ashes in the grate. "How is it possible that you do not know the whereabouts of your own daughter?"

"She sneaked away four nights ago. I thought perhaps she might return by now."

"You promised to deliver her to me today. Instead I get this written apology. You should have informed me sooner."

The earl had no reply.

Rushton strode to him. He was more than a foot taller than the old earl, and found himself looking at the top of the man's balding head, for his cowardly gaze was fixed on the floor as usual.

"Did you make the mistake of telling her she would become my wife?"

The earl nodded. Still he did not look up.

Rushton spoke in a low controlled voice, though it boiled with his wrath. "Why? You should have just stuck her in the carriage and brought her to me."

"I had to tell her," he replied. "She knew something was wrong."

"Well, now something *is* wrong," Rushton said. "My bride has run off and you are in danger of being exposed. If you want to prevent it, get your daughter back."

"I don't know where she went."

"You had best figure it out, Creighton, or you know what will happen. You have one week."

Never once lifting his gaze, the earl backed away and sank into a chair against the wall. He dropped his head into a trembling hand and began to weep.

Rushton felt no pity for the man. He could not. Creighton had brought this on himself, doing what he did to Serena that day at the rotunda. He deserved to go to hell for it.

Besides that, there were too many years of his own misery locked away in this house. It was why he had brought Serena here to tempt and lure the earl into his trap in the first place. If the man had not lost his head at the rotunda, Rebecca would not now be forced to be a part of this. Serena would have accomplished the task for her. She would have borne a male heir for Creighton, then Rushton would have moved in to take over from there.

But it hadn't worked out that way, had it? So now he needed Rebecca. His lip twitched with repugnance as he turned around and walked out.

Chapter 12

Devon glanced up from the paperwork on his desk when a knock sounded at his door and his mother entered his study. She wore a form-fitting gown of lavender silk, and looked as lovely as ever, though he could see from her expression that something was troubling her.

"Good morning, Devon. Do you have a moment?"

"Of course." He invited her to sit across from him by the window. "You haven't come to tell me I'm making the worst mistake of my life, have you?"

"No, nothing like that," she said with a smile. "To the contrary, I am thrilled for you, as I think very highly of Lady Rebecca. Charlotte and I have been fortunate enough to become acquainted with her over the past few days, and we both admire her very much. She is lovely. I could not have chosen a better bride for you myself."

"Not even Lady Letitia?"

His mother gave him a knowing look. "She was your father's choice, not mine."

"In that case, I am pleased you approve of the choice *I* have made."

She folded her hands together on her lap. "You might be surprised to hear it, but regardless of Lady Letitia's departure, your father could not be happier. He hasn't said anything to me, of course, but I know he is proud of you, and pleased that you have taken up your rightful position here at the palace again, so soon after your return."

He had not spoken to his father privately about his engagement. He had chosen to announce it publicly at dinner the night before. Everyone had applauded, and his father, who was seated at the head of the table, had risen and raised a glass and delivered an elegant and jovial toast. No one in a hundred years would have guessed the man was off his rocker.

Devon was simply relieved that he had not thrown a fit over Letitia.

"But I confess," his mother continued, "that I sense you are not completely comfortable with your decision. Are you having doubts?"

He leaned back in his chair and regarded her. "Do not worry, Mother. I am a man no different from any other, and as such have earned the right to have cold feet before my wedding day. Which is being planned with incredible haste, I might add. What man wouldn't be uneasy?"

"But you are *not* just any man," she replied. "And I know you too well. It's more than cold feet."

He gave up trying to appease her with jokes and lighthearted assurances. "You have always known it would be this way for me, Mother. You know how I feel about marriage and love."

"I know how you feel about your role in Vincent's tragic attempt at marriage."

He paused, then spoke in a low, gentle voice. "*Your* unhappiness has always cut my heart deeply, Mother."

He had always known his parents' marriage had been arranged, and later he had come to understand that she had once loved another. Though she would never speak of it.

She slowly stood up and turned away from him. "Please do not say such things. It would break my own heart to think that I was the cause of your unwillingness to find joy in your marriage." She faced him again. "Do not use Vincent or me as examples, Devon. We are poor ones. Especially me."

"Because you married for duty to your family? Isn't that what we all must do?"

"Not necessarily."

He gazed long and hard at her. "You know I am in an impossible situation, Mother. Father has already altered his will and he has an iron fist when it comes to what he thinks is best for everyone. I have already surrendered to my duty and proposed. There can be no turning back."

"I don't want you to turn back, nor do I want you to simply 'surrender to duty.' I want you to have more than that. I do not want you to feel as if you put everyone else's happiness before your own. I don't want you to feel as if you have made a mistake."

"Are you saying you made a mistake in marrying Father?"

He wanted to hear her say it.

She was speechless for a moment, but remained always the proper duchess and wife. "No, I will never regret the decisions I have made. I was meant to marry your father, so that I could have you and Vincent and Blake."

"And the twins," he added for her. "Charlotte and Garrett."

She lowered her gaze. "I was meant to have them, too, of course."

But they were the evidence of what she believed was her greatest transgression—her one brief flirtation with happiness, her children by another man. She carried the shame with her like a wedding ring.

No one ever spoke of it. It was one of those family secrets buried in the gardens of the past, where flowers grew from roots no one would ever see.

She sat back on her heels. Her voice was resigned and heavy with guilt. "Don't, Devon. I came here to discuss your future, not my past."

He leaned forward and took her hands in his, determined just this once to expose that wound she kept wrapped and hidden from everyone, and gently apply salve to it if he could. He spoke softly.

"Do not punish yourself, Mother. You are a saint. You seized one moment of happiness, which you deserved. You deserved it because you sacrificed your entire life to give your sisters and family a better future. You never thought of yourself. You still do not, and we all respect and adore you for that. You have set the finest example for all of us, so do not tell me to do something different from what you have done."

She gave him a warning look. "I am not a saint. I was unfaithful to my husband."

There—the words were out, the scandalous admission of her sin. It pained Devon to hear the disgrace in her voice, maybe because he understood it too well. Better than anyone.

She rose from her chair. "But as I said before, I did not come here to discuss my life. I came to discuss yours. You have your own regrets, too, Devon, and the guilt to go along with it. It is why I knocked on your door."

He sat back.

"You don't believe you deserve happiness either," she said, "and you are going to try to deny yourself, even when it is within your grasp."

"But is it *truly* within my grasp?" he asked, feeling angry all of a sudden. "I will never be able to forget what happened that day three years ago. Never. I will always regret my weakness and my impulsive passions. Yet here I am, rushing into marriage with a woman I barely know."

She knelt before him, placed her hands on his knees, and spoke with conviction. "I have a good feeling about her, Devon. You will be happy, if you will only let yourself. What happened with MaryAnn was tragic, there is no question about that, but you never meant for it to happen. You did your best. Her death was an accident."

"But her feelings for me were . . ." He paused.

"What she felt in her heart is not your fault either. You did what you could to discourage her and to be loyal to your brother. You need to forgive yourself."

He gazed into his mother's caring eyes. She was a wise and intelligent woman, but she did not know the whole story about MaryAnn. No one did. "Vincent has not forgiven me," he said.

"He will in time. Now that you are home."

"I am not so sure of that."

She sat back on her heels. "Please, Devon. It

is true that you have been pushed into this marriage because of your father's demands, but you can still open your heart to the possibility of love and happiness with the woman you have chosen to be your wife. Learn from my mistakes. Do not repeat them. Run toward love, not away from it. Don't resist what you feel for her. You could bring hope and joy back into this house. Lord knows we all need it here."

"That we do," he replied, feeling the weight of his responsibilities looming heavier than ever. "That we do."

That night after the theatricals in the grand saloon, the ladies said goodnight to each other, while some of the gentlemen decided to taste the brandy in the library and engage themselves in a few hands of cards.

Devon encouraged them to do so, ordered more brandy to be brought up, then discreetly slipped behind the crimson drapery in the saloon to the hidden door in the wall. He flicked the latch and entered the dark passageway, where a candle was waiting for him in a sconce.

As a boy he had explored these narrow corridors hundreds of times, and he and his brothers often escaped punishment when they'd been confined to their rooms by lock and key—at least until the new nannies discovered the secret doorways hidden behind movable bookcases or built-in wardrobes.

Their favorite places to explore had always been the subterranean passageways, for they were dark and damp and made of stone, and had once been used by the monks at the abbey before the king had dismantled the monasteries and turned them out.

That particular bit of palace history, along with the story of the prior who was murdered by his own canons, had provided Devon and his brothers limitless opportunities for ghost stories and trickery. That was how they had always managed to have *new* nannies. They could never keep one for very long after she'd been lured down to the foundations of the palace, where mice and cobwebs were always readily available in the pitch-black caverns, along with their own ghoulish howls.

But that was years ago. These days he used the passageways for a different kind of midnight game altogether.

He reached the secret entrance to Rebecca's room and paused with the candle in his hand, listening. His mother's maid had been assigned double duty to assist Rebecca until she found a permanent maid of her own, so he was careful to make sure Alice was not about. He heard a drawer open and close, but no one spoke, so he carefully pushed open the door.

He entered the well-lit room from behind the floor-to-ceiling portrait of one his ancestors, and stood briefly beside the bed, watching his betrothed stand before the mirror on the vanity, running a brush through her thick, wavy hair. She stood with her back to him and wore a white dressing gown, and was humming a melody he did not recognize.

As he watched her, he wondered why he had come. He had been working very hard to keep his mind fixed on his duties and responsibilities and all the practical details involved in planning a hasty wedding. He had been relatively successful in that regard, at least until his mother had knocked on his door earlier in the day and given him that speech about happiness. As a result, he had discovered that looking at his mother was like looking in a mirror. He had tried to convince her to let go of her guilt and shame and allow herself a better future. She had said the same to him.

After she left, he'd had no choice but to contemplate his own advice with a bit more care and reflection.

He glanced to the right and saw the diary sitting on the bedside table, and wondered if Rebecca had been reading it just now, or intended to read it when she climbed into bed.

Just thinking about some of the words on the pages of the book gave him a stir, so rather than continuing to fight against his unwieldy passions, he blew out the candle he held, set it on the table and slowly strode forward toward his betrothed.

She spotted his movement in the mirror and sucked in a breath, startled by his unexpected appearance. Whirling around to face him, she whispered hotly, "Don't do that to me! I thought you were a ghost."

"No ghosts in this house, darling, only randy fiancés who can't help sneaking around to see the objects of their desire."

She huffed. "Did you come through one of those secret passages again?"

"I did indeed."

He reached her and let his eyes wander down to her bare toes, then back up again.

Suddenly duty and responsibility had nothing to do with anything. He wanted sex with her, and he wanted it now.

She narrowed her clever gaze at him when their eyes met. "I beg your pardon," she said, playfully scolding, "but I thought that after our previous disregard for propriety, we were going to make this a respectable engagement and wait until our wedding night to properly celebrate our nuptials."

"But that's two days from now."

"You can't wait two days?" she said, incredulous.

"Definitely not."

She made a valiant effort to hide her smile, and walked past him toward the bed, stopping to turn around in front of the bedside table.

He raised an eyebrow and leaned to the side to see past her. She glanced over her shoulder.

"You want to read more of that diary, don't you?" she asked, with a teasing tone.

"Don't *you*?"

"I already know how it ends."

He strode toward her. "I, on the other hand, do not, and the suspense is killing me."

"I hardly think *that* is what's killing you."

How right she was.

He stopped a few inches away. She laid a hand on his chest, then slowly slid it down inside his trousers, wrapping it around his rock-hard erection, already standing stiffly at attention. "You just want to hear the naughty bits," she said.

"Aloud, if you don't mind."

He grinned wolfishly, realizing he adored this woman more with every passing second, and he was a very lucky man to have found her before anyone else had.

Perhaps there was hope for happiness after all—at least at night, after the sun went down, when he could forget about real life for a while. Maybe she was meant to be his oasis.

She looked him straight in the eye as she stroked

him with her warm, proficient hand, and the pleasure mounting in his loins compelled him to set a hand on the bed to keep from staggering sideways.

"Where did we leave off last time?" he asked, wanting to get down to business.

"Jess had not yet taken Lydie's virginity."

"Then perhaps we might skip ahead a few pages," he suggested, taking her into his arms so that she had to remove her hand from his pants. She grabbed on to his shoulders and he swept her up off her feet and laid her on the bed.

He stood over her, tugging at his tie to loosen it before he picked up the diary and looked carefully at the brown leather casing on the front cover. "In the mood for a little reading?"

"I'm always in the mood for a story."

He handed the book to her, and she flipped through the pages searching for a particular entry, while he sauntered around the foot of the bed, removing his dinner jacket and waistcoat and tossing them onto the upholstered bench.

He climbed onto the bed and lay down on his side facing her, his elbow on a pillow, his head resting on a hand, while he admired her lovely profile in the lamplight. Her skin was creamy white, her lips full and moist. When she began to read, her voice was smooth and intoxicating like wine. . .

"*Dear Diary,*

"*Tonight it happened and it was perfect, the most incredible day of my life. It was a gloriously hot and humid evening without a single breath of wind, and after dinner I could not contain my desires. My body was tingling with wanton urges, so I ran out the door and headed to the forest.*

"*My breasts were heaving with excitement, and in the warm, moist twilight, my skin became sticky and wet. I had never felt such burning anticipation. When I reached the clearing, I saw him. My dearest love, Jess. He had been sitting in a patch of purple wildflowers, but rose instantly to his feet when he heard my approach, and ran to meet me. I dashed into his strong, capable arms and together we sank down to the grass, our hungry bodies entwined, squeezing and thrusting, both of us sighing with delight and dreaming of erotic pleasures.*

"*He was eager tonight, more than ever before, and I knew I could not continue to deny him what he wanted. I parted my legs for him and boldly reached down to unfasten his breeches. He devoured my lips with his mouth while I pushed his breeches over his hips and kneaded his strong buttocks with my roving hands, pulling him firmly against my moist, open womanhood.*

"*If I had any lingering doubts about what we were about to do, they vanished instantly when*

*he paused and looked down at me, with the hazy
pink sunset reflecting in his eyes like firelight.*

*"'I love you, Lydie,' he said to me, tenderly,
and I knew I would spend the rest of my days
loving him with my whole heart and soul, and
that he would be my joy, my lover, my life, until I
took my last breath in this world . . ."*

"Stop," Devon said, for he had felt a sudden,
unfamiliar yearning in his gut, which was, quite
frankly, astounding to him. For so long, he had
been shunning the kind of all-consuming, romantic love that Lydie wrote about, believing it smothered common sense and resulted in eventual, inevitable ruin. He had always imagined he would
marry for duty alone, and would choose wisely
with his head, which is what he had set out to do
that night he met Rebecca at the ball. But somehow their relationship had very quickly snow-
balled into something more, and hearing her read
those passionate words tonight opened something
inside of him. There was such truth and honesty
and vulnerability in her voice, the very things he
had wished to avoid.

Driven by impulses he had not succumbed to
in a long time, he found himself reaching for the
open diary and lifting it out of her hands.

Bewildered, she watched him roll to the side
and place it on the table on the other side of him.

"You do not want to continue?" she asked.

He rolled toward her again and laid a hand on her flat belly. "I do, but I would prefer to do things our way tonight, not theirs."

He could not explain it, but he wanted to feel something real.

"All right," she said, lying very still.

He continued to admire the beauty in her eyes, the charming shape of her nose, and the soft texture of her skin. He ran a hand down the side of her curvaceous body and turned his eyes toward her long legs stretched out on the bed, one ankle crossed over the other beneath the lacey hem of her clean linen nightgown.

"You're so beautiful," he said.

"I'm glad you think so. I want to be beautiful for you, Devon. I want to give you everything and make you happy."

He remembered her confession—that she had come here dreaming of him in a romantic way, and for the first time he found himself actually wanting to be the devoted lover she desired.

Perhaps he could be that, if nothing else. It did not seem so impossible here on the bed with her, in the quiet privacy of this chamber where none of the palace madness could touch them.

And maybe this woman lying next to him was meant to be his respite from all of those hardships. His oasis. When everyone else expected him to solve their problems and save the palace and the dukedom, she only wanted to give him pleasure and love. She did not want anything from him, except love. It was a novel idea, to be sure. One he did not wish to shun, which again surprised him.

With careful tenderness, he lowered his mouth to hers and kissed her lips, meeting her soft warm tongue and feeling a heated stirring in his loins.

He wanted her now. He wanted to plunge into her depths and feel the heat of her body, but not just to satisfy his own sexual longings. There was something else at work here this evening, a desire for more than just pleasure—a desire he did not fully understand.

Whether it was because of what his mother had said to him, or if it was simply Rebecca slowly inching her way into his heart, he did not know. All he knew was that he wanted to let down his guard for once—tonight—and not be the man everyone depended upon. He wanted to strip bare and place himself in Rebecca's hands, to relax and simply let her love him.

Could he do that? Was it possible?

She sat up and pushed gently at his shoulder to roll him over onto his back, then lifted his shirt and dropped wet kisses across his stomach and below his navel.

"I'm glad we found each other," he whispered, enjoying the sensation of her long silky hair brushing over his skin.

"So am I," she replied, looking down at him. "I know it seems too soon to say it, but I love you, Devon, and I cannot wait to be your wife. I will be the happiest woman in the world."

She loved him.

God, she had said it, and he had not felt the need to retreat, nor had he dissolved into dust. A miracle. All of it.

"I hope those are your words," he said with a smile and a touch of humor. "And not Lydie's."

She took his face in her hands. "They are words spoken from my own heart. I want only to be yours."

"Then you shall be," he told her, pulling her down for another kiss while she swung a leg over him, straddling his hips.

Gathering her gown in both fists, he inched it up past her waist until he could cup her warm, fleshy behind in his hands. He groaned with need and thrust his hips upward.

"Can we do it this way?" she asked, "with me on top?"

"We can do it any way you like."

With eager hands, she unfastened his trousers, while he lifted his hips to allow her to pull them off and toss them to the floor.

"Your shirt, too," she said, lifting it over his head and tossing it aside as well.

She removed her nightgown and sat lightly upon him, swiveling her hips in tiny little stimulating circles. Then she took him in her hand, directing the round tip of his shaft to her primed opening. Bearing down, she covered him like a hot, magnificent sheath.

"You don't want to play a little first?" he asked, his voice shaky with desire.

Her eyes clouded with passion. "No."

She descended all the way around him, taking his whole rigid length inside until he felt the splendid suction of her interior. Her eyes fell closed as she began to pulse slowly up and down.

He held her hips in his hands, supporting her movements as she pleasured herself upon him. All he wanted to do at that moment was watch her in the lamplight and enjoy her expressions and reactions, but soon he became absorbed in his own blissful exertions, and he shut his eyes as they both worked faster, making love to each other with the full force of their desires and emotions.

He turned his head to the side, overcome with ecstasy, and drove into her with fierce intensity until she gasped and convulsed with rapture. When her shudders finally diminished and her sighs grew soft and faint, he sat up and turned her over onto her back, entering her sweet liquid haven again to bring the intimate union to completion.

Feeling lost beyond the reaches of his own mind, he drove into her as deeply as he could, kissing her and holding her and loving her until he became inflamed to such an unbearable point, he could hold back no longer. He gave in at last to the pounding ripples of orgasmic bliss and shuddered to a rich, powerful climax that shattered his senses.

Weak and spent, his brain almost numb from the violent onslaught of ecstasy, he sank his weight down upon Rebecca's soft, warm body on the bed, and lay there silent for some time, breathing softly and easily in the night, wondering how it was possible this woman could knock down all his defenses and make him forget everything that plagued him. He felt no heavy sense of obligation tonight. There were no reminders that he must do his duty and solve everyone's problems.

Rolling to the side, he lay next to her with his arm stretched across her hip. "I would like to stay a while," he said. "Here in your bed. I would like to sleep with you."

"Nothing would please me more," she replied.

And for the first time in his life he began to believe that genuine happiness just might be possible for the future Duke of Pembroke after all.

And perhaps curses *could* be broken.

Outside in the driving rain, somewhere between the Cotswolds and the village of Pembroke, Lord Creighton held tight to the side of the coach as it bumped and swayed ominously at a fast clip down a hill. His driver had freshened the horses a short time before, after searching the village inns at Corsham, and Creighton had instructed the man to push the team to its limit. There was not a moment to lose if he was going to find Rebecca and bring her home. Rushton was waiting, and he was not a patient man. He had said he would wait no longer than one week, and if Creighton did not deliver her by then, his own life and hers would be destroyed. He would have to endure the consequences of Rushton's threats—which were not idle ones—and Rebecca's future would never be the same.

The horses' hooves thundered noisily down the road, and Creighton rubbed at the pain in his temples. At least he had higher hopes for the next stop. He knew his daughter, he knew of her fanciful daydreams, and he had a feeling he would have better luck there. Yes, better luck in the village of Pembroke.

Chapter 13

"**I**'ll wager you never imagined," Blake said to Devon, who was donning his wedding attire shortly after breakfast, "that when you stepped off that steamship from America, you would be married within a week."

Devon looked at his reflection in the mirror while his valet adjusted his sleeves, and felt as if he were looking at someone other than himself—a confident groom, heir to a dukedom, a calm man who had all the pieces of his life under control and was about to marry his future duchess and ensure the continuation of his ancestral line.

Inside, however, he was not so calm. He was far from it, for he was wrestling with the terrible fear that he had fallen completely and hopelessly in love with his bride and had already lost all sense of reality.

There had been moments over the past few days when he'd actually felt happy, and he could not fight the fear that his feet were going to slip and slide out from under him, and he would soon, without warning, begin the agonizing tumble down the hill.

Nevertheless, he spoke to his brother matter-of-factly, not wanting to reveal what he was feeling. "I always knew I would marry eventually."

"And you are doing so now because you found a wonderful woman," Blake put in, seeming as if he were reminding Devon of the bright spot in all of this. His future wife. Rebecca.

He faced his very perceptive brother. "Thank you, Blake. And I should inform you that as soon as we are declared husband and wife, I intend to speak to Father about changing his will back to the way it was. As far as he is concerned, I will have done my duty to this family and he will soon have his heir. There is no need for him to pressure you or Vincent or Garrett. All three of you should be free to choose the women you want, when the time is right."

Blake eyed him carefully. "And you are absolutely certain that this is what *you* want? To be married today? For your sake, I hope it is."

Devon recalled the unexpected tranquility of sleeping with Rebecca all night in her bed, not to mention the blinding intensity of his sexual urges, completely fulfilled. "I have never wanted a woman as much as I want her." It was the truth.

Blake's shoulders relaxed slightly as he nodded. "She is perfect, Devon. Not the slightest blemish on her character. Everyone thinks so. You chose well."

"Strangely enough, despite all the insanity around this house lately, I believe I did. And I will forever be baffled by what seems to be a miracle at work here." He turned to the mirror again and adjusted his tie.

"What miracle?"

"The fact that no other man has claimed her before now, and that I was the one lucky enough to come upon her and her father in the woods that night years ago." He smiled cautiously at Blake. "I am hesitant to believe it, but perhaps there is not always a mud slick in one's future. Perhaps just occasionally, the path is clear."

For four long years, Rebecca had never dared to truly believe that she would one day stand inside the Pembroke Palace chapel with a bouquet of white roses in her hands, with Devon Sinclair beside her as her groom.

She had dreamed of it, of course, and in her dreams, she always imagined it would be the happiest moment of her life—that she would look into his eyes and marvel at the peace and contentment she would feel inside her heart.

Peace, however, was nowhere near her present

emotional state as she stood listening to the vicar's sermon, for since the moment she'd opened her eyes that morning, the only thing she knew was fear. It all seemed impossible to believe, and she was certain the bubble was going to burst at any second—that her father was going to come crashing through the doors, waving his cane and demanding to know what the devil was happening here. Or worse, that Mr. Rushton might rise from one of the pews at the back of the chapel and object to this marriage because he was her rightful groom.

Which he was not. He had never proposed to her directly, and even if he had, she would have refused him. It had been her father's promise, not hers, if that counted for anything.

She honestly did not know if it did. All she knew was that she was twenty-one years old today, and she would marry the man she wanted.

The vicar looked directly into her eyes. "I require and charge you both," he said in a deep voice, "as ye will answer, at the dreadful day of judgment, when the secrets of all hearts shall be disclosed, that if either of you know any impediment, why ye may not be lawfully joined together in matrimony, ye do now confess it."

The flowers began to tremble in her hands, and she lowered them slightly.

"And if any man can show any just cause," he continued, looking up at the small congregation, "why they may not lawfully be joined together, let him now speak, or else hereafter, forever hold his peace."

The muscles in Rebecca's stomach clenched involuntarily. She shut her eyes, listened to the silence in the chapel, prayed no one would speak. Seconds ticked by like minutes and hours. Someone coughed, and her heart squeezed with dread. She could hear her blood coursing through her veins in a noisy rush.

The vicar began again, terminating at last the long, unbearable silence.

"Devon Geoffrey Fitzgerald Sinclair," he said, turning to her groom, "wilt thou have this woman to be thy wedded wife, to live together after God's ordinance in the holy estate of matrimony? Wilt thou love her, comfort her, honor and keep her, in sickness and in health; and, forsaking all others, keep thee only unto her, so long as ye both shall live?"

"I will."

Rebecca blinked in disbelief, then focused upon the vicar's question directed at her. Her answer was the same. "I will."

Then the vicar cleared his throat and summoned the rings. Rebecca inhaled deeply, willing her heartbeat to slow down, otherwise she might faint and drop to the floor right here, and everyone would wonder what in the world was wrong.

The vicar delivered his final blessings, then declared them man and wife.

It was done. She was Devon's. She could hardly believe it.

She gazed up at the vicar with parted lips while he shook Devon's hand. *Please, do not let me find myself suddenly back at Creighton Manor, alone and fantasizing by the fire, with my shawl wrapped tightly around my shoulders to keep me warm. . . .*

But no, she was not going to wake up. She was awake now. The chapel was real, the vicar was real, and her husband had just taken hold of her hand and was lifting it to his lips.

"You're all mine now," he said with a seductive grin that melted away all her horrendous worries.

They turned around and faced the guests of the house party, who had remained at the palace for an extra day to celebrate the wedding.

Her husband leaned close and dropped a kiss on her temple, and the sweet, simple show of affection—chaste as it was here in the chapel before the vicar—poured relief through her trembling body and sent her heart reeling with anticipation for their future together, and more specifically for the night ahead, when he would come to her bed and consummate the marriage. Again. She could hardly wait.

And she was so pleased that the danger had passed.

Devon sat next to Rebecca in the formal dining room, where the table had been laid out with grace and flourish for their impromptu wedding break-fast. The room smelled of fresh flowers and cham-pagne, the sun was shining through the windows, making tiny rainbows through the raindrops still clinging to things, and all the guests were buoyant and cheerful, chatting amongst themselves.

It was a perfect morning, all the more so be-cause of the sun's unexpected appearance, which lifted everyone's spirits—no one more than Dev-on's father, the duke, who was so happy, his smile seemed glued to his face.

Shortly after the raspberry tarts were served, the duke rose from his seat at the high table and raised his glass. "Attention everyone! Hush now! Hush!"

Devon noticed an errant splotch of sugary red glaze on his father's chin, as well as a vacant look in his eyes, and glanced uneasily at Blake.

"It is my pleasure," the duke said, "to thank you all for coming to the palace for the duchess's fiftieth birthday celebrations. How impossible it seems that time could pass so quickly and she could be that old." He paused a moment and stared up at the chandelier over their heads, as if perplexed by the notion, then his eyes brightened and he continued. "And how timely the celebrations have been, because now you—my merry guests—have been fortunate enough to stay on for the hasty nuptials of my eldest son and heir to my title." He pointed a finger around the table, addressing a few of the ladies in particular. "And in case any of you are whispering—which I'm sure you are—there is no babe simmering in the stewing pot, at least not that I am aware of. It has all happened much too quickly for those kinds of shenanigans."

There was a shocked response from the table and a few disapproving murmurs, which went completely unnoticed by the duke.

"In that regard," he continued, "I am exceedingly pleased with my son's selection of a bride, for the gel does have an impressive form for child bearing, does she not?" The question was met with silence and stunned expressions. "So raise your glasses, if you will! To the bride's hips!"

While he tipped his glass up in the air and downed the entire contents in a single mouthful, the hush in the room slowly trickled into a reserved and somewhat confused murmur.

Blake immediately rose to his feet and lifted his glass as well. "Thank you, Father. And may I also convey my deepest congratulations to my brother, Lord Hawthorne, for he has found himself the loveliest of brides—Rebecca Newland, now Lady Hawthorne—a generous woman whom he was fortunate enough to meet four years ago. Their engagement was well worth waiting for. To Lady Hawthorne."

The more refined toast seemed to placate the guests, who nodded and agreed and raised their glasses to toast Rebecca, who bore it all with an easy stride. She even smiled up at Devon with amusement.

Later, after the wedding cake had been served, the guests milled about in the gilt drawing room, offering up their congratulations and sipping champagne.

Vincent approached Devon and Rebecca. "Congratulations," he said. "I hope you will be happy."

"Thank you, Vincent," she replied.

He bowed again, and turned to leave.

Devon followed him to the door. "Vincent, wait. Where are you going?"

"To London, where else?"

"Don't go yet."

His brother stopped just outside the drawing room and faced him. "What's to keep me here except for your toasts and revelry? No, I have other plans. I'm off to find a bride."

Devon strode forward. "I intend to speak to Father about that. I mean to approach him today when he is optimistic and convince him to change his will back to the way it was, so that you and Blake and Garrett will have your freedom. There is no need for all of us to be shackled by his demands."

Vincent gestured toward the reception room and laughed. "You're shackled now, are you? By that exquisite creature? I'm sorry, but you'll get no sympathy from me."

"That is not what I meant," Devon said.

Vincent eyed him shrewdly. "Oh, but I think it was. We all know your opinions on marriage. If it weren't for Father's will threatening your inheritance, you'd be a bachelor until your dying day. I'm surprised you even went through with this."

"Rebecca has changed my opinions on marriage," Devon informed him, "so do not mention it again. I intend to make a success of it. And you are hardly one to point the finger, Vincent. With your reputation lately, most would say the same of you, that you enjoy your bachelorhood."

"Only lately," Vincent stated. "There was a time when I wanted nothing more than the so-called shackles of marriage." He started off across the great hall. "It didn't work out, though, did it? So I suppose I'll just have to try again. Let us hope I won't be disappointed this time."

Devon watched his brother climb the staircase. "I will speak to Father," he said. "And I will send word if he comes around."

"No need," Vincent replied. "I don't need your

help. I just want my inheritance, so I can live my own life, somewhere far away from here."

Devon watched his brother until he was out of sight, then turned to discover Blake staring at him from the doorway of the reception room.

"I presume you heard that," Devon said. "He doesn't need my help."

Blake approached and patted him on the back. "Maybe he doesn't, but I think I can speak for Garrett and certainly for myself. If you still want to be helpful and speak to Father, we're behind you all the way."

"Not itching to be shackled just yet?" he asked.

"Not even close," Blake replied. "But that is not why I am here. There appears to be a gentleman in the library who wishes to speak to you."

"Did you tell him I am in the middle of my wedding celebrations?"

"Yes. I invited him to join us in fact, but he did not wish to intrude. He nevertheless insisted on speaking with you. Alone."

"Who is it?" Devon asked.

Blake stopped and drew in a deep breath. "I'm afraid it is none other than your new father-in-law, Lord Creighton. And I must warn you, Devon. He looks rather pale for a man recently returned from India."

Chapter 14

Devon entered the library to find Lord Creighton pacing back and forth, tapping his cane across the floor. The instant he became aware of Devon's presence in the room, he halted and looked up—though his shoulders remained hunched forward. His gray eyebrows drew together with concern, and he bit down on his lower lip.

Devon greeted him warmly. "Lord Creighton, welcome to Pembroke."

The man was smaller and more frail than he remembered. He stared speechlessly at Devon for a moment, as if he did not know the proper thing to say.

Devon studied him, then made another attempt at a greeting. "What marvelous timing you have. May I presume you are here to bestow your good wishes?"

At least he hoped that was what his father-in-law was doing here. But the fact that he did not wish to intrude upon the celebrations did not indicate all was well. Devon could not help but be on his guard.

Creighton cleared his throat and spoke shakily. "Am I correct in my assumption that the wedding ceremony has already taken place?"

"Indeed it has," Devon replied. "Just over an hour ago. I presume Lady Saxby's letter about our impending nuptials reached you?"

But even as he spoke the words, he knew it could not be so. Rebecca's aunt had posted a letter to the earl immediately following the announcement of their engagement, which was less than a week ago, and she had posted it to India.

Creighton cleared his throat again. "No, I received no letter. I did not even know my daughter had come here."

Devon pondered the earl's pronouncement. "To be honest, sir, I did not expect you to know, and I am surprised to see you. It was my understanding that you were abroad, traveling in India, and could not easily be reached."

The earl's brow furrowed with distress, and he almost appeared to be fighting a complete breakdown. "India? Is that what they told you?"

"Yes."

The frail man backed up and sank into a chair, while Devon struggled to hold on to his calm, for clearly there was something afoot here, which he did not fully understand. And he did not enjoy being kept in the dark.

He took a few seconds to gather his wits about him. "You are obviously surprised by what has transpired, sir, as I am equally surprised by your unexpected appearance, not to mention your reaction to all of this. May I ask what is going on?"

The earl collected himself, then looked up into Devon's eyes. "Nothing. It is nothing. I am simply taken aback, that is all. My daughter left home without telling me where she was going, and I did not expect to discover that she had become a married woman."

Not entirely convinced the earl was telling him everything, Devon nevertheless spoke with understanding. "I believe it is always a surprise to any father, to see his daughter as a wife."

"Yes, exactly." But the man's eyes were darting around the room in a panic.

Devon slowly moved to the sofa and sat down. "I apologize, sir, for the suddenness of this, but I would like you to know that I discussed the matter in some depth with Lady Saxby, who assured me you had entrusted Rebecca into her care. She assured me also that you wished to see Rebecca happily married. I expressed my desire to speak to you directly about my intentions, but was informed it was not necessary. Rebecca is twenty-one today, as you know."

"Yes, I do know." He paused for a moment.

"But to marry so quickly . . . Did you have an arrangement before? Did you plan it? Have you been secretly writing to each other?"

Devon frowned. "No, I had not seen or heard from your daughter since that night on the old coach road four years ago. In fact, I was in America until very recently."

"So there was no previous arrangement?" he asked again, as if he could not quite believe it and needed further clarification.

"No," Devon replied. "We simply . . ." He did not quite know how to say it. "I believed we were a good match."

The man's shoulders relaxed slightly, though he still appeared distraught. "I suppose I shouldn't be surprised she came here. She often spoke of you over the years since that night. It was my impression that she considered you very heroic. I believe she idolized you."

The earl continued to sit with both hands folded over the handle of his cane, his posture curled forward, his expression forlorn, while Devon felt a rather urgent need to have an immediate conversation with his new bride.

"Allow me if you will, Lord Creighton, to go and fetch Rebecca. I am sure she would like to see you. It is her wedding day after all."

The man considered it. "No, no, I do not wish to impose."

"It would be no imposition."

"No, I really . . ." He hesitated. "I beg your pardon, I am certain she would not wish to see me."

Devon narrowed his gaze at the earl. "Because of your . . . *disagreement*?"

"So you *do* know the circumstances," he said. "I suspected as much. It explains the hastiness of your wedding."

Devon made no reply. He simply sat in silence, waiting for the man to explain himself.

"I suppose, in that case," the earl said shakily, looking all around the room, appearing more and more distraught with every passing second, "that she was right to come here. You *are* her hero, destined to be her rescuer and protector." He stood up and strode to the window. He was breathing very hard. "Perhaps I should try not to be so distressed by this. Perhaps I should be thankful, for you have succeeded where I have failed. At least she will be safe with you."

Safe.

Devon listened to all of this with a throbbing ache in his gut. He was to be her hero? Her protector?

What was going on, and what had she wanted from him, which she did not disclose?

He felt that weight bearing down upon his shoulders—the weight of everyone's mistaken notions that he could take care of them and solve all their problems. He had come home to a family who thought he could not only deal with his father's madness, but could stop a family curse and prevent a flood from sweeping them all away. Now to learn that the one woman who seemed to be a respite from all of those lofty expectations had expectations of her own as well. . . .

She had come here to ensnare him for some reason, so that he could protect her from something. God only knew what.

"Lord Creighton, I suggest you start at the beginning and tell me what I am protecting your daughter from, because contrary to what you think, I know nothing."

The earl turned instantly to face him. "I beg your pardon. Did you say you do not know?"

"It appears your daughter is very good at keeping secrets."

Creighton covered his face with a hand and squeezed at his temples. "Damn my life," he whispered irritably as he limped back to the sofa and sat down again.

"Sir, I require an explanation," Devon repeated.

"Yes, it seems you do, and I will give you one. My daughter came here to escape a future she did not want—more precisely—to escape her betrothed."

Devon returned to the reception room and stopped just inside the door. He let his gaze pass over everyone in the room and spotted his wife conversing with Charlotte and a few other guests. They were standing by a bouquet of daffodils. Rebecca was holding a cup of tea in her hands and smiling, as if she hadn't a care in the world.

He placed a hand over the knot in his gut, not wanting to believe what he had just heard. Surely it was a mistake. It could not be true. His bride, his Rebecca, could not have used him for her own purposes, to escape a man she was engaged to marry. And who was this man? Was he the real reason she was not so very innocent? Was it because of him—his hands, his touch?—that she knew what she was doing in the bedroom? And how had a betrothal come to pass? The earl would not say. He had become agitated and felt ill, and had walked out on Devon before answering any of his questions.

Just then, Rebecca threw her head back and laughed at something someone said, so Devon set out to get the answers he needed, steeling himself for the worst as he strode across the room to her.

"My dear wife," he said, "may I have a word with you in private?"

The conversation skidded to a halt, and the smile in her eyes died away while everyone gaped at him. He supposed his tone had been terse, but there it was.

"Of course," she replied, laboring to sound

lighthearted when it was clear—at least to him—that she was unnerved. He wondered if she had any idea that her father had been there.

Offering his arm, he escorted her out of the reception room, through the center of the house and out the back doors onto the terrace overlooking the former Italian Gardens. The area was still a sea of muck and overturned rocks. The sky, however, was a perfect blue, and the sun was shining brightly overhead.

"What is it, Devon?" she asked.

He was not in the mood to dance around the subject or even broach it gently. He only wanted to know the truth, and to hear it from her.

"Your father was here," he said, taking note of her sharp gasp. "We had a most enlightening conversation in the library before he left the palace, exceedingly agitated and in a hurry."

Her lips fell open. "*Just* my father? No one else?"

Devon strove to keep his breathing under control while he wrestled with the strange complexity of his emotions. He was angry, to be sure. What man wouldn't be? His bride had been engaged to another man and she had hidden it from him, while she'd cleverly wrapped him around her delicate ring finger in less than a week.

He felt something else, too, however, which was not anger exactly. There was a burning in his gut over the fact that there was another man somewhere in the world who had a prior claim upon her. A man who still, at this very moment, believed she belonged to him and would be his wife. He was probably out searching for her, because he was not yet aware that Devon had put a ring on her finger that very morning.

He thought of the diary suddenly, and wondered if she had read it to this man, too. A muscle in his jaw clenched.

"You were expecting your betrothed," he said at last. "Why didn't you tell me about that, Rebecca?"

"Because there was nothing to tell," she insisted. "And he was *not* my betrothed. At least not in my mind. He never proposed to me, and even if he had, I would have turned him down in no uncertain terms."

Her plain anger assuaged some of his, so he strove to at least listen to what she had to say before he crushed all feeling for her, which is what he wanted to do. He wanted this escape—this diversion from the tender affection he had never wanted to feel, because God help him, this was the slipping and tripping he had feared would come.

But he would keep his footing this time, damn it. He would not fall backward and go sliding down that long, slippery slope.

"Your father sees it differently," he said. "He told me that this gentleman understood you were to be his wife. Who is he? What's his name?"

"What does it matter?" she asked.

"His name, Rebecca."

Her eyes clouded over with indignation as she ground out the words. "Rushton. Maximillian Rushton. And my father made those arrangements without ever consulting me. But I was not about to be shepherded into my future like a meek little lamb. I have a mind and a will of my own, you know."

"That's quite obvious," he said. "So you took matters into your own hands, disobeyed your father, and came here instead. Under your terms."

"Exactly."

"So this is what I have to look forward to," he said. "A headstrong, willful wife who will do whatever she pleases? A woman who will use any tactic necessary to get what she wants?"

"What do you mean?"

"The diary, Rebecca. You used it to lure me into your bed, didn't you? To trap me."

She gave a choked cry of protest. "No, that is not true."

He turned away and strode to the balustrade, where he stood for a long moment looking at the statue of Venus while he fought to contain his temper.

"I cannot deny," he said with a note of bitter sarcasm, "that I must at least admire your spirit. That is what drew me to you in the first place, I suppose—that fire in your eyes. Which is probably what drew *him* to you as well." He turned to face her. "What bothers me is the fact that you came here to secretly use me for protection from another man's intentions, without ever telling me. I do not appreciate being used and manipulated."

"I did not manipulate you."

"No?" Antagonism lit in his veins. "What would you call it then? You came to the ball looking irresistible, flirting up a storm, and on the third day of your visit, began quoting from an erotic diary. It was enough to make any man lose control of his senses and cross the line. All the while, you had an ulterior motive which you did not disclose to me."

"May I remind you," she said heatedly, "that you had an ulterior motive as well. Your father was pressuring you to find a wife."

"But there is the difference, you see. I told you. That moment in particular would have been the perfect opportunity for you to confess your true motivation to me. I would have liked to know I might have to defend my actions to a man who will no doubt believe I acted dishonorably and stole something from him."

He realized suddenly it was the second time in

his life he had stolen another man's fiancée, and neither time had it been his conscious intention to do so. On both occasions, he had been the object of a spirited woman's desires, and his passions had overwhelmed his intellect.

At least this time, he had not known there was another man. He had not known he was doing anything dishonorable.

But what was worse—dishonor or stupidity?

She blanched—her anger fading somewhat to reveal a hint of anxiety. Over what? he wondered. That he would turn her out? He could hardly do that now, could he, after speaking vows before God a short time ago. Not to mention the fact that she could already be carrying his child in her womb.

"I wanted to tell you," she implored. "Truly I did. I thought about it many times, but I was afraid you would withdraw your offer if you knew. And when the marriage was within my grasp, I just couldn't do anything to jeopardize it. I didn't want to lose you."

He scoffed. "To lose your safe haven, you mean. Your protection from *him*."

"It wasn't just that," she said. "Everything I said to you over the past week has been true. I wanted you, Devon, with every breath in my body and soul. I've been dreaming about you since the night we met in the woods four years ago. I fell in love with you then."

He almost wanted to laugh. "You fell in love with a fantasy, and you've been living in one ever since, sheltered in your father's house, reading another woman's diary. You don't know anything about me if you think I am your hero. I was not looking to be anyone's protector. I do not need another burden of responsibility, especially when it involves a woman's safekeeping. I simply needed a future duchess."

"But you *are* a hero," she said, sounding almost perplexed to hear otherwise. "You are the future Duke of Pembroke. You are powerful and honorable. That's more clear to me than anything."

"You think I am honorable, do you? You don't even know me."

She bristled. "I know enough."

"No, you do not. All you know is one night four years ago when I led a few horses out of a bog, and more recently a week of good sex. Trust me, neither one of those things was terribly difficult, especially with you waving that diary in front of my face. What you do not know is that in reality I am a man who would betray his own brother, but more importantly, a man who could lead a woman to believe he could keep her safe, then cause her death. Maybe you would have been better off with this Rushton fellow."

She stiffened and said nothing for a long moment. "Who are you talking about? What woman?"

He almost enjoyed the surprised look on her face. The realization that she might not be so right about him after all, that she had in fact married a stranger. Because that's what they were. Strangers. She was certainly a stranger to him.

"There, you see?" he said. "You have no idea what I'm talking about, and I suppose since we are now man and wife, and secrets and lies are being revealed, it's time you heard the whole story."

Chapter 15

Rebecca fought the sickening jolt of regret in her stomach. She had wrecked it. She had wrecked everything. He was disenchanted with her now, and it was all her fault. She should have told him sooner. She should not have come here planning and conniving to hook him into marrying her, like some sort of devious fugitive. She should never have encouraged him to make love to her before any promises were made. In that regard, she had indeed forced his hand.

She walked to the bench and sat down, clasped her hands together on her lap. She supposed he was right in one other respect. They did not know each other very well. Maybe she had been in love with a fantasy hero—because in all her romantic dreams of him, there had never been any other women in his life. There had only been the two of them, as if the outside world did not exist.

It truly had *not* existed for her while she'd lived secluded in her father's house, safe from danger, wrapped up cozily in her daydreams. The only time there had been any threat to her dreams was when she learned she was to marry Mr. Rushton.

And since she'd arrived here, she'd always felt like the only woman in Devon's life. He had made her feel that way with his attentive behavior and constant flirtations. They had never once discussed his personal life before her arrival here, or what he had been doing in America for three years. It was as if they were living in a bubble. For all she knew, he, too, could have been engaged or even married. Perhaps he was still in love with this woman he had just mentioned, who was now dead. Perhaps she had been the great love of his life and he would always love her.

She felt slightly nauseated at the thought.

Devon sat down beside her on the bench, then spoke with a strange show of pleasure, as if he enjoyed proving how wrong she had been about him.

"The woman I am referring to," he said, "was Vincent's fiancée."

Vincent's fiancée. The nauseous feeling in her stomach swelled. "And she died," Rebecca said.

He nodded.

"Is that why you and he do not get on well?"

"That is an understatement. My brother despises me, and for good reason, which is why I cannot hate him in return, despite his many attempts to make it so."

"What reason does he have to despise you? What happened?"

He looked directly at her and spoke without emotion. "His fiancée, MaryAnn, was in love with me."

She swallowed uncomfortably and squeezed her hands together so tightly, she could feel her nails digging into the skin. "Did this happen before they were engaged, or after?"

He considered the question for a moment. "I only became aware of it after the engagement. I suppose it's a rather complicated story because there was a history between the three of us. MaryAnn's father was a lifelong friend of our father's, and we had known her since childhood, playing games on the estate. Vincent had always fancied her, and I knew it. I also knew she liked to pester me constantly, but I never thought anything of it until much later."

He stopped talking and gazed off in the other direction, as if he were recalling specific moments in time, those moments from childhood that gain clarity from years of reflection.

"How did she die?" Rebecca asked, wanting to steer him back to the point of all this.

"It was a week before their wedding," he said, "and she sent me a letter."

"Declaring her feelings?"

"She told me she could not marry Vincent when I was the one she truly loved and always had. She intended to call off the wedding and asked me to meet her at the treehouse beyond the lake, where we used to play hide-and-seek as children. I rode out there to convince her that she was making a mistake—that she would be better off with Vincent because he loved her and I did not. But it was a lie. I did have feelings for her, terrible passions that consumed me, and I didn't know what would happen when I got to the treehouse and was alone with her."

"What did happen?"

He sighed deeply. "I gave the letter back to her and told her it could never be. She cried and pleaded with me to return her feelings, and I was weak. I took her in my arms."

He bowed his head, and Rebecca sensed it was much worse than that. "Did you make love to her?"

He did not answer for a long time. "Certain things happened that I am not proud of. But when I realized what we were doing, I put a stop to it. She was very distraught and confused, so I attempted to bring her home to my brother."

Rebecca frowned. "Attempted?"

He stood up and walked away from her, but she did not rise. She waited patiently for him to return.

A moment later, he came back and sat down. "She was climbing down the treehouse ladder when she caught her skirts, fell to the ground, and injured her ankle."

"But that was not your fault," Rebecca told him, for she was anticipating the gist of all this.

"I realize that," he said. "I did what I could. I helped her up and carried her down the path and lifted her onto my horse, then we started back to the palace. She was in a great deal of pain and was urging me to hurry while she clung to my neck and cried and told me that she loved me, that I was the most extraordinary man she'd ever known, and that she knew I could take care of her better than anyone, including Vincent." He paused. "They were words that will haunt me until the day I die."

"Why?"

"Because that was the moment I wanted to be free of her. All I wanted was to get her back to the palace and deliver her to my brother, then turn around and disappear. I wanted her to forget me and realize that Vincent was the better man. He loved her and was devoted to her and wanted nothing more than to make her happy every day for the rest of his life, while I never really wanted to marry her. It killed me to think she preferred me, and that I had encouraged her affections. So I took a shortcut. I steered my horse off the path to travel through the woods and over a ridge. I should have known better."

"Why?"

"The hill was slick with mud because of the spring rains, which was not unusual. I knew I was taking a risk, yet I forged ahead, and even when Asher resisted and bucked against my commands, I ordered him on. All I knew was my impatience, my guilt, and my desire to get MaryAnn back to Vincent where she belonged. But Asher lost his footing and neither he nor I could gain control after that. The three of us started sliding backward down the hill, through the muck and slime, while Asher scrambled to stay on his feet. Then we all went down. My foot was tangled in a stirrup, MaryAnn was clutching onto me, and I watched as Asher rolled over her, crushing her body before he rolled over my leg and broke it."

A suffocating sensation squeezed in Rebecca's throat. "It must have been terrifying."

"It was the most horrific moment of my life, but it did not end there. I was knocked unconscious, and when I woke, Asher was lying beside me, bruised and broken, writhing in pain in the mud slick, and MaryAnn was face down, dead. I had to make my way back to the palace with a broken leg to face my father and brother. I was crawling by the time I reached them. I told them where she was, then I lost consciousness."

"Did you tell Vincent why you were with her?"

"No. The fact that she and I were alone in the woods together was enough."

"But did you tell him you tried to discourage her? That you told her to forget you and marry him?"

"After he returned from the ordeal of bringing her body back, yes, but he knew me too well. He saw the guilt in my eyes."

"And your horse?"

"Shot and killed. Vincent did that, too, after he found and read the letter in MaryAnn's pocket, which I had given back to her."

Rebecca listened to all of this with a steady, persistent drumming in her ears. She understood now why Vincent was so bitter about his brother's return, and why today he had been quiet and sullen during the wedding celebrations. She also understood why Devon had left England three years ago and stayed away so long. He had blamed himself for what happened and could not face his family.

"This is all very tragic," she said to him. "I am so sorry it happened to you."

"It didn't just happen to me," he replied. "At least I am alive to talk about it."

"But you cannot blame yourself for MaryAnn's death. It was an accident. It was not your fault she fell from the ladder and hurt her ankle, or that Asher slipped in the mud."

"But it was my decision to take the shortcut when I knew it would be dangerous. All I was thinking about was my own selfish need to get her off of my horse." He looked straight at her. "All the while, she was telling me I was her hero. She was very wrong about that."

Rebecca shifted uneasily on the hard bench.

"I see now why you felt a need to tell me this today, and why you were angry to learn of my situation. You think that is the only reason I am here, to have you as my protector, when you do not want to be responsible for another person's well-being."

His voice was hard like stone. "People have expected that of me all my life, and it is a heavy weight to bear. One I did not ask for. What they don't seem to understand is that I do not have all the answers, and I don't *want* to be head of the family. I did not ask to be born first."

"But you *are* head of the family, and it has nothing to do with the fact that you were born first," she told him. "There is just something about you that inspires people's trust and confidence."

"Falsely."

"No. MaryAnn was right. You are an extraordinary man. You are also only human."

He stared at her for a moment, then spoke without tenderness, only single-minded resolve. "Your father seemed very distraught about our marriage," he said, "which makes little sense, considering my rank. One would expect him to be pleased. So is there anything I should know about this man who believes himself to be your future husband? Does he have some hold over your father? Will he be difficult?"

"No hold that I am aware of, but he is not kind," she replied. "He has an intimidating demeanor. I believe that is why my father has always feared him and why he could not refuse his demand to have me as his wife. It is why Father came looking for me today—to drag me home. I'll wager he was very surprised to learn he could not."

Devon's gaze narrowed. "You are *my* wife now, Rebecca." He rose to his feet. "And this man who has intimidated your father will not intimidate me."

She looked up at him, so tall and masculine before her. *There, you see?* she wanted to say. *And you wonder why people feel safe in your presence.*

"I suggest you write to your father right away and ask him if he requires assistance in dealing with this difficult neighbor. If the man does have some control over your father, I would like to know about it."

"So would I." She rose to her feet as well. "I am sorry, Devon, that I did not tell you this before. I did not mean to spoil things. I hope you can forgive me."

There was no warmth in his pale blue eyes. "What's done is done. We are married now."

"But do you forgive me?" she pressed.

He offered his arm. "I suppose I have no choice. We are bound together, till death do us part. We will soldier on."

They were words intended to put this unpleasant conversation behind them, but she knew with despair that their marriage was no longer a union of joy and passion and love. Reality and truth had come crashing down, and it was now, for him, merely another burden and obligation.

And he was probably wishing that he had chosen Lady Letitia instead of her. At least she would not have disappointed him so completely in every way.

Chapter 16

Devon escorted Rebecca back to the reception room in silence, dreading the continuation of the wedding celebrations. He had done enough talking today, and he did not believe he could paste on a smile for the guests. He had managed it before Rebecca's father had arrived, certainly, but did not think he could manage it now. Not after he'd dealt with the fact that Rebecca had come here because she believed he was her hero, and that she'd been engaged to another man and had kept it from him. Not to mention the fact that he had dredged up agonizing memories about Mary-Ann and relived that wretched day in the woods.

He was beginning to think his father was right. Perhaps this palace was cursed. It seemed no one here was permitted to be happy. Teased with happiness, yes, but only briefly before that happiness was abruptly snatched away.

He thought suddenly of Lady Letitia's embittered warning. *You chose the wrong woman to be your wife. And I will wager my grandmother's diamond tiara that one day, you will live to regret it.*

He could not bear to think that she was right, or that he might have made a mistake—that he should have chosen her instead. Despite everything, he did not want to believe that.

They soon arrived back at the reception room. Devon was immediately approached by his father, who came marching across the room with Mr. Beasley, the portly village banker. They were hooting with laughter, jolly as a couple of Christmas fiddlers. Before they reached him, however, the duchess approached also, asking if she could borrow Rebecca for a few minutes to take her and the other ladies to the conservatory to see the orchids.

Naturally Devon agreed, then turned to his father and Mr. Beasley, who was staggering to and fro, clearly in his cups, despite the fact that it was barely past noon.

"My son!" his father said. "A married man at last. Come with us, we have something for you."

With mischievous, mumbling laughter, the two of them led Devon out of the room and across the great hall, through the south corridor and up the stairs to his father's study. They were chortling the entire way, congratulating Devon on his choice of a bride, his rosy future, nudging him in the ribs, and reminding him of his proper husbandly duty that very night. He did his best to be patient and humor them, and not to reveal his grim mood.

They entered the study and closed the door, and Mr. Beasley staggered like a wide, sloshing water barrel across the room to the bookcase behind the desk.

"I brought something for you," he said, lifting down a small box. "It's a wedding gift."

Devon glanced briefly at his father, who watched the box with eager eyes.

Beasley set it down on the desk and lifted the lid. He withdrew a clay plaque with an image impressed upon it. Devon looked more closely to discover a lewd depiction of the sexual act—a man poised behind a woman on her hands and knees, his tremendous erection largely out of scale, the size of a tree trunk. Sharp beams of sunlight rained down upon them.

"It's a fertility stone," Beasley explained, swaying drunkenly. "If you put it under your pillow tonight, it will bring you luck and put a child in your bride's womb the very night her maidenhead is broken."

It was a little late for that, Devon thought.

Beasley chuckled and nudged Devon in the ribs again. "You're an efficient lad, aren't you? I thought you might appreciate the gesture."

Devon raised his eyebrows and picked up the flat stone, turning it over in his hands.

Beasley, who was enjoying himself tremendously, wagged a confident finger. "It's a powerful thing, my boy."

Devon glanced again at his father, who reached for the stone and held it like a treasured family heirloom.

"Beasley, you are a good man to bring this here," he said. "The palace will benefit."

Beasley exploded with laughter. "I think the lad here will be the one to reap the benefits," he said. "It being his wedding night and all that."

Devon took a deep breath, willing himself to ignore the man's playful teasing, for he knew he meant no harm.

"Thank you, Beasley," he said. "I appreciate the thought." He turned to his father and spoke meaningfully. "Though I have never been a superstitious man."

The duke glared at Devon, his brows pulling together with frustration.

Mr. Beasley, in his drunken state, was oblivious to the tension between them. "Neither have I, when it comes right down to it. It's just a bit of fun, my boy. Promise me you'll at least give it a try, and maybe your bride will find it amusing. Show this to her and she'll at least know what to expect." He took hold of the stone and examined the fornicating couple, pointing specifically at the man's monstrous instrument of pleasure. "On the other hand, it might send her screaming from the room."

He slapped Devon on the back and laughed again. "Shall we head back to the reception room? I believe I left my brandy on a windowsill."

"You go on ahead of us," Devon replied. "I require a few minutes alone with my father."

"Ah, yes, father and son must have their moment to look to the future and all that. I'll leave you two to share a drink." He started off toward the door. "Congratulations again, my boy. You've made your family proud."

As soon as the door clicked shut behind him, Devon set the stone back into the box and lowered the lid.

"I'll have that sent up to your bedchamber," his father said. "And you must use it tonight. I will have your word."

"I will promise no such thing, Father. This is nothing but superstitious nonsense. It has no magic power and I will ask you again to let go of your silly belief in a family curse."

The duke pressed his shoulders back. "I thought you believed."

Devon shook his head. "No. I have been very clear about my opinions on the matter."

"But you did what I asked and chose a bride." He waved a hand toward the window. "Look.

The sun is shining today. Surely that is enough to convince you."

"It is a coincidence, nothing more. The sun was bound to shine sooner or later. It could not continue to rain forever."

"But it *could*," his father argued, "and it would have, if you had not heeded my warnings. But you did, thank God. You did well, marrying that gel today. The sunshine is our reward. You have made me very happy."

"Happy enough to change your will back to the way it was?" Devon asked pointedly.

His father frowned at him. "No."

"But if it is a grandchild you want, I will give you that. I have already proven my willingness to remain here and fulfill my duty to this family by taking a wife. There is no need to force the others into marriages they do not want. At least give them time."

"I told you before, there is no time. The flood will come."

Devon fought to keep his frustration in check. "The only thing that will come will be misery for all your children, if you force them to abide by your ridiculous demands."

He knew the truth of that all too well.

The duke slapped his open palm upon the desk. "They are not ridiculous! And I will not alter my will!"

Devon cupped his forehead in a hand. God help

him, talking to his father about this curse was like talking to a brick wall.

He drew in a deep breath and counted to ten, then tried to appeal to his father's compassionate side, if he had one. He certainly hadn't shown any compassion to Devon three years ago when the surgeon was setting his leg.

"This family has seen difficult times, Father. Vincent and Charlotte especially. They deserve happiness."

"Charlotte's cooperation is not required. She can marry tomorrow or never. It makes no difference to me."

Because she is not of your bloodline.

"Then perhaps you do not require Garrett's cooperation either," Devon pointed out, speaking openly for the first time to his father about the twins' true parentage.

His father's face flushed red with shock, but Devon was indifferent to it. The time for sweeping secrets under the palace carpets was over. If there was a chance he could free just one brother, he would take it.

"No," his father said flatly. "That boy needs to learn some responsibility. He is an embarrassment to me, living the way he does, mixing with those people."

"They're poets, Father. They are free thinkers."

"I can't stand the defiance. Especially from him, after I have given him so much."

"You gave him your name and a roof over his head. That is all."

"Well, my name is worth a hell of a lot!" he shouted. "As yours will be when you are duke."

Not yet willing to give up just yet, Devon strode closer to his father and placed a hand on his arm. "I am begging you, Father. *Please*. Change your will. Don't force your sons into hasty marriages. I will give you the grandchild you want. A whole nursery full of them. You could even consider it a wedding gift to me."

The duke slapped Devon's hand away. "No, no, no, no, *no*! And I already gave you your gift."

"A silver tea service."

"Brand new. And did you notice the pattern of engravings? They are tiny little oak trees. Hundreds of them on the teapot and creamer and sugar bowl."

His eyes brightened and his voice rang with fascination. Devon's heart sank, for he knew his father's mind was skipping around and toppling off the track. Their discussion about the will was over.

"I've never seen a tea service quite like it," his father said. "Have you? Not that a gentleman takes notice of such things," he said with a chuckle. "It's the woman's domain, to be sure. But I do love a good strong cup of tea." He looked around the room as if he were suddenly confused. "What time is it? Is it teatime?"

Devon worked hard to let go of his frustration. "No, Father. We just had breakfast. The wedding breakfast. Remember?"

"Oh, yes, yes. Your bride is lovely, I dare say." He ran a finger under his nose and his eyes darted about for a moment. "But who is pruning my rosebush? I don't want it pruned."

Devon realized he was becoming accustomed to the challenge of keeping up with his father's thought processes. "No one is pruning it, Father."

"But it's getting smaller."

Devon watched his father stare with concern at the sunny window.

He spoke in a gentle, reassuring voice. "Your rosebush is doing fine. It just looks smaller because you moved it to a larger space."

"I moved it?"

"Yes. A week ago. The day I returned home. Remember?"

The duke's expression became strained, revealing the intensity of his concentration, then at last he raised his chin. "Oh, yes."

A quiet wave of sadness and regret moved through Devon, distracting him from his irritability over what had happened with Rebecca. He moved to take his father's arm.

"Let us go now," he said. "It's time to return to the reception, and when we get there, we'll get you a cup of tea. A nice strong one, just the way you like it."

They walked out of the study together. "You are a good son, Devon. I don't know what any of us would do without you. We'd never manage."

"You would manage just fine," he assured him, wondering for the first time if they really would.

Rebecca strolled around the conservatory with the duchess and the other ladies, working hard to hide her troubles from them, while they examined the rare orchids and the many indigenous plants and flowers. It was a well-known fact that the duke had a passion for horticulture, and his commitment was more than evident in this enormous, lush, green, sweet-smelling conservatory.

"But what of the Italian Gardens?" Aunt Grace asked, as they wandered leisurely around the bubbling stone fountain.

"Yes, what does he intend to do with the garden?" Mrs. Quinlan asked. "It must be something marvelous. A complete transformation I expect."

The duchess strolled ahead of them. "It's his well-guarded secret, I'm afraid. But I believe he means to . . ." She paused, as if taking the time to choose her words with great care. "I believe he means to take England by storm."

The ladies expressed their fascination with bright smiles and flattering comments.

"If anyone can accomplish that," Mrs. Quinlan said, "it is your husband, the duke. He is a true genius when it comes to the beauty of flowers and all things that come from the ground."

"His mind is indeed a mystery to me," Her Grace replied.

While the ladies moved on, Rebecca took her time bringing up the rear, strolling at her own pace to look at the plants and flowers, for she needed time to think about what had happened that morning.

Not only was she devastated that her husband was displeased with her and she had lost his trust, but she could not stop thinking about her father. He had not wished to see her that morning. Was he so very angry with her for her defiance? Were they now permanently estranged?

She stopped and touched the leaves of a red ginger plant. With a painful rush of grief, she recalled the many dark nights as a child when she had been frightened by the wind outside rattling her windowpanes. She would call out to her father, and he would always come. He would tuck her back into bed and sit in the chair by the window until she fell asleep again. Sometimes she would wake up in the morning, and he would still be there, curled up and snoring.

She'd been a little girl without a mother, but she had never felt abandoned. She had loved her father dearly in those days, and now her heart ached over what had become of their relationship. He had changed so much over the years. His illness and pain had caused him to recoil inside himself. He had become a stranger to her.

She worried suddenly about him having to face Mr. Rushton and deliver the news that she was married to another man. Mr. Rushton would not be pleased, that was certain. But surely, once he learned that she had married the Marquess of Hawthorne, he would withdraw and leave her father alone, for he could never imagine he was any match for her new husband.

Or perhaps it would play out differently. Perhaps, knowing that he was now connected to a very powerful family, her father would find the courage to show some grit and stand up to Mr. Rushton. How she longed for him to be a man of strength and integrity—for his own sake and happiness, as well as hers, for he still had to live near that horrible man.

"Rebecca," the duchess said, stopping ahead to wait for her.

Rebecca realized she had fallen behind the others, who were already making their way past the jungle of Mediterranean palms and up the stone steps that led out of the conservatory and back to the main part of the house.

"Are you all right?" the duchess asked. "You seem distracted."

Rebecca's first instinct was to smile brightly

and say she was fine, but as soon as she looked into her mother-in-law's eyes, she found herself quite unable to lie.

The duchess linked her arm through Rebecca's. "Come and walk with me," she said. "I think it's time we got to know each other better."

They walked to the door at the opposite end of the conservatory which led outside to the South Garden and the Arboretum beyond. "Let's walk to the maze," she suggested. "With all the rain, you haven't had a chance to see it yet, have you?"

"I've seen very little of the estate, Your Grace. But I'm looking forward to exploring, as I enjoy the outdoors."

"Devon does as well. You are a good match."

Rebecca was quiet for a moment. "I hope so."

"You're having doubts?" the duchess asked, though it seemed she already knew the answer and had even been anticipating it.

"I confess I am."

They walked down a stone path toward a rose arbor. "Was it something that my son said or did?" the duchess asked. "Or is it just a general feeling in your heart which you cannot explain?"

Rebecca sighed. "It is both, but I suppose this kind of thing is to be expected, considering how quickly we were wed. Perhaps we should have taken more time to get to know each other."

Her mother-in-law squeezed her arm. "May

I ask, did he put pressure on you to marry quickly?"

"No. If anything, I was the one in a hurry."

They stopped on the path and faced each other. "I am surprised," the duchess said.

"I truly was not even aware that Devon was searching for a wife," Rebecca explained, "because I was too wrapped up in my own wishes and desires. I feel rather ashamed of myself, as a matter of fact."

Her mother-in-law inclined her head. "What do you mean?"

They began walking again, slowly, side by side. "I almost do not want to tell you, because I do not want you to think badly of me. I hold you in the highest regard, Your Grace."

The duchess gave her a warm smile. "First of all, you must no longer address me as Your Grace. We are family now, Rebecca, so call me Adelaide. Second, I could never think badly of you. You are simply a woman who is in love with my son. Don't look so surprised. It's as obvious as the nose on your face. I would never have supported the marriage if I didn't believe that."

Feeling some relief, Rebecca nodded at Adelaide. "I do adore him. I fell in love with him the first time I met him when he helped my father and me on the road four years ago."

"We've all heard the story of his daring rescue,

so rest assured, I applaud you for your efficiency in winning his heart. You must have said and done all the right things."

Rebecca thought of the diary she had read aloud to him, winced slightly at her scandalous tactics, and of course chose not to mention it to her mother-in-law.

"There is more to it than you know," she said to Adelaide, "which is why I was distracted just now. I am afraid Devon is unhappy with me today."

"Why?"

"As I said, I was in a desperate hurry to become his wife—but not just because I adored him. I've adored him for years from afar without ever once leaving my father's home to do anything about it. Until now, when I was forced to take action."

"Forced?"

"Yes. My father had promised me in marriage to someone else."

The duchess stopped abruptly. "I presume you did not love this man."

"No, I did not."

"Was it a very advantageous match?"

"Only for the man in question," Rebecca replied. "He is wealthy and owns property, but he is not a member of the aristocracy. His father was once a successful merchant in West London, but from what I understand, he lost everything in a gamble. His son has been working his entire life not just to regain their social position, but to surpass it. Which is why he wanted me."

They arrived at the maze.

"So that is why you came here hoping to marry my son, and why you were in such a hurry?"

"Yes." Rebecca accompanied her mother-in-law into the gravel path between the hedges. "The problem is that I did not disclose this to Devon, and he found out today when my father arrived looking for me."

Adelaide stopped at a junction. "Your father was here? When? I was not told and did not receive him as I should have. Is he still here?" She gestured toward the house, looking as if she wanted to return.

"I am sorry, he is gone." Rebecca strove to explain. "He is not a very . . . *sociable* man, Adelaide, as I am sure you have heard, which is why I am concerned. He would never have come here if he were not very distraught about my disappearance, and the fact that he left so quickly after learning of my marriage without even speaking to me . . . I can only conclude he was very angry."

"Angry? One would think a father would be overjoyed to learn his daughter has married the heir to a dukedom. He couldn't actually *prefer* that you marry this neighbor of yours, could he?"

"I believe he would prefer it, Adelaide, which is

why I fled, and why I am still so angry with him for agreeing to such a thing."

"But why would he agree? Is it possible this man has some control over your father?"

Rebecca hesitated. "That is what Devon suggested. I confess, up until now, I believed that my father made the arrangements because he has been living too long in isolation with his pain. I believed he lost his grip on reality. He has never seemed to realize there is a whole world of opportunity outside our estate. All he knows is his own small world of intimidation, from a neighbor who enjoys beating down those who are weaker than he. But after his visit today, I have begun to wonder if there is more to it than that. I am going to write to him for answers."

Her voice trembled slightly, and she realized with distress that she had not once cried over her father's betrayal. She had only been enraged and focused on her escape. And upon winning Devon's affections.

"It is not easy when we cannot understand those we love," the duchess said. "Especially when that person is a man—not to mention a peer of the realm—and we are expected to honor and obey him. Come."

Adelaide took her arm and led her through the maze to a wooden bridge in the center. They climbed the steps together. It provided a fine vantage point from which to see a way out.

Adelaide took hold of both Rebecca's hands. "I understand what you did more than you know, for I, too, was forced to marry one man, when I loved another."

Rebecca took a breath to ask about that, but Adelaide raised a hand. "No, dear, that's a story for another day. It is your marriage we must focus on now. I know you care for my son. That is without question. I also know that forced marriages between strangers can result in disaster and a lifetime of unhappiness. In that regard, rest assured that you did the right thing, to refuse the other man and stand up to your father. As far as Devon is concerned . . ." She paused. "Well, there are things that have happened in his life which make him wary of happiness in any form. Our family certainly has its warts."

"He told me about MaryAnn," Rebecca said.

Adelaide's eyebrows lifted. "Did he? Then he must care for you if he shared that."

"He did not tell me because he wished to open his heart to me," Rebecca admitted. "He told me as a warning, after he learned I had come here seeking protection from another man."

"Ah. That is because he does not want to be responsible for other people. He is afraid he will fail them."

"That is exactly what he tried to tell me. Obviously he entered into this marriage believing it was based on . . ." She hesitated a moment. "Based on duty and our surface attraction to one another. He feels duped, Adelaide, and I cannot blame him. I will never forgive myself."

"Did he openly accuse you of 'duping' him?"

"He used the word manipulated, and was angry with me for having an ulterior motive."

Adelaide gazed down at their hands clasped together and seemed lost in thought, then she sighed. "Perhaps it is not my place to interfere," she said, "and I might live to regret it, but you are going to find out sooner or later, so I might as well tell you now."

"Tell me what?"

"That Devon needed a wife, Rebecca—and fast—because his father had threatened to withdraw his unentailed inheritance if he did not marry."

Rebecca rested a hand on the wooden rail to steady herself. She was so surprised she could not speak.

"So, perhaps," Adelaide continued, "my son needs to be a bit more forgiving about your so-called ulterior motive. And perhaps you need to understand that if there are problems between you, they are not all on your shoulders."

Rebecca shook her head with dismay. "Why are you telling me this? To make me angry with him?"

"No, I am telling you because I know my son. He will use any excuse to retreat from loving you or anyone else. But someone has to fight for your happiness together. Someone has to tell him he's being stubborn and thickheaded."

Rebecca chuckled. "And that someone is me."

"Yes. Do not give up on him, dear. Just love him, unreservedly, however long it takes. Prove to him that it is possible to be happy for more than just a moment."

Rebecca gazed out over the complicated network of hedges below. "I don't think loving him will be difficult," she said. "The challenge will be holding back my foot, when what he really needs is a good swift kick for that secret he kept from me—the bit about the inheritance. Honestly."

Adelaide smiled. "Go ahead and kick away, dear. And the sooner the better, I say."

Chapter 17

Shortly after three, the wedding breakfast and reception drew to a close, the houseguests began to pack their belongings and prepared to bid farewell to the bride and groom, as well as their hosts, the duke and duchess. For a time, pandemonium ensued, while footmen scurried up and down the palace stairs with trunks and bags. Carriages lined up outside the front entrance, pulling away one by one with organized, ceremonial aplomb.

By teatime, the palace itself breathed a sigh of relief. The rooms settled back into a quieter, sleepier atmosphere. The chairs sat empty, the fireplaces went cold, the champagne was all gone.

After saying goodbye to Aunt Grace—and convincing her that all was well now that the earl had learned the truth about her marriage—Rebecca retreated to her room to pack her own things, for she was to move to different lodgings in the family wing, not far from her husband's. The duchess's maid, Alice, continued to assist her.

Alice was folding Rebecca's dressing gown and gently placing it into her trunk, when a knock sounded at the door. Rebecca crossed the room and answered it.

There in the corridor stood her husband, still dressed in his wedding attire, and despite everything, she responded immediately to his stark beauty, the mesmerizing lure of his confident stance and moody expression.

It galled her that he could have this effect on her after everything that had occurred between them that day, but she supposed he would always be that impressive man she had first seen on a big black horse in the forest. The man who had awakened her to her passions.

She stepped aside and invited him in. He directed his gaze at Alice. "The duchess needs you," he said.

"Yes, milord." The maid hurried from the room and swung the door shut behind her.

Rebecca strolled to the upholstered bench at the foot of the bed and sat down.

"It appears we have something to discuss," she said, not bothering to hide the anger and resentment she felt over the way he had treated her earlier, when he had been keeping a secret, too.

He casually unbuttoned his jacket as he moved toward her. "I thought we did enough talking this morning."

"Did you indeed? Then what are you doing here?" She was already fully aware of what he wanted, however, and was infuriated by the traitorous rush of excitement coursing through her veins as he stood tall and powerful before her.

"If you will recall," he informed her, as he shrugged out of his jacket and tossed it clear across the room to the chair by the window, "we were married this morning, so I believe a consummation is on the agenda. We are to soldier on, remember? And duty decrees an heir."

"If *you* will recall," she said with a sharp bite to her voice, "we already consummated the marriage. So you may at least strike *that* off your list."

He grinned wolfishly. "I seem to recall you mentioning your desire for such pleasures again and again."

She glared at him with burning, reproachful eyes. "That was before I found out you were a hypocrite."

His fingers froze on the buttons of his waistcoat, and his expression darkened with suspicion. "How so?"

"*Who, sir, was using whom?*" she asked, her tone ice-cold with accusation. "You might have told me you were being pressured to marry, but you did not tell me why. Do not bother to play innocent. I know all about your father's will."

For a long moment he stared down at her, then

he tore at his necktie, pulled it off and tossed it lightly onto the bench beside her. "Then it appears we have everything out in the open now, doesn't it? You wanted me to save you from marrying your neighbor, and I wanted you to save me from losing my inheritance. We trapped each other, plain and simple. So now we can move forward with this convenient marital arrangement without pretenses or romantic expectations. There are no more secrets. At least I hope that is the case."

"It is."

"You're sure?" he asked, pulling his shirt off as well, so she was forced to look at his smooth muscular abdomen, directly in front of her face. "Because I still have my doubts." He tossed the shirt to the chair with his jacket.

"There is nothing to doubt," she replied, realizing she was somehow on the defensive again. "I've told you everything."

He bent forward and braced his knuckles on the bench on either side of her, his face a mere inch from hers. "But do I *believe* everything, is the question."

Her breath was coming short, and she was very close to losing her composure. For the longest time he remained there, brushing the tip of his nose over hers, wetting his lips. . .

"What does he look like?" he asked.

"Who?"

"Your betrothed."

She huffed with annoyance. "He was never my betrothed."

"I'm sure he would argue with that. I would most certainly put up a fight if I had been told you were mine, then another man took possession of you."

"I am no one's possession."

"Yes, you are. You're mine."

She should have been offended. She should have slapped his arrogant face. But she was capable only of sitting on the bench, using every ounce of will she possessed simply to hide how shaken she was in the presence of such ostentatious masculinity. He was a powerful, imposing man. It was what had knocked her off her feet to begin with.

"Surprised to hear that from your perfect-gentleman hero?" he asked, looking like he was enjoying this far too much.

"Not in the least," she replied. "Didn't I say you were a scoundrel that first night in the ballroom?"

"Indeed you did." Appearing somewhat amused, he straightened and stood over her, looking down. "Perhaps occasionally, you do know how to judge a man with some accuracy."

She let out a long-held breath, relieved when he backed away, then moved around the bed. She did not turn around, but heard the bed creak and knew he had climbed onto it.

"Incidentally," he said, "I didn't marry you to keep my inheritance. I married you to appease my father so that he would not require my brothers to be rushed into hasty marriages."

She stood up and turned to face him. He was lying back with one leg crossed over the other, his muscular arms tossed behind his head on a soft, feathery pillow, recently fluffed.

Gazing freely at his thick biceps and his toned, strapping body, she found herself able to focus on little else but the shivery thrill dancing down her spine.

"So you are a martyr," she replied. "A sacrificial lamb, forced to give up your independence and chain yourself to a life you never wanted. No, wait, you are a *hero* to them," she added with sarcasm. "Isn't that what they think?"

His blue eyes clouded over with disdain. "Not all of them."

"No, of course not." She moved gracefully around the bed, closing a hand around the ornately carved bedpost, running her open palm over the smooth, flowing grooves in the mahogany. "Vincent would never thank you for anything, would he? And he's the only one with any sense, isn't that right?"

She stood over him, taking in his tempting virility while she remembered her mother-in-law's advice. *Just love him. . .*

She pulled the pins from her hair and shook it loose down her back, then climbed onto the bed. "I know what you're doing, you know." She straddled her husband's hips and sat down upon his enormous erection, swiveling her hips, rubbing against him. "You're trying to make me hate you, trying to prove you are right and I am wrong, that I was mistaken to believe you were good and reliable, and that our marriage is doomed like every other."

He took her hips in his hands and thrust himself about, meeting her smooth, erotic undulations with proficient movements of his own.

"Maybe I am," he said, "but admitting that doesn't change anything. We still deceived one another, and we both have very good reason not to trust much of anything in this marriage. So there we are. Doomed."

"Forever the pessimist."

"There will be fewer disappointments that way."

She wiggled and squirmed over his amorous erection, growing harder by the second. "And fewer joys." Leaning forward, she pinned his arms over his head. "I might as well inform you now," she said. "I am not going to let you do what you are attempting to do."

"And what is that?" He lifted his head off the pillow and tried to kiss her.

She pulled back, just out of reach. "To spoil this marriage by pushing me away."

"I'm not pushing you away at the moment, darling. I would very much prefer it, actually, if you would come closer."

She did as he asked. She leaned down and kissed him, letting go of his arms so he could cup the back of her head in his hand and thrust his tongue into her mouth.

"And how exactly do you intend to keep me from spoiling this marriage?" he asked, when she dragged her lips from his.

"I'm going to allow you to make love to me."

He laughed. "Allow *me* to make love to *you*? I'm not the one on top."

Then his eyes narrowed, and he flipped her over onto her back and reached down to unfasten his trousers.

"Who's on top now?" she asked, while she wriggled her hips and tugged her skirts up to her waist.

He shoved his pants down. "I am, and don't forget it. You are mine now, Rebecca. No other man shall ever have you. Unbutton your bodice."

She understood what he wanted and needed from this. He wanted to prove that she belonged to him, that he was still in control of his emotions and his life and the future of this marriage.

Perhaps she could have been more sensitive to that, or more resistant, but all she wanted was to give herself to him body and soul, because it was all true. She *did* belong to him, and she wanted him to know it.

"Give me a chance to get my skirts out of the way," she said breathlessly. "You *could* help, you know."

Panting with impatience, he leaned to the side on one elbow while he unbuttoned the bottom of her bodice, working his way up while she started at the top.

As soon as it was free, she sat up and yanked it off her shoulders. At the same time, he was unfastening her skirts and drawers and wrenching them down over her hips.

At last, their clothing was out of the way. Very quickly he positioned himself between her legs and moved until he found the precise location for his purposes, then thrust inside, smoothly and easily, for she was slick and wet and ready for him.

She gasped with unrestrained lust, aching for more as he plunged deep and hard, again and again. He worked in and out of her, pounding furiously, moving inside her with voracious passion.

"I cannot understand this," he said, squeezing his eyes shut, surprising her with the passionate confession. "This madness. I cannot fight it. I must have you, Rebecca. Completely."

Nor could she understand it, as sensation overwhelmed reason. She could not even begin to contemplate the forces at work in this room. She had been so angry with him earlier for his arrogance and the withdrawal of his gentler affections, and for his lack of forgiveness, when he was as guilty as she.

Yet she still wanted him and would do anything for him. All she knew at this moment was the tremendous power of her impending orgasm, coursing through her nerve endings to the very center of her being. Pleasure assailed her, and she released a muffled scream into her husband's mouth as she felt at the same time the hot gush of his climax pour into her.

He collapsed heavily upon her, and they lay there in the dazzling afternoon light, their desires fulfilled, their bodies damp with perspiration, limp and weak, but magnificently sated.

"I *am* yours," she whispered in his ear as she ran a finger up and down his smooth, slick back. "I was never Rushton's."

"Don't say his name again," he softly said. "Ever. Just the sound of it infuriates me."

She could barely breathe under the tremendous weight of him. "Nothing would please me more than to never say it again, or hear it. But you must promise me something, too."

He rolled to his side and faced her, waiting in silence for her request.

"You must promise to at least try and forgive me for our unfortunate beginning, as I will forgive you. I want you to love me in return," she said. "If not today—someday."

He rested his head on his arm. "We are still strangers, you know."

"But we won't be forever. Every day will bring us closer if you will let me love you, which you must, because no matter what has happened between us, now that I have found you, I cannot live without you."

He rolled onto his back and looked up at the ceiling. "Do not rely on me for your happiness, Rebecca. You must find other things to occupy yourself besides me, because I cannot be responsible for all that."

She sat up. "You are not responsible for my happiness."

"But you just said you cannot live without me."

"It was an expression of love," she told him, "and I warn you, I will say other things like it in the future. I want us to be everything to each other."

He spoke in a calm voice, his gaze steady. "That is not the kind of love I ever imagined myself wanting."

"What other kind is there?" she asked, unable to understand how he could think or feel any other way.

He stared at her for a long time. "I honestly don't know, and I am not sure I wish to find out. It is not a question I wish to explore."

Chapter 18

Every morning for a week, Devon woke to the sound of wind and rain pelting against his window, rattling the panes. The river had risen higher than anyone remembered in fifty years, and he heard from a servant, who had gone into the village the day before, that a bridge had collapsed in the next county and a farmer crossing over it on foot was swept away.

The duke was not taking the news well. He was pacing constantly, whether in the privacy of his own bedchamber or in full view in the drawing rooms. He wandered the corridors, loitered in the gallery, and even skulked about in the servants' wing. Occasionally he would look up at a portrait of an ancestor and apologize in a vague, disturbing way, which the family took note of with concern.

"Do you think we should summon the doctor again?" Blake asked, late one afternoon, while he and Devon were alone in the study, working on estate matters.

Devon was seated at the desk inspecting the ledgers, which he had been spending a lot of time on lately, for it kept his mind off the two things that were a constant concern to him: his father's madness, and the antagonism he still felt regarding his wife's former engagement.

He wished he could let it go, but for some reason he could not. It still incensed him on a daily basis. Every time he looked at her, he thought of that other man who had believed she would be his, and found himself wondering what conversations they'd had in the past, what this man knew of her, and how he had reacted to the news that she was now another man's wife.

"Devon?"

He blinked a few times, then laid down his pen and looked at his brother. "I'm sorry. . . . Yes?"

"Should we summon the doctor again?" Blake asked, repeating his earlier question.

Devon labored to bring his mind back to the subject at hand. "Dr. Lambert has not been helpful in the past. He would no doubt continue to tell us this behavior is normal, which I suppose it is, if it is simply old age."

"But perhaps he could give Father a tonic or something to ease his mind or help him sleep."

Devon leaned back in his chair. "I am of the

opinion that it is time to call on someone new, someone who has some experience with this kind of thing. Someone who does not expect to be named in the will."

"Someone from London?"

"That is what I am thinking." He leaned forward and picked up his pen again. "Didn't Mother work on a hospital benefit last Christmas? Perhaps she would know someone."

"It is worth a try," Blake said.

Just then, the door swung open and hit the wall, and the estate steward, Mr. Jacobs, entered with their father, who strode across the room in a wild frenzy.

"*Devon,*" he said. "*Devon . . .*"

Startled by the abrupt interruption and the panic in his father's voice, Devon rose from his chair. "What is it? What has happened?"

Mr. Jacobs inclined his head and spoke in a calm voice. "Good afternoon, Lord Hawthorne. There is some news about the fields to the east."

"News!" the duke shouted. "It is not news, it is the end!"

The steward's gaze darted uneasily to the duke. "I thought you should know, my lord," he said to Devon, "that some of the fields require attention. The drainage ditches are not performing as they should."

Devon glanced at his father, who was having

difficulty breathing and was now tugging at his cravat.

"You are here to tell me," Devon said, "that the fields are flooding?"

"Yes, my lord."

Wonderful.

"Do you hear that?" his father said, pointing at the steward. He gazed incredulously at Blake. "What the blazes are you doing here? Why aren't you in London with Vincent looking for a bride? And where is Garrett? Have you reached him yet? Does he know? Why has he not returned?"

"I have posted a letter," Devon assured him, "but it will take some time to reach him, and it will be longer still, before we hear a reply."

"But what are we going to do in the meantime?"

Devon moved out from behind the desk and went to pour a glass of brandy. He handed it to his father. "There is no need to worry. Blake and I will accompany Mr. Jacobs to the east fields now and assess the damage, then find a solution. We will dig new drainage ditches ourselves if we have to. Everything will be fine, Father."

"But that will only buy us time," he replied, sucking back a deep swig of brandy.

Devon placed a comforting hand on his father's shoulder. "Maybe time is all we need."

The duke looked into his eyes and stared blankly,

then his breathing calmed. He strode to a chair. "Yes, I'm sure you're right."

Mr. Jacobs watched the duke with further uneasiness, then cleared his throat and spoke to Devon. "My lord? Do you wish to see the fields now?"

"Yes. Blake and I will accompany you. Have a groom ready the horses."

Blake followed him out of the library, but glanced over his shoulder at their father, who was finishing off the brandy in record time.

"Maybe we should skip the horses, Devon, and take a rowboat instead."

Devon gave him a warning look. "Blake, I swear, if you tell me you're starting to believe in this ridiculous curse, I will respectfully suggest that you go stick your finger in a dyke."

"Point taken," his brother replied. "Horses will do."

Darkness had already descended upon the estate when Devon and Blake returned from the fields. They were both soaked through to the bone, their feet numb from the chill, their hands shaking with fatigue, blistered after working with the tenant farmers to dig extra drainage ditches where they were needed.

The butler met them at the door and took their wet coats and hats, then they each ordered hot baths and brandy in their rooms. They took a glass together in the study while they waited for the baths to be drawn, then scaled the steps wearily and headed toward their private lodgings, each of them intent upon collapsing with all due haste as soon as they cleaned the grime from their skin.

Devon said goodnight to his brother and started down the long corridor. A wall sconce flickered wildly as he passed by, then blew out.

He stopped in his tracks, then started again. Reaching the next sconce, he kept his gaze fixed upon it. Thankfully it remained lit, illuminating one of the many palace portraits of his ancestor, the first Duke of Pembroke.

Devon stopped in the corridor and looked up at it. It was disturbingly lifelike, as were all the paintings of that man. No wonder their father was obsessed with them and talked to them in the night.

At last Devon reached his door and turned the knob to discover a fire roaring in the grate and a tub full of hot water waiting for him. He closed and locked the door, then stripped off his wet clothing and stepped into the steaming bath. When his hands touched the water, however, his blisters burned like hot pokers, so he rested his arms along the brass rim of the tub, palms up.

His entire body was aching, his mind in a fog of exhaustion. The fields had indeed been flooded, and if his father had seen them for himself, he would have collapsed in a hysterical fit. Something had to be done, but for the life of him, he didn't know what.

Tipping his head back, he closed his eyes and tried to relax. It wasn't a moment before he felt that pleasant feeling of floating as sleep approached, but a dripping sound pulled him from that place and compelled him to open his eyes.

"I must be dreaming," he said, recognizing his wife sitting beside him, leaning over the tub, dipping a cloth into the water and squeezing it out over his knees. "Because I see an angel."

Indeed, an angel she was, dressed in her flowing white nightgown, her red hair spilling in graceful waves down her back.

Over the past week, they had made love every night, reading from Lydie's diary when it suited them, but more often than not, leaving it in a drawer and exploring their own particular tastes and desires with enthusiasm and curiosity. Their lusty appetites were always in harmony, and the sex was, without question, superb.

Rebecca was adventurous in every sense of the word, and he was thankful for that. It gave their relationship a clear dynamic, for they were both open about what they wanted in bed and had no reservations when it came to the use of titillating words and lusty language. They were each determined to satisfy and be satisfied, and it was the one thing they had in common—the daily anticipation of sex, and the question of when and where they would have it next.

Devon knew their lovemaking was distracting them both from the secrets they had kept from each other before their marriage, as well as his unwillingness to surrender to the kind of love she wanted him to feel.

Every night she said the words to him—*I love you*—and every night, he answered with a kiss. He simply could not return the sentiment. He was not capable of letting his emotions go free in that way, nor could he lie to her and say it just to please her.

All of it was acceptable to him. He was quite happy to continue on in that way, enjoying sex but never speaking of more intimate matters of the heart. He suspected, however, it would just be a matter of time before Rebecca would want something more.

"How did you get in here?" he asked, determined to enjoy things the way they were, for as long as he could.

"You're not the only one who knows about the secret passages in this house," she said. "Charlotte has been taking me around."

He glanced at the tall wardrobe by the bed with its double doors ajar. "Alas, my secret is no longer a secret. Where else did she take you? Have you seen the mice in the old south passage yet?"

"The abbey underground? No, she refused to take me there. She said it gave her nightmares as a child, because she thought it was haunted by the monks."

He puckered his lips. "I think the nightmares came from her unscrupulous brothers, who told her terrible ghost stories about those monks." His brow furrowed as he recalled certain, specific details from his boyhood. "Maybe there was a spider or two involved," he added.

She shook her head with disapproval, then changed the subject. "I heard you worked very hard today."

"Yes, and I will work my fingers to the bone again tomorrow, and the day after that if this weather continues."

"Not all landlords would do what you did," she said, sounding wistful and pensive. "You picked up a shovel and worked side by side with your tenants. I am sure you won much respect and loyalty today."

He slid down and dunked his head, remained under water for a moment, then surfaced and wiped the back of a hand over his face.

She noticed the blisters and calluses. "Oh, Devon." She took hold of his hand and kissed it.

"I'll survive," he said. "I am not so sure about the fields though."

"The rain *will* stop," she assured him. "It's just a bad spring, that's all. Summer will soon be here, and we will all be roasting in the sunshine, praying for a cloudy day."

He tipped his head back upon the smooth rim of the tub. "I hope you're right. For my father's sake."

"Of course I am."

She reached for the soap and lathered it between her palms, then stood up, moved behind him, and began to wash his hair. He closed his eyes and relaxed while she massaged his scalp and stroked his temples firmly with her thumbs. He reveled in the sound of swabbing lather, enjoyed the sensation of his genitals swelling pleasurably beneath the water.

"You are a goddess," he said.

"No, I am your wife. Now rinse." She kissed his forehead, then moved around the tub and picked up the cloth again.

He slid down and dunked his head, came back up and wiped his eyes, then lay back while she rubbed the lathered cloth over his neck and chest and shoulders, then down to his navel and lower still.

She had only to look into his eyes to recognize the need coursing through his body and the errant thoughts on his brain.

"Would you like me to get in there with you?"

she asked. "Or would you prefer to come out here with me?"

"I think I would like you to hand me a towel."

Smiling, she reached for it and held it out. He rose from the hot tub, water sluicing down his naked body and dripping noisily into the tub, his skin glistening in the firelight.

"I should apologize in advance," he said. "After the day I've had, I doubt I'll have my usual stamina."

"I'll have enough for both of us."

She held the towel up while he stepped out, but he did not make use of it. He took it from her and dropped it carelessly onto the mat, dripping water and leaving shiny footprints behind him as he followed her, naked, to the bed.

"You're going to get me wet, aren't you?" she asked, backing up toward it.

"Undoubtedly, so you better take that off." He pointed at her dressing gown.

With a mischievous glimmer in her eyes, she pulled it off over her head and stood before him, also naked.

He stopped where he was, letting his eyes feast upon the graceful swell of her breasts and the curve of her hips and the enticing triangle of curls between her thighs.

He thought again of their argument the day of their wedding, and how he had felt when her father had informed him that she'd been engaged to another.

Devon had told her everything about MaryAnn that day. Well, almost everything. He had left certain details out.

He wondered in turn, with a hint of unease, what details he did not know about *her* former life.

He strode toward her and rested his hands on her hips. "Tell me something. Did he ever touch you?"

Her elegant eyebrows drew together in a frown. "Who?"

"Rushton."

She looked disappointed that he had interrupted what they were about to do by bringing that up again. "Why does it matter?"

"Just tell me."

"Why? What good would it do for you to know something like that? And why do you want to know?"

He realized suddenly that he was now the one digging for information about intimate matters outside of their sexual encounters, and the thought was disturbing to him.

Not, however, as disturbing as the fact that she would not answer the question.

She sighed and climbed onto the bed, completely uninhibited about her nudity, as always.

. She patted the spot next to her. "Come and lie down with me."

He joined her on the bed. "Tell me, Rebecca. I want to know."

She hesitated, then finally began to explain. "Mr. Rushton used to come to our house and have tea with us. It was always very strange and silent and awkward. He would look at me in a way that made me uncomfortable."

Suddenly agitated, Devon inched closer to her. "Did he ever touch you?" he asked again, more demanding this time.

Her slender throat bobbed with a swallow. "Once."

Devon braced himself for whatever she was about to tell him, and began in advance to subdue the anger he knew would come. "What happened?"

She hesitated again. "It was a year ago. I did not know he had come to visit. I was in the stables after returning from an afternoon ride. He came up behind me, grabbed hold of my skirts, and tore them as he pulled me toward him. He tried to kiss me, but I fought him and scratched his face and ran into the house. I never told Father."

"You should have."

"I don't know that it would have made a difference. Father would never have confronted him, and I did not want to place that burden of guilt on him."

Devon was surprised that his principal reaction was not anger, but his need to reassure her that she was now safe here at Pembroke Palace—that nothing like that would ever happen to her again. He touched his lips to hers.

"Neither he, nor any other, shall ever touch you that way again, Rebecca. If any man does, you shall tell me, and I will not hesitate to confront him. In fact, I will hunt him down tirelessly in order to do so."

She nibbled at his lips. "I thought you did not wish to be my protector."

She was challenging him, meaning to prove that he was wrong to think he was not born to be her hero.

"It is my duty as your husband to protect you."

"Just duty?" she asked, eyeing him intently. "Does it have nothing to do with passion? Jealousy? Love?"

His heart was beginning to pound in his chest. He shifted uncomfortably. "Sometimes we have no choice about the things we must do."

"Do you regret the choices you have made?" she asked, referring, of course, to their marriage.

Growing more and more uneasy with the direction of this conversation, he rolled on top of her. "I regret nothing. But tell me, do you think Rushton will ever try to see you again?"

"Why are we talking about this tonight," she

asked, "when you have avoided the subject all week?"

"I don't know. I am always surprised by the things I feel when I am with you."

She wiggled her hips invitingly, beckoning him, pushing against the throbbing tip of his erection. "I doubt he will come here. This is Pembroke Palace, and you are the future duke."

He thrust gently into her heated folds, but paused. "If I were him, I would want matters resolved once and for all—perhaps an apology from you for leaving without a word. I would also want to meet the man who stole my fiancée."

She cupped his buttocks in her hands and pulled him in closer and tighter. "I told you before, I never agreed to be his fiancée. He knows that. He will simply have to let the matter go."

Devon pushed and entered her in a single, deep thrust. She sighed with rapturous delight, while he began to lose sight of life beyond this bed, his raging arousal sliding in and out. She gyrated beneath him, and he quickened his stroke.

Soon, passion obliterated everything else. They made love eagerly, changing positions often, exploring different sensations and responses. In the end, shortly after they both climaxed, they lay flat on their backs with their heads down at the footboard, struggling to catch their breath in the fading firelight.

"That was wonderful," Rebecca said in a breathless sigh of release.

"As it has been every night," he replied.

They lay quietly, exhausted. He was just drifting off to sleep when she spoke.

"Why did you want to know those things about Mr. Rushton? Do you still believe there are things I am keeping from you? Do you suspect there was something more between us?"

"I confess, part of me still wonders."

"There was nothing, Devon. *Nothing.*"

He turned his head to look at her. "And yet, there is something inside of me that feels rage when I imagine you reading that diary aloud to him."

"I never did. You must believe me about that."

He looked at the ceiling again. "I suppose I do. I just hope to God I never meet him. For his sake."

Chapter 19

Maximilian Rushton arrived in Pembroke Village by coach at half-past four on a Tuesday. He entered the Pembroke Inn, complimented the hostess on her gown, and procured the most luxurious room in the establishment. He then ordered a bottle of their finest brandy and retired to his lodgings.

Weary but unwavering in his determination, he poured a glass before he even bothered to remove his coat. He raised it to his lips, took a drink, then set it down upon the table and began to ponder the situation.

He had important plans to carry out now that he was here, and it was crucial that he think everything through with great attention to detail. He could not dwell on his anger. He could not think of his discontent, or how sick he was of this frustrating uphill battle.

It was important that he remember the past and

why he was here. He had come so very far in his lifetime, earning his fortune with a keen sense of business, improving his manners and speech, but he had met resistance in recent years. Ever since he acquired the house that bordered Creighton Manor, the obstacles had reached intolerable heights. He had hit one wall after another, which was all the more exasperating, after coming so far.

He could not allow this to go on. Yesterday, at a small village inn, he'd looked at the miniature of his mother, which he kept with him at all times, and was overcome by a rage so severe, he tore his room apart in a fit of temper. Just thinking of it now lit a hot ball of fire in his gut. All he'd ever wanted to do was avenge her death.

And all he wanted now was his due—the final glory, which he deserved. His mother and father deserved it, too.

He thought of the Creighton ballroom suddenly. The present earl did not make use of that room. It stood empty all year round, the crystal chandelier covered in dust, the small number of furnishings hidden under white sheets like ghosts.

The previous earl had used it, of course—that despicable, foul rotter. He was the one who had built the ballroom with funds from the sale of the Rushton home and family business. That man, with the world at his fingertips, had won all that in a card game, and the very next day, had come to collect his winnings. He had tossed the family out onto the dirty streets of West London without a backward glance or a single care as to how they would survive. He did not care that the house had been in the family for four generations, or that Maximilian's mother was expecting a child.

He ground his teeth together with loathing. His mother had died three weeks later, giving birth to the child who would have been Maximilian's brother. That same day, the earl had sold their house. He'd used the funds to build the ballroom.

Maximilian had decided long ago that he would own that room. He would open it up and hang a portrait of his father and mother on the center wall. He had planned to do so when he became lord of the manor, and had come very close to that end only two short weeks ago.

But of course, as always, there had been another setback. There had been further frustration because Creighton—that spineless old lord—had not been man enough to keep his daughter under control.

Maximilian looked down at the brandy glass again. Deciding that he would not be denied his due a second time, he raised the glass to his lips and downed the whole drink. He picked up the brandy bottle to pour another, watched the amber liquid gush forth, and carried the glass to the bed.

Yes, he had let Rebecca slip away because he

had been too patient and easy on the earl, and had not expected any resistance. Not from the old man, at any rate, considering the history they had together. Rushton had assumed the earl's daughter would simply arrive on his own doorstep, dutiful as always, dressed for her wedding.

Evidently, he had underestimated *her*, which he now knew had been a mistake. He should have expected something like this, especially after the incident with the dogs.

He had been overconfident, he supposed, as he lay down on the bed, still wearing his coat and boots. He was convinced that he could snap her spirit like a dry twig once she was living under his roof. As it turned out, there was far more spirit and gumption than he had bargained for.

Not an unattractive quality in a wife, he decided, as he tipped his head back upon the thick pillows, for at least he could be sure their son—the future heir to the Creighton title—would not be a weak-willed jellyfish like the present earl. Maximilian's son would be taught with a firm hand never to whimper, and he would grow up to be a powerful man, hold a seat in the House of Lords, and Maximilian would enjoy a new position in society.

Yes, after all he had been through, it was time he reaped his due. If there was any justice in the world—and he could not accept that there was not—the Creighton earldom would repay its debts, both financial and otherwise.

Maximilian didn't care that Rebecca had married a marquess, for he still had the power and means to take her away. She would discover that very soon.

A fine, cold mist put a chill in the air the day Rebecca and Charlotte ventured out to visit the milliner. Their coach pulled up in front of the shop and slowed to a halt, and a footman hopped down from the page board to lower the step. He assisted them both out of the coach, and Charlotte led the way inside.

They were greeted by the milliner herself—an older woman with plump, dimpled cheeks and spectacles. She wore a gown of dark green foulard with Russian pleating, and appeared with a smile from behind an elegant display of hats.

"Lady Charlotte," she said, "how wonderful to see you. Have you come to view the new selection? I have a number of fashionable designs this week. Or if you would like to see the fabrics . . ."

Charlotte beamed. "Yes, Mrs. Sisk, I want to see everything. But first I must present you to my new sister-in-law, Lady Hawthorne. Rebecca, this is Mrs. Sisk, the most gifted milliner in England."

The woman placed a hand over her heart, then curtsied. "I am honored, your ladyship. I hope I can be of service to you in the future."

"Thank you, Mrs. Sisk," Rebecca replied. "I can see by looking around at your beautiful inventory that I will be visiting your shop often. This is spectacular." She gestured toward a stylish cap of embroidered batiste, edged with Mechlin lace and trimmed with lilac ribbon.

Mrs. Sisk turned to the hat in question. "You have exquisite taste, Lady Hawthorne. You may try it on if you wish, and if it does not fit perfectly, I can make you another exactly like it."

So followed an hour of delightful millinery pursuits, with both Charlotte and Rebecca experimenting with different colors and styles, while Mrs. Sisk spared nothing in tending to all their needs, whether it was in the presentation of hats and bonnets, or the arrangement of cookies on a tray, and tea with milk and sugar.

They were sitting on the sofa later in the afternoon, enjoying their cookies and cakes, when Charlotte glanced toward the window.

"Look at that man out there on the street, Rebecca. He has been pacing back and forth for quite some time. You don't suppose he is up to some kind of mischief, do you?"

Rebecca set her teacup on the table and turned.

"What is it, Rebecca? Do you know him?"

Her heart began to pound.

Rising slowly, she walked to the glass and spoke slowly, with disbelief. "It is the man my father wanted me to marry."

Charlotte set down her teacup as well and joined

Rebecca at the window. "Mr. Rushton?" They continued to watch him as he looked in the shop windows across the street. "What was so terrible about him?" she asked. "You never really put it into words."

Rebecca swallowed uncomfortably. "He is cruel. He beats his dogs and horses, and he is ruthless in his ambition. He preys on those who are weaker than he—those he believes will permit him to be superior."

Charlotte wrapped her arm around Rebecca's. "In that case, I am very glad you came to us when you did."

Just then he turned and looked their way.

"Good Lord," Charlotte said. "He's seen us. We should not have been staring."

Rebecca strove to remain calm while her former neighbor started off across the street toward them. "I believe he saw us long before we started staring," she said. "My guess is that he has been watching us for the past hour."

"That is a rather disturbing notion." They both remained in the window, watching him approach. "What shall we do?"

"There is nothing else to do," Rebecca answered, working hard to steady her nerves, "but wait here until he comes through the door, at which time we will discover exactly what he wants."

Chapter 20

Devon had just sat down in his study to answer some letters of estate business, when the butler knocked and entered. "There is a Dr. Thomas to see you, my lord."

"Do send him up," Devon replied, relieved that the man had finally arrived. He set the letters aside.

A moment later, the butler returned and announced the doctor, then left and closed the door behind him. Devon took in the man's appearance and demeanor. He was fair-haired, slender, and appeared to be in his midfifties. There was a clear mark of intelligence in his eyes.

"Dr. Thomas, it is a pleasure to make your acquaintance," he said, rising and coming out from behind the desk, "and it was good of you to come on such short notice."

"It is an honor to be of service to you, Lord Hawthorne." They shook hands.

Devon invited the man to sit. "I presume my mother explained the particulars to you in her letter?"

The doctor moved to the sofa. "Her Grace said the duke has been unwell. She mentioned symptoms of insomnia, anxiety, and some possible delusions?"

Devon regarded the doctor steadily. "That is correct. All this is confidential I presume."

"Of course, my lord."

He paused a moment, watching the doctor's eyes, then sat down in a facing chair. "My father wanders the palace corridors at night talking to himself—or rather, he talks to the portraits of his ancestors, the first duke especially. He has let his appearance go—his valet has had a difficult time lately—and he often seems nervous, agitated, frightened."

"Frightened of what?"

Devon paused again. "I shall be forthcoming with you, Doctor. He believes the palace is under some kind of curse. He believes also that if all four of his sons are not married before Christmas, a flood will sweep us all away. He has even gone so far as to change his will to force us to comply, and if a single one of us does not, *none* of us will receive our portion of the unentailed fortune upon his death."

The doctor's eyebrows lifted. "I see. And you

are certain he is not simply trying to scare each of you into growing up? Sometimes obstinate fathers can go to great lengths. You're sure he is truly delusional about this curse?"

"I am sure."

"And you do not believe in it."

Devon chuckled. "No, I do not believe in ghosts or sorcery."

The doctor glanced around the room at the paintings on the walls. "And the rest of your family feels the same?"

"Of course."

"What about your younger sister? Is she being forced to marry as well?"

"No."

"So your brothers . . . Do they all plan on following in your footsteps and doing as he asks?"

Devon began to explain. "As it happens, my brother Vincent is in London at this very minute searching for his wife-to-be. He does not wish to lose his inheritance. Blake, however, is in no great hurry, but he is never one to panic. A calmer man there never was."

"What about your third brother?" the doctor asked, leaning forward slightly. "Your sister's twin. He is abroad, is he not?"

Devon eyed him shrewdly, noticed he was a very handsome and dignified man, then glanced up at his mother's portrait on the wall. "That is correct, sir. Garrett is traveling in the Mediterranean. He is artistic and enjoys his freedom."

The doctor leaned back. "Does he know about his father's illness?"

"I sent a letter a week ago. I doubt he has even received it yet."

"Ah, well, that is not my business, I suppose. I am here to examine your father. Is he expecting me, or will this be a surprise?"

"We have not told him of your visit, Doctor, as he refuses to see anyone but his own physician, who always gives him the diagnosis he asks for."

"That is not uncommon," Dr. Thomas replied, "especially when a physician does not have a firm diagnosis to begin with. Diseases of the mind are sometimes the most challenging of all."

"Indeed."

The doctor stood. "If you will present me to the duke, Lord Hawthorne, and leave us alone for a time, I should be able to draw him out and see what is happening inside his mind."

Devon hesitated a moment. "I beg your pardon, Doctor, but I must have your word that you will not harm or humiliate him."

The doctor's expression softened with understanding. "You have my word, Lord Hawthorne. I only intend to speak with him."

Devon rose from his chair. "Then I shall take you to him straightaway."

* * *

Charlotte and Rebecca stood inside the hat shop window, watching Mr. Rushton cross the street toward them. He walked into the shop, bold as a bull, paused just inside to peer obnoxiously at them, and said only one thing.

"*Rebecca*."

Rebecca had never given him permission to use her Christian name before, and just the sound of it on his lips made her skin prickle with aversion.

Charlotte's eyes turned toward her questioningly.

"Mr. Rushton," she replied in a polite but cool tone. "What a coincidence, meeting you here."

"But it is hardly a coincidence," he said. "You must have known I would come to Pembroke in search of you."

She bristled at his familiar tone and squared her shoulders. "You should have called upon me at Pembroke Palace," she said. "My husband and I would have been pleased to receive you."

He looked at Charlotte while he spoke. "*Your husband*. Yes, your father informed me of your marriage. As you can imagine, I was surprised to hear it."

It was clear he wished to communicate something to her—that he was angry or felt betrayed? She was not yet sure which it was. All she could do was wait anxiously for him to say what he came here to say, and hope it would satisfy him and he would leave.

Charlotte cleared her throat.

Rebecca fought to remember her manners. "Forgive me, Charlotte. Allow me to introduce Mr. Maximilian Rushton, my father's neighbor. Mr. Rushton, this is Lady Charlotte Sinclair, my sister-in-law."

He bowed to her. "Delighted to make your acquaintance."

"Good afternoon," she replied, with a notable degree of reserve.

He turned his gaze to Rebecca again. "But surely your sister-in-law knows that I am more to you than just your father's neighbor."

Rebecca flinched at his candid words and assumptions. "She knows exactly what I have told her—that you are my father's neighbor, nothing more, because whatever arrangements you had with him do not concern me. I am a married woman now."

"But it *should* concern you," he said. "You were promised to me, yet you did not explain yourself or even say goodbye."

She could not believe he had the audacity to confront her about this at all, let alone in front of Charlotte. How she wished Devon were here. "I owed you no explanation whatsoever."

Charlotte carefully interrupted. "Perhaps I

should see if Mrs. Sisk has found the right fabric for that hat we were discussing earlier." She pointed toward the back room. "I am sure she wouldn't mind if I just went to see if—"

"You do not need to go anywhere," Rebecca said. "Mr. Rushton was just leaving."

"Please, my dear," he said in a beseeching tone she'd never heard him use before. There was an actual hint of vulnerability in it. "If I could only have a moment of your time. I would like to understand what happened between us, so that I can put this painful experience behind me."

She could almost feel the pity from Charlotte's soft heart floating into the air between them, while her own heart was squeezing with distrust.

"There was no *us*, Mr. Rushton. There never was, so perhaps that is enough of an explanation."

"Please tell me that is not true," he persisted. "I have been paying calls to you and your father for years. Surely you knew that my feelings had become involved. And that day we met in the stables . . ."

Charlotte coughed and cleared her throat again. "My, my, I dare say it is warm in here. I believe I would benefit from a brief walk and some fresh air. If you will excuse me."

"No, Charlotte, that is not necessary!" Rebecca stepped forward, but before she could do anything to stop her sister-in-law, she was out the door and Rebecca was standing in Mrs. Sisk's hat shop, alone with Mr. Rushton.

She glanced at the door to the back room and could hear the woman puttering around. She wondered if she was listening.

"Lady Charlotte is very astute," he said, the façade of vulnerability vanishing like a drop of water on a hot stove. "She was very good to give us some privacy."

"I do not want privacy with you, sir, for there is nothing of any consequence to say. You already know that I have married the Marquess of Hawthorne, the future Duke of Pembroke."

She hoped he was intimidated.

"Mm, yes, and you entered into that marriage very hastily, without a thorough understanding of the situation."

"I understood enough," she said. "I know what kind of man you are, and for all I know, you beat my father into submitting to your wishes. And because he was weak and ill, he made promises on my behalf which were not acceptable to me."

He smirked. "Weak and ill? That is precisely what I am talking about. You lack insight, Rebecca."

She laughed at him. "No, it is you who lacks insight. I am married now, and I have nothing more to say to you."

She walked past him out the door to find Charlotte.

He followed her onto the street. The door slammed shut behind him.

"Excellent idea," he said. "We shall take a walk together in the mist and clear the air."

"I am going nowhere with you." She looked frantically up and down the street, but Charlotte had disappeared, presumably into another shop, and their coachman had not yet returned to pick them up.

"And why is that?" he asked. "I suppose you think I am going to try to kidnap you, or knock you over the head with my walking stick and stuff you into my coach. That would be rather dramatic, if I may say. Foolish, too. Your husband would pursue us without a doubt."

She stopped and faced him. "Good day, Mr. Rushton."

"But you cannot say good day to me yet," he replied, continuing to follow her when she started off again. "You haven't heard me out."

Barely able to contain her fury, she stopped and waited for him to explain whatever he wished to explain.

He strolled leisurely to the corner and leaned against a lamppost. "I am not going to knock you over the head and kidnap you because there is no need for force on my part. I am quite certain you are going to recognize the error you have made, and come home to me under your own free will."

She strode toward him, chuckling scornfully at his preposterous suggestion. "You cannot possibly be serious. I am in love with my husband."

"Which is precisely why you are going to leave him."

All at once, sickening dread seeped into her core. "Leave him? I would never do that. Not in a thousand years."

His brown eyes darkened with resolve. "I have been waiting a long time for you to be my wife, Rebecca, and that is how things are going to be. You are going to leave your husband tonight and ask for an annulment."

"An annulment! You are mad to even suggest it!"

He pushed away from the post and approached her slowly. "A divorce, then. I don't care. And I am not mad. You are going to do what I ask, and do it without a fight, or else your husband will be involved in the scandal of the decade, along with you—and worst of all, your father."

"What scandal?"

She thought of the letter she had written to her father, asking why he was afraid of Mr. Rushton. She had not yet received a reply.

He leaned closer and rubbed the back of a cold finger down her cheek. "Here is your insight, darling. Your father is not the sick, weak man you believe him to be. He is in fact a cold-blooded killer, and if you do not leave your husband and return to Creighton Manor to be my wife, I will expose your father, and I might even hear about some unfortunate accident involving your husband's early demise. Or any other member of his family, for that matter."

Her entire being wrenched with horror. "You are threatening to kill my husband, the heir to the Duke of Pembroke, or members of that esteemed family? I shall report you to the magistrate this very instant."

"That would be pointless," he said, unruffled. "I'd only deny it, and a day or two later, evidence of your father's ghastly crime would appear on that same magistrate's desk. Then the esteemed Pembroke family would not be quite so well regarded, because of their connection to you."

She shook her head. "There was no crime. There could not have been."

She wished her father had answered her letter.

Rushton handed her a note with the Creighton family crest printed at the top. It was the stationery from her father's desk, dated five years earlier. Written upon it was a note to a jeweler, asking about repairs to a bracelet. It was signed: *Miss Serena Fullarton . . .*

"What is this?"

"It identifies the victim," he casually said. "Your father gave that bracelet to her, and she is buried with it on his estate. I know exactly where."

Her stomach clenched. "Is this your handwriting?"

She knew it was not her father's. . .

"No, it is hers."

A sickening lump lodged in her gut as he plucked the note out of her hands and slipped it back into his pocket.

"Accept it, Rebecca. You do not know everything about your father."

She had no answer to that.

"If you want to protect your husband," he said, "leave him. Flee the palace in the night like you did when you left home, and write him a letter explaining that you made a mistake, and that you love me."

"And you think he will just let me go? Has it not occurred to you that I might be carrying his child—the ducal heir?"

Mr. Rushton turned away and started walking toward his coach, parked on the other side of the street. He glanced over his shoulder as he spoke. "For your sake, and for your father's, you better pray that you are not. And if you are, it had better be a girl. But do not worry. There will be other heirs in your future. I will see to that. Now off you go. You need to go home and pack your things."

He stepped into his coach, and the driver closed the door behind him. As soon as the man climbed up onto the seat, the door opened again, and Mr. Rushton peered out at her.

"By the way," he said, "I liked the hat with the yellow feathers. Purchase it when you go back inside and bring it home with you. I expect to see you wearing it with a smile, at my door, by tomorrow, midnight."

With that, he shut the door, and his shiny black coach rolled away.

Chapter 21

That evening after dinner, Devon made his way through the dimly lit palace corridors to his wife's bedchamber. Rebecca had been quiet and without smiles at the table during the meal, and afterward had insisted on speaking with him privately. He knew something was wrong. He intended to find out what it was.

Arriving at her room, he knocked gently. There was no answer, so he knocked a second time. He waited, then lifted his fist to knock a third time when the door finally opened, and his gaze fell upon his beautiful wife, already dressed for bed. He was relieved to see her, though he did not quite understand why.

"I've decided I prefer the secret passageways," he said. "When I use them, I do not have to wait so long at your door."

With notable wariness, she stepped back and invited him in.

He entered the room. A hot fire was blazing in the hearth. He stood for a moment looking at the flames, then turned to her.

"Rebecca, you were not yourself at dinner this evening."

She closed the door behind him, went to the bed and climbed onto it. "I know."

He studied her tentative posture, her fingers fiddling with the coverlet, the absence of light in her eyes. "Tell me what is wrong," he said. "It is obvious you are troubled. Whatever it is, I will fix it."

She frowned at him. "I thought you did not wish to be my hero, yet here you are offering to rescue me again."

A dozen misgivings began to spin through his mind. "Is there something you need to be rescued from? Or some*one*?" he added, feeling that familiar spark of obsession and jealousy, which he did not welcome. It made him feel like he was not in control.

She slid off the bed, covered her cheeks with her hands, and strode to the opposite corner of the room. "It is not easy to say. I am so afraid of what you will think, Devon, but I know I must tell you." She faced him. "I am in a terrible bind, and I do not know how to resolve it."

"What bind?" he asked, incredulous that something was distressing her so, and that she had not yet told him what it was.

"I . . . I encountered Mr. Rushton in the village today."

His jaw clamped together. "He spoke to you."

"Yes."

"What did he want?"

She stared uneasily at him, then dropped her hands to her sides. "Me. He still wants *me*."

Devon labored to keep his breathing under control. "But you are my wife."

"That doesn't seem to be much of an obstacle as far as he is concerned. I think he is insane."

Devon paused, swallowing hard. "Why did you not tell me about this sooner?"

"I am telling you now."

"But why did you not tell me *before* now?" He heard the irritation explode in his voice and knew she heard it too.

"You were gone out to the fields when I returned," she explained, "and I couldn't bring it up at dinner."

"You should have sent a groom out with a message to me the minute you returned from the village! I would have gone immediately after the man. I would have caught up with him and instructed him never to come within a ten-mile radius of you again. I would have educated him as to how my wife—the future Duchess of Pembroke—is to be treated and esteemed."

She stood silent, staring uncertainly at him, her

face as pale as candle wax. "I wasn't sure how you would react."

"*That* is how I would have reacted, had I known. But now there is nothing I can do but stand here and interrogate my wife."

Suddenly he wondered what would be happening presently if her father had not come to the palace on their wedding day and revealed the truth to him about her previous engagement. Would Devon even know about it? Would Rebecca *ever* have confessed, and if she had not, would she be telling him that she had met her former fiancé in the village today? Or would he never know?

He remembered how she had answered his earlier question, and something inside him wrenched with dread. "What is this *bind* you are in?"

Was she confused about her feelings? Was she torn?

God help him, he had thought this marriage was a straightforward affair. Rebecca had seemed enamored with him and eager to be his wife. From what he understood, she had lived her whole life sheltered in her father's home. He had assumed there would be no complications, that he was marrying an innocent without a history. He had even allowed himself to become enamored with her in return, despite the fact that he knew how painful and disappointing love could be, and had never intended to venture near such perilous affections again.

He thought of his mother suddenly, how she had suffered through her marriage because she had been forced to marry a duke, when the one she truly loved was lost to her. Was that how Rebecca was feeling, or was he being completely obsessed and unreasonable?

Rebecca touched a trembling finger to her mouth. "He accused my father of something terrible, and he told me that if I do not leave you, he will reveal my father's crime to the world."

Devon closed a hand into a fist, while he carefully directed his thoughts and emotions to the practicalities of what she had just told him. "What is the accusation?"

She hesitated, then spoke in a near whisper. "Murder."

He stared at her in disbelief.

"It cannot be true," she insisted. "My father may be many things, but he is not a killer."

"So you believe Rushton is lying."

There was a slight faltering in her tone. "He must be. At least, that is what I am telling myself."

"But you are not sure."

She bit her lip and looked away. "To be honest, I do not know. I thought I knew my father. He was everything to me when I was a child, but over the years he has changed, and when he promised me to Mr. Rushton, I realized I did not know him at all." She met his gaze again. "What kind of father forces a daughter to marry a man she despises, when that man is not only a bully, but beneath her in rank?"

Devon spoke in a matter-of-fact voice. "A father who is being blackmailed for murder."

She shot him a look. "So you think he is guilty."

He strode across the room to stand before her, and spent a long moment studying her glistening green eyes, her moist, cherry lips, and her creamy white complexion. He found himself aware of her anguish and vulnerability, but in light of what was happening, in light of his own anguish and dismay, he strove to ignore that awareness, to crush it and cling to the particulars of the situation.

"What I really want to know," he said, "is why Rushton is so fixated on you. Why he cannot let go of his desire to have you as his wife, and would blackmail an earl for that purpose, despite the fact that you have already married another man and have shared your bed with him. Tell me, Rebecca, are you sure you never once encouraged his affections?"

He thought of the diary. He remembered how she had surprised him that night in the gallery with her knowledge of all things sexual. How she had known so much and been so naïve of the sexual power she wielded.

He found himself wondering where she had really gotten the diary.

She glared at him. "Are you suggesting there

was something between us, and that I have been lying to you? Why can't you believe that I have only ever been devoted to you? If I were not, I would be taking the easy way out. I would be doing what he asked me to do—which, for your information, was to flee the palace tonight. If I did not want to be with you, you would be reading a letter of farewell from me at this very moment. But no, instead, I am taking a deadly risk. I have just done exactly what he warned me not to do. I have told you everything, Devon—everything— and now I must face the possibility that he will expose my father for something, which I am not entirely sure he did not do."

Her emotional outburst should have broken through the hard wall of Devon's resolve, but instead, he found himself fortifying that defense. "What exactly does he expect from you, and when?"

"He wants me to leave you tonight and arrive at his door by tomorrow, midnight."

Devon imagined such a thing. "You are not to leave your room tonight," he said curtly, "nor will you set foot outside the palace tomorrow. Do you understand?"

She turned her face to the side, almost as if he had slapped her, and responded with ice-cold derision. "Yes."

"I will put a footman outside your door," he

said, "in case your former betrothed grows impatient and decides to come and fetch you directly."

She glared at him. "You're sure it's for my protection? Perhaps imprisonment is a better word."

He stood motionless, staring at her. *Was* it a better word? Was it rage, jealousy, and obsession that had inspired his unfeeling instructions? Had he wanted to punish her for making him fear the loss of her? Or did he simply want to protect her?

"Get some rest, Rebecca. We will discuss how to deal with this in the morning." He moved to leave.

"I never wanted to be a burden to you," she said.

He felt a stab of regret, but he already had one hand on the door. "I know," he said, without turning around, because he did not want to surrender to his emotions. "You thought I would enjoy being your knight in shining armor. But you did not know me very well, did you? Nor I you."

With that, he walked out and did not stop until he reached the end of the corridor, then he came to an abrupt halt, squeezed his eyes shut and tapped his forehead against the wall.

God help him. He had just done it again. He had dealt with her in a cold and unfeeling manner—just as he had on their wedding day—when he should have shown her some compassion and eased her fears.

Her father had just been accused of murder, and she had trusted him with that secret. She had *trusted* him! Even when she knew he could turn her out, or turn her father over to the authorities.

He had responded callously. He'd even suggested she had given Rushton false hopes. He had smothered his tender feelings for her and had not permitted the fear of losing her to take hold—because that's what he was afraid of, wasn't it? He knew it. He understood it. Just the thought of Rebecca leaving him for another man made him want to put his fist through the wall.

Touching the heel of his hand to his forehead, he managed to recover himself and started off down the corridor. He reached his own bedchamber and only then did he realize it would be the first night of their marriage they would not make love.

Chapter 22

Dear Diary,

It is true, as I have always known it would be one day. I am doomed. Perhaps this is the punishment I feared would eventually descend upon me for my wicked thoughts and desires, for the sinful pleasures I have sought, and because I gave my body freely to a man who was not my husband.

Was it of no consequence that I loved him with all my heart and soul—that I would have died for him and would die for him still?

But what does love matter now, I suppose, when I am to be dragged to the altar to marry another? In one hour, my father will come for me, and I will leave this dirty London inn for the church.

And what of Jess? Is he even alive? Two days ago, my brothers beat him before my eyes and took him away. Where, oh where, did they take him?

Please, dear God, I will do anything if you can spare his life. I will marry this man and repent my wicked desires, if only you will let my darling Jess go on living.

Rebecca slammed the diary shut and wondered if she should deliver the book to Devon and mark the next page, for there were so many similarities to her own situation. If only her husband could believe that love like that truly existed. If only. . . .

But she was not going to take the book to him, because, for one thing, she was not supposed to leave her room. More importantly, she did not want to see him. She was far too angry. He had treated her like the criminal in all of this, when *she* was the one being threatened and mistreated.

If anyone deserved her husband's wrath, it was Mr. Rushton, for he was seeking to break up a marriage for his own selfish ambitions, while Rebecca could do nothing but worry about her father and live with the possibility that her entire life had been a lie—that she had sacrificed her happiness all these years for a killer.

But no, that could not be true. She could not believe it. She could not even bear to think of it.

Was her husband incapable of pity? Could he not see past his own skepticism and understand that she was in agony right now?

She supposed he could not, and he had proven tonight that he was not so very different from Mr. Rushton. To him, she was a possession, and he had been overbearing and controlling because his power and authority had been threatened. He had told her she could not leave the palace, so it seemed she was indeed his prisoner.

Devon woke at dawn the next morning, still uncertain about what to do. He lay in bed staring up at the ceiling. He supposed he could simply do nothing and let Rebecca's father be exposed. Rebecca might not agree with that plan, but if her father was guilty of something heinous, it was only fair that he face justice.

On the other hand, if he is innocent, the truth would prevail. There would be a scandal, yes, but at least Rushton would no longer hold any power over them, and Rebecca would be able to distance herself from it, here at Pembroke Palace.

Devon looked toward the window. The sky was growing brighter. There were raindrops on the panes, more evidence of the wretched family curse, which his father would no doubt take to heart.

At least Dr. Thomas had been helpful the day before. He had spent an hour with the duke and had spoken to Mother about it afterward, shedding new light on the duke's fears and agitations. The doctor noted an intense fixation with the past, his own childhood, and a delusional view of history, going as far back as the Dissolution of the Monasteries. As far as Dr. Thomas could ascertain, the duke believed the curse originated with one of the monks of Pembroke Abbey, and that that monk was still haunting the corridors.

The doctor promised to return again in a few days for further analysis. He told the duchess that if the family desired it, he could recommend that the duke's new will be rendered invalid on the basis of their father's insanity. That would, however, require an official declaration that their father had gone mad.

Devon and the rest of the family would have to take some time to consider the broader ramifications of such a course of action, and they had yet to receive word from Garrett.

But that was not Devon's first concern this morning. His first thought was to speak to Rebecca again and decide what must be done.

He rose from bed and dressed without calling for his valet, then left his bedchamber and walked through the quiet palace. He passed a maid with a feather duster who seemed startled to see him at such an early hour. She quickly backed up against the wall as he passed.

He turned the corner and spotted a footman pacing in front of Rebecca's door. The young man stopped when he spotted Devon.

"Good morning," Devon said.

"Good morning, my lord."

Devon knocked on the door. There was no reply, so he knocked again, louder the second time.

Still no answer came, so he turned to the footman. "No one has come or gone since I left?"

"I was posted here only an hour ago, my lord, but I understand it was a quiet night."

Devon turned the knob, but the door was locked. He knocked louder and more insistently, and his heart began to beat faster as a sense of panic cut through to his bones. She wouldn't have done anything foolish, would she? She wouldn't have used the passageways to leave him. . .

He turned to the footman. "Go and get a key from Mrs. Callahan."

"Yes, my lord." The young man ran down the corridor toward the stairs, while Devon waited impatiently. A moment later, the housekeeper appeared with the footman.

Mrs. Callahan fumbled with her keys. "Good morning, Lord Hawthorne," she said, as if nothing were amiss, but she was quick to insert the key into the lock and open the door.

Devon entered Rebecca's bedchamber and found it empty, though the covers were in disarray. At least the bed had been slept in. He went to the dressing room and peered inside, but there was no one about. He looked at the portrait on the wall, slightly ajar.

Where had she gone, he wondered? If she had left the palace, he would have a hard time finding her, and pray God she didn't leave to confront Rushton alone or surrender to his demands. If she did, Devon would have only himself to blame. He had offered her no help or support. He had made her feel like a prisoner.

He turned from the room and met the footman and housekeeper waiting in the corridor. "If you would be so kind," he said, "as to help me locate my wife. If you find her before I do, tell her I wish to speak with her in my study."

"Of course, Lord Hawthorne."

He strode off and went from room to room. He searched the library, the gallery, the breakfast room, the saloon, each of the drawing rooms, but she was nowhere to be found.

With growing panic, he went back upstairs to his study, hoping the housekeeper had already brought her there, but the room was empty like all the others. Bloody hell, had she left? Had he been that much of a brute the night before? Oh, he knew he had. That was without question. But surely she would not have been so foolish and impulsive to actually leave without telling anyone. . .

What if she had? What if he had lost her?

He ran back down the stairs again to find the housekeeper, but passed a footman carrying a pot of coffee. "Where are you going with that?" he asked.

"To the breakfast room, my lord."

"Someone is up at this hour?"

"Yes—"

Devon turned and ran in that direction, and burst through the door. Lo and behold, there she was—his precious, lovely wife—sitting at the white-clothed table with a book, dressed for the day and looking completely at ease in a sunny yellow gown with lace around the collar.

He had never been so relieved to see anyone at breakfast in his life. If anything had happened to her . . . If he had lost her. . .

What? he asked himself with a frown. What would he have done? How would he have felt?

It was pointless to deny it. Despite all his worthy efforts to avoid falling hopelessly and desperately in love with his wife, despite his intentions to focus on his duties, not his heart, his heart was in pieces in her pretty lap.

"Where have you been?" he asked, struggling to recover from the panic still searing his brain. "I've been looking everywhere for you."

She frowned at him and lowered her book. "You did not make it entirely clear, Devon, whether that footman was posted at my door to keep unwelcome visitors out, or to keep me in. And I confess the mere *idea* that I was not permitted to leave my room was offensive to me in every way. Did you actually think—for one single minute!—that I would run away in the night and submit to Mr. Rushton's attempt to blackmail me?" She slammed a fist onto the table. "You forget I have a will of my own, Devon. I will not be forced to do something I do not wish to do! And I am not stupid!"

The footman walked in at that moment with the coffee pot, saw the fire blazing in her eyes, her fist on the table, then promptly turned around and walked out.

Devon realized he was short of breath from running up and down the stairs, not to mention the disconcerting effects of walking into this room just now and discovering his heart was not as impervious as he had thought.

And now—after listening to Rebecca's very impressive tirade. . . .

Damsel in distress? Clearly not.

How could he ever possibly win the fight against loving her? He could not. It was as simple as that. He was conquered, defeated, done for.

"I apologize," he said, "for not being clear on that point. The footman was intended to keep unwelcome visitors out. You are of course free to move about the palace at your leisure."

She leaned back in her chair, appearing somewhat satisfied to hear it, even though it was a bald-faced lie. He had in fact wanted to keep her locked inside, because he *did* fear she might wish to save her father and would leave without a word. Without him at her side to. . .

To do what?

Protect her?

Be her hero?

Choke the very breath out of Rushton's throat?

He approached the table. "It's time we discussed what must be done about the situation."

"You actually wish to discuss it with me?" she asked with a note of scorn in her voice. "You don't intend to make the decision on your own, and simply inform me of it after the fact? If in fact you plan to do anything at all."

He deserved her open hostility and he knew it. He had not been sympathetic to her problems before now. He had been thinking only of his own fears. He was thinking of them still.

He also knew he could not control what he felt. He could only control his actions and his words.

It was clear she deserved some courtesy. She was not a burden. She was self-reliant. "I have a suggestion," he said, "as to how we should proceed."

He pulled out a chair and sat across from her at the table. The footman returned and set the coffee pot on the sideboard, then more servants entered and set plates of eggs and sausage on the sideboard as well.

As soon as they were gone, Rebecca leaned forward. "I am listening."

He leaned forward, too. "You told me Rushton wants you on his doorstep by midnight tonight."

"That is correct."

"Then that is where you shall be," he said. "I will deliver you there myself, and I will stand at your side when you knock on the door."

She frowned. "What then?"

"The man believes he has all the power because you cannot see his cards. We must deal with this man head-on, and knock those cards out of his hands."

"How?"

"With knowledge. We must find out what your father did or did not do. We *must* know whether or not Rushton is lying."

She sat quietly for a moment, then rose from her chair and walked to the sideboard, saying nothing while she poured herself a cup of coffee. At last she turned.

"What if he isn't? What if it is true? What if my father is guilty of something?"

"Do you suspect he is?"

She took a long time to answer. "All I know is that Rushton has a note about a bracelet which implicates Father, and he claims the note was written by the victim, Serena Fullarton."

"Did you see this note?"

"Yes, and Rushton also claims the woman is buried on my father's estate—wearing the bracelet."

Devon leaned back and inhaled a deep breath.

"There is something else I have not yet told you," she said, "and if we are to face Mr. Rushton tonight, you must know everything."

"I'm listening."

"He warned me yesterday that if I did not do exactly as he said, not only would he expose my father, he would somehow arrange for you or other members of your family to meet with . . . a fatal accident."

"He has threatened not only you, but my family as well?"

"Yes."

If there was one emotion he was willing to surrender to this morning, it was rage toward that man.

Devon crumpled the napkin in his fist and stood. "Go and pack your bags. We will be leaving the palace immediately, and God help Rushton when I finally lay eyes on him."

Chapter 23

It should have not have come as a surprise to any of them that the rain would not let up during the ten-hour journey to Creighton Manor. They were cooped up inside the coach the entire way—Rebecca, Devon, and Blake, who had insisted on accompanying them, after Devon had explained the situation to him.

The trip was cold and damp and endless. Water poured down the coach windows and the horses trotted through miles of puddles and muck. Rebecca sat next to her husband, but they could speak of nothing personal. She could not ask him if he forgave her for all the trouble she had caused, as Blake was always present.

Even if he had not been, something would have held her back from more intimate communications with her husband, for he was preoccupied and gravely silent. He was determined to solve the immediate problem of Mr. Rushton's attempts to blackmail her and her father.

By the time they arrived at Creighton Manor, it was past dark. The coach pulled up at the front entrance, and though Rebecca was exhausted from the journey, she could barely keep from stepping out of the coach and running inside to see her father.

She had not said goodbye to him before she left almost a month ago, and though she had been furious with him and continued to be uncertain of him now, he was still her father. He had once been the center of her life.

Which was why none of this made sense to her, and why she felt as if the entire world was crumbling to pieces under her feet.

The door of the coach opened at last, and Rebecca waited for her husband to step out and offer a hand. He escorted her to the door, and she rapped on the knocker.

The maid answered. "Lady Rebecca!" Mary lunged forward and threw her arms around Rebecca, then spotted Devon and Blake behind her. "Begging your pardon, it's Lady Hawthorne now, isn't it? Good heavens, would one of these gentlemen be your husband?" She let go of Rebecca and stepped back.

"Yes, Mary. This is Devon Sinclair, Marquess

of Hawthorne, and his brother, Lord Blake. We have come to see Father."

Mary curtsied to both of them and took their coats. "Welcome to Creighton Manor," she said.

"Go and fetch him right away, please," Rebecca said. "We will wait by the fire."

"Yes, your ladyship."

Mary picked up her skirts and dashed up the stairs, while Rebecca led the way to the stone hearth in the great hall. She held her chilled hands out to warm them over the fire.

Devon and Blake crossed the hall slowly, looking up at the high timber ceiling, the stone walls and sparse furnishings.

"What a magnificent house," Blake said.

Rebecca managed a smile. "Thank you. Father has always been reluctant to modernize it, so it still shows its medieval origins, though the south wing is new. My grandfather had a ballroom added with crystal chandeliers. Unfortunately it's never been used. At least not in my lifetime."

Devon and Blake reached the fire and stood beside her to warm their hands as well.

"It is good to be here," her husband said, lifting his exhausted gaze to meet hers, and for the first time that day, he gave her a small nod of encouragement. It was not much, but it was something, and it revived a tiny fragment of hope.

His gaze turned upward and swept around

the expansive hall, which had once been used for feasts and banquets. "This place is very different from Pembroke Palace," he said. "I can see why you felt secluded."

Just then she heard that familiar tapping upon the winding staircase. Her father's cane. She turned.

He took the final step and reached the ground floor. His white hair had not been combed, his clothing was shabby and wrinkled, as if he had not donned a fresh shirt in days. How old he appeared, as he hobbled across the hall toward her.

Suddenly she was overcome by despair, and walked straight across the room into his arms. "Father, I am so sorry."

But what did she have to be sorry for? She had only been trying to save herself from a life of misery.

And what of the accusations? She could not bear to think of it being true.

"No, my dear," he replied, wrapping his frail arms around her. "*I* am sorry. I have been weak. I failed you."

She pulled back to look into his eyes. She wanted more than anything to understand what he meant. Was he implying he had committed a terrible sin? Or was it simply an apology for arranging a marriage she did not want?

She turned around and looked at her husband, who was watching her.

"If you wish, Blake and I can see to the horses."

"No, Devon, please stay." She turned to her father again. "We have come a long way to speak to you."

His brow crinkled with apprehension. "I understand." He limped toward the fire.

"Lord Creighton," Devon said, "allow me to present my brother, Lord Blake Sinclair."

They shook hands.

Her father gestured to both men. "Look at you, brothers without a doubt. The same dark features and self-assured demeanor."

Rebecca was quick to interrupt. "Father," she said, "we must speak to you about Mr. Rushton. He came to Pembroke Village, and he is not prepared to give up his intentions to have me as his wife."

The flames from the fire reflected in her father's eyes as he glanced uneasily at each of them. "You spoke to him?"

"I did," she replied. "He has made some grave accusations."

He paused, then spoke harshly. "What has he told you?"

Rebecca could not bring herself to say it. She was thankful when Devon answered for her. "He has threatened to expose you as a murderer, sir."

Her father backed away from them and sank into a chair. He cupped his forehead in a hand. His fingers were trembling. "Lord help me."

She went to him and knelt, resting her hands on his thin knees. "Is it true, Father? Tell me it is not."

At last he dropped his hand, and she could see his face. "Did he try to use this to force you to leave your husband?"

She nodded. "He expected I would obey him to protect you. But you must tell me, Father, is there anything to protect? I cannot accept what he says as true. Tell me he is lying."

She stared into her father's eyes, searching for the truth.

"Of course it is a lie," he told her. "You know I am not that kind of man."

For the longest time, she sat and stared at him. She wanted to believe it, truly she did, but something inside her was not yet satisfied. She thought of the note about the bracelet.

"Mr. Rushton says you gave a bracelet to a woman named Serena Fullarton. In fact, he has a letter that she allegedly wrote, and he claims that she is your victim, and is buried here on the estate."

His hands were shaking as he looked up at Devon and Blake. "I do not know that woman, nor do I know how she obtained my stationery. Perhaps Rushton stole it in order to frame me, so that he could have you."

"But did you know about the letter?"

He hesitated. "No, I swear it."

None of this was making sense to her. She wanted to shake her father. She was having a hard time believing any of what he was saying. "If you are innocent, why did you give in to him? Why did you not stand up to him and defend your honor and protect my happiness? Why did you not refuse his demands? Or send for the police?"

There was pleading in his tone. "I have not been well in recent years, Rebecca. You know that. I am not young and strong like your husband. I did not have any fight left in me." Tears pooled in his eyes, and he covered his face with a hand. "I am a coward, afraid of everything, even leaving this house."

"Do not say that, Father."

She could hear the shame and humiliation in his voice.

"You have been so good to me," he said. "So devoted. I should have fought harder to keep you here with me."

"But I could not remain here forever," she said. "I am a woman now. I needed to live my own life."

She felt a hand on her shoulder—her husband's hand, squeezing gently. "It is almost midnight," he said. "We must go."

"Where?" her father asked, taking hold of her wrist as she tried to stand. "What are you going to do?"

"Rushton expects your daughter at his door tonight," Devon explained, "and he has threatened to expose you as a killer if she does not obey. I mean to confront him, sir, and inform him that she will never be his. She is my wife now. This blackmail must stop."

Her father stared for a long time at Devon, blinking up at him, then at last he spoke. "This is the second time you have offered your assistance, Hawthorne, when I have found myself in a difficult predicament. I am grateful."

"It is more than a difficult predicament, Father," Rebecca said. "The man has accused you of murder."

Her father's Adam's apple bobbed. "He is a villain. He has always been so, you know it yourself. He is obsessed with you and will do anything to have you. I have not been strong enough to oppose him, but it is clear your husband is very different from me." He stood and limped to Devon and grabbed hold of his wrist. "I have had enough of this pain and turmoil. Do whatever you must to protect my daughter. She deserves happiness, and Rushton will destroy any hope of that. *Please, do what you must . . .*"

Rebecca recognized a look of comprehension in her husband's eyes as he took hold of her arm and led her toward the door. She, too, understood her father's message.

He wanted Rushton dead.

Chapter 24

The Pembroke coach pulled up in front of Mr. Rushton's country house shortly before midnight. It was a large home of Dutch design, flanked by two pavilions, which gave it balance and breadth.

Though the rain had stopped, a thick, heavy fog blanketed the land and put a damp chill in the air. Devon stepped out of the coach, offered his hand to Rebecca, and walked with her to the front entrance. Blake followed a few steps behind, carrying a pistol.

Before Devon knocked on the door, he looked into his wife's face and saw her distress, for she did not know whether her father was lying or telling the truth. Quite frankly, neither did he.

Leaning forward, he kissed her on the cheek. "We shall get to the bottom of this. You have my word."

She only nodded.

Devon rapped the heavy brass knocker. Blake stepped to the side and pressed his back against the wall, remaining out of sight.

The door opened, and Devon faced a well-dressed gentleman who was clearly not a servant. He wore a dark jacket and looked to be in his mid-forties with strong facial features, a long, straight, patrician nose, and golden brown hair. He was fit and slender. There was confidence in his smile. It was Rushton, without a doubt.

His smug smile disappeared, however, the instant he met Devon's gaze.

"I thought you were going to leave him," he said to Rebecca, his blatant arrogance causing Devon to squeeze his hand into a tight fist. "Was he not willing to let you go?"

During the brief coach ride from Creighton Manor, they had discussed exactly what needed to be said, but suddenly Devon was hard-pressed to hold to the plan, when what he really wanted to do was walk in, grab the slimy worm by the throat, and toss him out a window.

"I am not leaving my husband for you or anyone else," Rebecca said. "Go ahead and expose my father if you must, but I think you will have a difficult time proving anything, because I shall be the first to appear as a witness and tell the court how you issued threats against the Marquess of Hawthorne and his family, in order to pressure me to become your wife. If anyone has a history of wrongdoing, sir, and a motive for misconduct, it is you."

A contemptuous frown set into Rushton's features. He looked at both of them as if pondering how best to proceed, then he glanced over their shoulders at their coach.

"I don't think you understand what is at stake here," he said. "Why don't you both come inside, and I will ring for tea. We will discuss the matter in some depth."

"No," Rebecca said. "There is nothing to discuss. I came here only to tell you that—"

But now that Devon was here, seeing for the first time the man who had once torn his wife's skirts and attempted to force himself upon her, he could not simply walk away. He stepped forward and pushed the door open, forcing Rushton to step back onto the black and white checker floor and make way.

"I beg your pardon, darling," Devon said to Rebecca. "I've decided I would like to hear him out after all."

He could almost feel Blake's grimace just outside the door, for they had not intended to enter the house, and now his brother would have to wait in the chilly darkness or somehow sneak inside.

Standing nose-to-nose with Rushton, Devon kept his gaze fixed on the man's brown eyes. He was aware of Rebecca stepping quietly into the hall behind him and waiting in silence for the two of them to step apart.

Rushton backed away first, then turned to the footman across the hall. "Bring tea."

The young man made himself scarce, and Rushton escorted them to the drawing room, which was adorned in blue and yellow drapes and furnishings. Once inside the room, Devon looked up at a large family portrait in a gilt frame over the fireplace—a mother, father, and son. They were dressed formally. The mother wore a blue satin gown, pearls and diamonds around her neck, and a tiara on her head.

"My parents and me," Rushton said. "I had it painted last year. The artist was able to copy our likenesses from our individual portraits, and create this masterpiece."

But Rebecca had once mentioned Rushton's father was a merchant. "Where is your family now?" Devon asked.

"Dead, for twenty-five years."

"My condolences." Devon strolled around and looked carefully at the furnishings and other paintings on the walls. "You wish to enlighten us about the situation . . ." he prompted.

"Yes. I don't believe you understand the significance of it." He sat down and crossed one leg over the other. "Please, sit down. Would you care for a biscuit?" He casually pointed at a plate of cookies on a side table.

Rebecca dropped her hands to her sides in obvious frustration. "Do not continue, sir, with this ridiculous attempt to arouse our apprehensions by keeping us in suspense. Come out with it, if you please, or I will walk out of here this instant."

He smirked. "You've obviously had your hands full with her," he said to Devon, "while I have been missing out."

Devon's blood went cold at the mere insinuation that there could ever be anything between them. "You heard my wife," he said. "Say your piece."

"Very well," Rushton replied, rising from his seat. "Five years ago, I became acquainted with a woman named Serena Fullarton at some local gatherings in the village, and discovered she was having a secret affair with your father."

"I find that difficult to believe," Rebecca said. "My father has always been a very private person. I would have known of it."

He glared at her. "Ask him."

"I did. He denied it."

"Then he's lying."

She was taken aback. Devon merely watched and listened to all of it with great scrutiny.

Rushton continued. "I saw them together on numerous occasions at your father's rotunda by the lake, where I often went walking on warm days, and on one particular afternoon, I heard them arguing. The young lady was distraught, and I could not help but move closer and listen to their conversation, uncertain about whether or not I should intervene. Consequently, what followed will haunt me forever. I remained too far away, you see, and could do nothing but watch from a distance as your father wrestled the young lady to the ground and strangled the very life out of her. I, of course, hurried to the scene, but was too late. When I arrived and pulled your father to his feet, she had already expired."

The color bled from Rebecca's cheeks. "I don't believe it."

Devon went to her side.

Rushton continued. "Your father confessed to me that Miss Fullarton was carrying his child and demanding that he marry her. He did not want her as his wife, however, only as his mistress, so he lost his temper. Once the ghastly deed was done and he collected himself, he buried her there by the rotunda, where she lies to this day without a headstone. I can even attest to the fact that she was buried wearing the bracelet your father gave to her. I am sure the magistrate will find it a pleasant challenge to trace the bauble to its purchaser."

Devon looked at Rebecca whose brow was knitted in disbelief, and strove to focus on the details.

"How would you even know the bracelet was from him? Perhaps it was you who killed her."

He shook his head. "As I tried to explain, I had become acquainted with her in the village, and she had revealed some of her secrets to me." He approached Rebecca, who was breathing heavily. "Perhaps what you need to do is question your father about all of this again, and watch the color drain from his face when he is reminded of the gruesome details. Then you will know the truth, won't you?"

Just then, a noise from the hall diverted their attention, and they turned. Lord Creighton came hobbling into the room with his cane in one hand, a sword already drawn from its scabbard in the other.

Rushton immediately withdrew a pistol from his jacket. Devon grabbed hold of Rebecca's arm to pull her out of the way, and Blake came running into the room, his pistol aimed at Rushton.

"She shall have the truth *now*," Creighton said. "You sir, are a villain and a blackmailer, and I will not permit you to cause my daughter further anxiety. She has chosen her husband and will not be bullied."

"Pity you missed it," Rushton replied, "but I have already delivered the truth to her, so you are too late with your attempt at heroism. She knows what you did."

The earl raised the sword, but his stiff, misshapen hand could barely keep it steady. The tip of the sword dipped low. Rushton aimed his pistol at Creighton, then at Blake, then back at Creighton.

"Give her the *whole* truth," the earl said.

Rebecca tried to go to him, but Devon held her back. "Father, tell me it is not true," she said. "Tell me you did not kill anyone."

The earl glanced briefly at her. No one made a move or uttered a word for a long, tense moment. Then at last he answered in a tremulous voice, his whole arm shaking from the weight of the sword. "I was in love with Serena, and I was with her that day at the rotunda."

"But what happened?" Rebecca asked. "Did you kill her?"

The earl seemed barely able to form words. "Not on purpose."

"Father . . ."

Devon moved to take her hand, but she was distracted.

"I confess, I was involved quite improperly with her, and we argued that day."

"Over your bastard child in her womb," Rushton put in.

The earl raised the sword again and garnered his strength. "No, sir. It was *your* bastard child she carried. I always understood that, which is why I would not marry her."

Suddenly he strode toward Mr. Rushton, aiming the sword at his heart.

"Father, no!"

Devon dashed forward, but Rushton fired his pistol and the shot rang out before anyone could stop the earl from his useless attack.

Creighton dropped the heavy sword and crumpled to the floor.

"Father!" Rebecca flew to him and dropped to her knees beside him.

Rushton scrambled to reload his pistol, but Devon lunged at him and knocked it from his hands, sending it clattering across the shiny floor, while Blake stood back with his own pistol aimed and ready to fire.

Devon pinned Rushton down, but somehow the man swung a fist and punched Devon across the jaw. A shrill, sharp pain rang inside his skull.

"You had no right to marry her," Rushton ground out. "She was already spoken for."

"She was not given the chance to speak for herself," Devon ground out in reply, landing his own punch to Rushton's side.

They rolled into a table and knocked it over, then Rushton straddled Devon and wrapped his hands around his neck. He began to choke him. "That pistol shot was meant for you."

Gasping for breath, fighting to suck in air, Devon swung a fist and knocked Rushton over with one blow. The man rolled to the side, picked up the sword, knelt behind Rebecca and pressed the point into her back. She froze on the floor at her father's side.

"No . . ." the earl pleaded, clutching the dark stain of blood on his stomach.

Devon slowly, carefully got to his feet. "Don't hurt her." He should have kicked the sword away. Why hadn't he?

All at once, he was sliding back down that muddy hill again, helpless, out of control, and regretting all the little decisions he had made that had brought him to this horrific moment in time. He should have knocked Rushton in the other direction just now. He should have brought his own pistol. He should never have brought Rebecca here in the first place. But he had, and now he was forced to face the possibility of a loss greater than any he had ever known. If Rushton drove that sword into her heart and took her life, it would take Devon's soul.

Rebecca was still watching her father, who was groaning in pain. "Let me help him," she pleaded, struggling. "He's in pain."

Rushton gestured toward Blake. "Tell your brother to drop the pistol and kick it to me."

When Blake held firm, Rushton pushed the sword against Rebecca's back, and she lurched forward with a cry of agony.

"Blake, put it down," Devon ordered, his eyes trained on Rushton's.

Blake set the pistol on the floor, but kicked it to the side.

Rushton frowned. "I spent all my life fighting to recover what was taken from me—my home, my family. The Creighton name owes me that at least, and this woman was going to give it to me."

"*Why* do we owe you that?" she asked.

The earl tried to speak. "Rebecca, your grandfather . . ." But he could not go on.

"Just lie still, Father. *Please.*"

Rushton continued the explanation for him. "Your grandfather won my family home in a card game twenty-five years ago, and came to claim it the very next day, turning us all out onto the street. My mother died two weeks later giving birth to my younger brother in a boardinghouse, then my father, in his grief, took his own life."

Rebecca looked down at her father. "Is that true?"

He closed his eyes and nodded.

She turned her head to the side to address Rushton. "I am very sorry to hear that," she said shakily. "Perhaps we could offer you some compensation."

Devon had been listening to all of this with increasing fury at the sight of that sword at Rebecca's back, and her father lying injured on the floor. She had come here with him believing he was her hero, and he had intended to protect her.

Rage—so powerful that it burned away every regrettable thing he'd ever done in the past—flooded his head. He could not repress the violent instinct to retaliate. It was festering in his gut, shuddering in his bones. He felt like a wild animal in a cage—captive, threatened, and vicious.

"If it's compensation you want," he bluntly said, "go ask your dead father. He's the one who gambled away your home."

Rushton's gaze turned to him in shock, and Devon shot forward. He threw his body into Rushton's. The force of the assault carried them both flying through the air to the other side of the room. The sword dropped with a clatter. They landed with a crash, and Devon's chin hit the ground.

He scrambled to his knees and bashed his fist into Rushton's face, then straddled him and grabbed his whole head with both hands. He smacked it once, hard, against the floor.

Shocked and disoriented, the man blinked a few times, parted his lips as if to say something, then fell unconscious.

In the meantime, Rebecca had torn off her cloak and was trying to stanch the flow of her father's blood.

Blake seized the pistol and hurried to Devon. "Are you all right?"

"I am," Devon replied, barely conscious of

what he had just done. He accepted his brother's hand and let him pull him to his feet.

Blake aimed the pistol at Rushton's heart, should the man awaken and wish to make another move. Devon met Rebecca's gaze. He knelt down beside her. She was gently stroking her father's head. The earl's breathing was ragged.

"We have to do something!" she cried.

"I'm sorry," the earl whispered. "I never meant to hurt you, but you must know, the child was Rushton's. Serena was going to pass it off as mine. I don't know what happened to me that day. I couldn't control my anger. I pushed her down and she hit her head. Her death was my fault. It has haunted me ever since."

"Try to calm yourself," Rebecca said. "You're still bleeding."

"I did care for her," he tried to explain, "but she was his lover. He wanted his son to have my title." He began to gasp for each costly breath. "I have come to realize that he would have killed me after the child was born, then married her. But when she died, he turned his ambitions toward you."

"Why didn't you tell me any of this?" Rebecca asked. "I would have stood by you. You should not have given him that power over us."

"I was ashamed and ridden with guilt. And the scandal . . . I couldn't face the disgrace of a trial, the destruction of my family's good name." He squeezed her hand. "It was wrong of me. I should never have believed you would be safe with him. In my fear I was not rational. But you are free now. No need to protect me. I was brave tonight. At last. Brave for you."

He gazed at her for a moment, then a shadow passed over his eyes, and they fell closed.

Rebecca bowed her head and wept.

Devon placed a hand on her shoulder to offer what comfort he could, then turned to see the young footman watching from the door, his eyes wide as he held a silver tray with tea.

"Go and instruct the driver outside to fetch the magistrate," Devon said.

The young man nodded, set down the tray, then turned and ran out.

Rebecca buried her face in Devon's shoulder. He held her close.

Chapter 25

It was nearly two in the morning when the magistrate and local officers dragged Rushton out of his house and shoved him into a coach bound for Newgate. The coroner had been there, too, and had taken charge of the earl's body, which would be delivered to the Manor the following day. Rebecca requested also that the magistrate and coroner locate Serena Fullarton's remains and take the necessary steps to find and notify her family.

Afterward, Rebecca, Devon, and Blake returned to Creighton Manor. They explained to Mary and the other servants what had occurred, and the members of the household were grief-stricken to learn of the earl's demise.

Blake was shown to a guest chamber, while Rebecca and Devon were shown to her former room. The bed was freshly made, and Mary warmed the sheets with the copper bed warmer.

Rebecca looked upon her room with exhaustion and sorrow. She was here with her husband—the man she had dreamed about countless times in this very bed—but everything was different now. She'd learned things she had never suspected about her father, one very terrible thing, and now he was gone.

And tonight she had become the Countess of Creighton, a peeress in her own right.

"Thank you, Mary," she said. "That will be all."

"You won't be needing anything else, my lady?"

Rebecca shook her head. All she wanted was to be alone with her husband.

"I am so sorry," he said, closing the door behind Mary. He took Rebecca into his arms and held her for a long time. She closed her eyes and rested her cheek on his chest.

When she was ready to let go, he helped her unbutton her bodice and folded it with her skirts, and set everything carefully upon a chair. While she stood in somber silence, he removed the pins from her hair and brushed it, smoothing it out with his hands and stroking it away from her face.

When that was done, she went to the wardrobe and opened the doors to find all of her clothes still hanging there, just as she had left them. Her chest of drawers had not been touched either, so she was able to find a favorite nightdress. She put it on while Devon undressed, and a few minutes later, they both slid into the warm bed with a candle burning beside them on the table.

"Are you all right?" he asked, lying on his side, facing her in the dim, golden light. "Is there anything I can do?"

She touched his cheek. "You have done so much for me already. I could not ask for anything more."

"But your father is gone. Perhaps if I had acted sooner. . . . Or if I had come here alone to face Rushton . . ."

"No, you must not think that way, Devon. None of us can control how life plays out. Nor can we look back on things and wish we had done them differently. All we can do is our best at any given moment, and risk making mistakes, for the alternative is to sit back, always afraid, and do nothing."

He spoke softly in the quiet room. "But in my desire to avoid being your hero, I left matters alone that should have been attended to. It was wrong of me to work so hard to keep a distance between us."

She gazed into his eyes. "May I ask you something?"

"Of course."

"On our wedding day, you told me you did

not want to be my hero because you had failed MaryAnn that day in the woods. Please tell me the truth, Devon—did you love her?"

A shadow of regret passed over his features. "She was my brother's fiancée, and yes, I did."

Rebecca digested the words with a surface calm, while inside she was wishing desperately that the answer had been different. But at least now she understood her husband's emotions surrounding that ordeal, and why he had always exercised restraint when it came to his emotional involvement within their marriage.

Love had not been a friend to him in the past. It had caused him heartache and shame. It had destroyed his relationship with his brother. "What happened between you?"

"It was the letter she wrote," he replied. "Until then, I had denied my feelings for her and buried them as best I could. But the letter was what made me go to see her alone. I had every intention of convincing her to forget me, and that she should be with Vincent. I was not going to reveal how I felt, but she was persistent, and I was weak. I desired her, and we did things I regret."

"Did you make love to her?"

He paused. "I went as far as a man can go before complete ruination, but stopped in the nick of time. Even so, I had never felt more ashamed." He closed his eyes. "I remember telling her harshly to get dressed, while I fastened my breeches with hands that would not stop shaking. It was a nightmare, and it is why I was in such a hurry to return her to the palace. To Vincent. I wanted to erase what I had done, and in my haste, I was grossly incompetent."

She sighed. "You had enough to worry about at Pembroke, after coming home from America to face your brother again, then to learn of your father's illness. Then you suddenly found yourself with a new bride who was pushing for your love—a bride who had kept secrets from you. I should not have expected you to solve all my problems, Devon. It was wrong of me to come to Pembroke assuming you would."

"But thank God you did come," he said, pulling her close. "How I needed you. You will never know how badly I wanted to be your hero tonight. With every inch of my soul, I wanted to protect you and keep you safe, not only from Rushton, but from everything unpleasant in the world."

She snuggled closer. "You *were* my hero."

"Perhaps a better word is 'ally.' You were very brave tonight. You've always been brave."

She managed a small smile. "I had the strength and courage to confront Rushton because you were at my side, and if not for that, my father would still be living in fear and shame. And perhaps your family might have been in danger."

"I am so sorry about what happened to your father."

"I am, too. But it was his choice to confront his enemy. I believe he needed to do it, and now I understand that it was his guilt and fear that changed him in recent years. He was no longer the father I remembered from my childhood."

Devon kissed the tip of her nose. "But he was brave tonight."

She nodded.

"As for you and me," Devon said, "we shall share the heroics by agreeing to be comrades, because when we are together, Rebecca, you rescue me from all the madness of my life, and I suspect you are going to be a great comfort to me in the coming months—when I will no doubt need your support in dealing with my father, and possibly a few spur-of-the-moment weddings."

Rebecca wet her lips. "I will do whatever I can to ease your burdens."

He inched a little closer. "And may I have permission to envision you riding to my rescue on a magnificent white horse?"

She raised an eyebrow. "Why would you need my permission to envision that?"

"Because you are naked on the horse." He squinted with humor, then laid a light, tender kiss on her lips.

"In that case, you have my consent."

He continued to gaze at her in the candlelight, then his expression became serious again. "Will you be able to forgive your father," he asked, "now that you know what really happened?"

"I am devastated to know what he did, but I shall have to find a way to forgive. I only wish I had known the whole story sooner. Perhaps I could have helped him do the right thing, and Rushton would never have had the power to bully him for so many years."

"Your father found his courage in the end. And none of it is your fault. You didn't know."

She felt a painful lump in her throat. "Everything you say is a help to me, Devon. You do ease my pain with your kindness. I am a lucky woman."

He ran a finger down her cheek, then kissed her again. "*I* am the lucky one. The most exciting, exquisite woman in the world fell straight into my lap. I will be forever grateful that I traveled through the forest that night four years ago, and that I was able to be your hero. I love you, wife."

He pressed his lips gently to hers and held her close in his arms all night long, until sunlight shone through the window in the morning. A clear, new day beckoned to them, and when they rose from bed and pulled the drapes open, there was not a cloud in the sky, nor a single drop of rain.

* * *

Rebecca, Devon, and Blake remained at Creighton Manor for a few days, long enough to see to
the earl's funeral, which was a private family affair. He was entombed in the mausoleum on the
hill, where all the Creighton earls had gone before
him.

As for Creighton Manor, it belonged to Rebecca now, and she and Devon decided they would
spend their summers in residence after the close of
the London Season, and enjoy the autumn hunting season there as well. And when—God willing—they brought their children, they would deliver life and laughter back to those quiet, empty
rooms.

Promising to return soon, Rebecca and Devon
said goodbye to the servants and stepped into the
Pembroke coach with Blake.

The journey back to Pembroke passed quickly,
for the sun was shining through the coach windows and both Devon and Blake were in high spirits. The sky had been clear for three days straight,
and the weather, they believed, was sure to alleviate some of their father's anxieties regarding the
family curse. Perhaps in time, he would realize
they were not in danger of being swept away by
raging floodwaters, and the hasty weddings could
be put off.

Perhaps also a grandchild would bring him some

peace of mind, Devon thought, feeling hopeful as he gazed at his lovely wife sitting next to him in the coach. He wondered how soon they would be able to call themselves expectant parents. He had never in a hundred years imagined he would anticipate such an event with joy. He supposed anything was possible—and that very simple notion boosted his spirits further as they drew closer to the palace and waved at the villagers in the fields. Everyone was in high spirits it seemed. Sunshine, he supposed, had a way of spreading cheer.

By the time they arrived at the palace, the sun was low in the sky and the whole estate was twilight-pink.

"It is good to be home," Devon said, feeling a sense of warmth and completeness he had never known before. He had his wife with him and his brother, and he would soon see his sister, Charlotte, and their mother.

He wanted to see his father, too. He wanted to hear that he was no longer fearful of a flood and a family curse, for the sun was shining.

All at once the yearning to see the man, who had once callously turned him out, affected something in Devon's heart. He remembered his cautious return to the palace not long ago. He had not believed the shattered pieces of his life could ever be put back together and mended. But they *had* been mended, in some ways, at least, for he felt a deep, soulful compassion toward his father, and a genuine desire to ensure that he was well cared for, no matter what the future held.

The coach pulled to a smooth stop and a footman lowered the step and opened the door. Charlotte and their mother came down the stairs to greet them.

Devon stepped out, into the fresh air. His mother wrapped her arms around him. "Welcome home," she said.

He hugged Charlotte as well, then turned to assist Rebecca out of the coach. The duchess embraced her and held her close for a long moment. "My dear, I am so sorry about your father."

"As am I," she said solemnly. "But he is at peace now."

Just then, the duke appeared at the open palace doors waving a letter over his head.

"What is that?" Blake asked, looking suspiciously up at their father.

Adelaide sighed heavily. "It is a letter from Vincent. It arrived yesterday."

"And what about Garrett?" Devon asked. "Has there been any word from him?"

"No, nothing, but your father sent a man to Greece two days ago to hunt him down and bring him home."

"Garrett won't be pleased," Blake said. "He's likely to toss the messenger into the Mediterranean."

The duke came hopping down the steps in his slippers.

"Has Dr. Thomas been back yet?" Devon whispered discreetly to his mother.

"No," she replied. "But he is coming tomorrow, thank goodness."

"Devon!" the duke called out. "How wonderful that you have returned! And your beautiful wife. You are a work of art, dear girl."

"Thank you, Your Grace," she replied with a smile.

"I see you have a letter from Vincent," Devon said.

"Indeed I do." The duke handed the letter over. "And just look at the sunset, will you? I dare say, we are doing well."

Devon exchanged a curious look with Blake, then read the letter. A knot tightened in his gut, and he ran a hand down over his face.

"Surely not," he said, holding the letter out to Blake.

Blake read it, too. "Good God. No, he can't be serious. He's engaged?"

"Yes!" the duke said, dancing about on the steps. "Oh, Vincent, I am so proud. I shall give him my best shotgun for hunting. Or maybe that pair of boots he sometimes borrowed without asking. And look at the weather, would you, please?"

They all turned and looked at the colorful sunset on the horizon.

"Who is the lady?" Rebecca asked, while Devon was still unable to speak, for he was in shock.

Blake handed her the letter.

"Good heavens," she said. "It is Lady Letitia, the Duke of Swinburne's daughter." She looked at Charlotte, who was biting her lip. "She will be our sister-in-law."

"Vincent has acted too hastily," Devon said. "He has not given it adequate thought."

"When did adequate thought ever get a man to the altar?" his father asked. "A young, robust man needs to listen to his John Thomas. Eh? Eh?"

Blake sighed. "She is a handsome woman. That was probably enough for Vincent, under the circumstances."

"She is the perfect young gel," the duke said cheerfully. "I shall adore her. He is bringing her home tomorrow."

Devon inhaled deeply and looked back toward the sunset. Rebecca laid a gloved hand on his arm, expressing her understanding.

"So it appears the curse has been thwarted again," he said, with a notable sense of defeat as he looked into his wife's lovely, knowing eyes.

"Indeed, thwarted again!" his father shouted triumphantly. "Now, do tell me, what time is supper? I'm hungry for beef."

"Shall we enjoy the diary tonight?" Devon asked, pushing through the large portrait on the

wall in Rebecca's bedchamber and closing it behind him. He stopped and turned around, however, to swing the portrait open and closed a few
times. "These hinges need to be greased."

Suddenly his wife leaped onto his back and
wrapped her legs around his waist. He laughed,
and she dropped to her feet on the floor, pulled
him around to face her, and crushed his lips with
hers.

"Where were you?" she asked, after a deep and
tantalizing kiss. "I thought you would never get
here."

He somehow managed to get an apology out
between laughter and more kisses. "I'm sorry—
Blake kept me late in the library."

Rebecca pulled his shirt out from inside his
breeches and lifted it up to his chest, then went
down on her knees, kissing his bare stomach along
the way, probing his navel with her hot, wet tongue.
He was instantly, overwhelmingly aroused.

She looked up at him with a wicked smile as
she unfastened his trousers. "I shall read to you
from the diary tonight," she told him, "but this
will be the last time."

"Why the last?"

"Because after tonight, we shall contrive our
own fantasies and write our own future." She
pulled his breeches down to his ankles and rose
to her feet, while he ripped his shirt off over his
head.

"But before we put it away for good," she added, "I thought you might like to know what happens to Lydie and Jess." She pulled off her nightdress, tossed it to the floor, and climbed onto the bed.

"I admit I've been curious."

She rested her cheek on a hand and beckoned him with a smile. "Come here, then." She patted the spot beside her and pulled the book out from beneath her pillow. "Now, where did we leave off?"

He slipped under the covers, naked and stiff as a post, and faced her.

"I'm happy to listen to anything you wish to read to me."

She flipped through the pages, then settled on an entry toward the end. "In that case, lie back and listen."

He obeyed her command—all ears as she began to read.

"*Dear Diary,*

"*Today I learned an important lesson, the most important of my life.*

"*He came, as I hoped and dreamed he would. I had only just finished writing my last words to you, when I heard a commotion downstairs at the inn. It was my love, Jess, who had followed my father's coach and found us in London. He came bursting through my door like a white knight. He*

*faced my father with a sword and demanded my
hand in marriage, and my father could do nothing but submit. He let me go, and Jess took me
away. My brave hero, Jess, who did it because he
loves me."*

Devon laid a hand on Rebecca's arm, touching
her with his own love. She continued reading.

*"That was one week ago, and we were married
today. I love him more than life itself, and I know
we will be happy. We will have children together
and raise them in a happy home, and I will forever be thankful for the day we met.*

*"So my lesson, Diary, is this: One must always
believe in what the heart knows, and never give
up on it. Jess is the world to me, as I am the world
to him. We are everything to each other. This is
bliss."*

Rebecca closed the diary and placed it on the
bedside table, then faced Devon without a word.

For a long time he looked at her, then he inched
closer and wrapped his arms around her waist. "I
am glad they found their bliss," he said. "I have
found mine, too."

"Oh, Devon." She took his face in her hands
and kissed him.

"I would not have understood those words a

month ago," he told her, "for I did not know what bliss was until you entered my life. But now everything is perfect."

"But what about the pain you once knew, Devon? You had not forgiven yourself for what happened between you and Vincent four years ago, and you used your guilt to put distance between us. Are you able to truly let go of that now?"

He touched her soft face and ran a finger over her hair. "I will always regret what happened, and I will always feel pain when I think of it, but I will not continue to feel dead inside, as I have for the past three years. I have come home and my heart has come back to life. I have found happiness again, thanks to you. And perhaps someday, I will earn Vincent's forgiveness, though it will not be easy with Letitia as his wife. The woman despises me for choosing you. She will encourage his bitterness."

She kissed him in the lamplight, and he rolled her over onto her back, using his lips and mouth to express his love for her with tireless devotion to both her emotional and erotic pleasures. For an hour he delighted her senses, sent passionate jolts of excitement to her core, and filled her with a yearning he had every intention of fulfilling.

When he finally entered her in the darkness, she cried out and pulled him close, and he made love to her gently and tenderly, looking into her eyes the entire time, moving with great care and attention to detail. He used every skill he possessed as a man to work her up to a powerful climax, and the instant he felt her body tremble and shudder beneath his own, he, too, surrendered to his own orgasmic pleasures, feeling the shimmering heat of absolute love fill his whole being.

They fell asleep for a short time with his body still inside hers, then they woke to make love again, when he grew hard within her.

It was almost dawn when they finally surrendered to sleep, their bodies drained and sated, and if not for the knocking at their door at daybreak, Devon would have slept until noon.

But it was not to be that morning. He was forced to rise and pull on his trousers. He left Rebecca sleeping and crossed the room to answer the persistent caller. When he opened the door, there stood his mother with a sleeping infant in her arms.

"What is this?" he whispered, not sure if he might in fact be dreaming.

"We have a problem," she said flatly, in a quiet voice so as not to wake Rebecca. "A woman just left this child on the doorstep. A few of the footmen are out searching the grounds at this very moment, hoping to catch her."

"There is no indication who the woman was?"

"We have this." She handed him a note, and he

blinked sleepily, willing his eyes to focus on the elegant penmanship. It was too dark to read any of it in the corridor, so he carried the note to the bed and lit the lamp, then read what it said.

He turned to face his mother, who was still standing in the doorway.

Rebecca sat up, clutching the covers to her neck. "What is going on?"

"We don't quite know," the duchess said. "This baby was just left here, and I do not think Lady Letitia is going to be happy about it when she arrives to have her engagement announced later today."

Rebecca squinted drowsily at the baby. "*It's Vincent's?*"

"So the letter writer claims," Adelaide said.

Devon sank down into a chair. "If that is true, this is *his* bed. *He* made it. *He* will have to lie in it."

At that moment, the baby began to babble in the sweetest, most adorable manner, and Rebecca leaped out of bed with the sheet wrapped around her, and joined the duchess in the doorway to indulge in a very maternal round of doting, coddling, and cooing.

Don't miss Vincent's story in the next install-
ment of the Pembroke Palace Series, coming to
you in Summer 2008.